"Funny, adventurous, passionate, and especially poignant, this is a great beginning to a new series . . . Bradley mixes suspense and a sexy love story to perfection."   —*Romantic Times BOOKreviews*

"A wonderful start to a very looked-forward-to new series . . . once again showcases Celeste Bradley's talent of creating sensual and intriguing plots filled with memorable and endearing characters . . . A non-stop read."   —*Romance Reader at Heart*

"Danger, deceit, and desire battle with witty banter and soaring passion for prominence in this highly engrossing tale . . . Bradley also provides surprises galore, both funny and suspenseful, and skillfully ties them all in neatly with the romance so as to make this story more than averagely memorable."   —*Road to Romance*

"A fantastic read . . . Bradley successfully combines mystery, intrigue, romance, and intense sensuality into this captivating book."   —*Romance Junkies*

THE CHARMER
"Amusing, entertaining romance."   —*Booklist*

"Bradley infuses this adventure with so much sexual tension and humor that you'll be enthralled. You'll laugh from the first page to the last . . . The wonderful characters, witty dialogue, and clever plot will have you wishing you were a Liar too."
—*Romantic Times BOOKreviews*

THE SPY
"Only a clever wordsmith can make this complex, suspenseful tale work so perfectly. Bradley pulls us into the wonderful world of the Liar's Club and gives us a nonstop read brimming with puzzle after puzzle."   —*Romantic Times BOOKreviews*

"With its wonderfully witty writing, superbly matched protagonists, and intrigue-steeped plot, the third of Bradley's Liar's Club historicals is every bit as much fun as *The Pretender* and *The Impostor*."   —*Booklist*

"A must for readers of the Liar's Club series and a good bet for those who haven't yet started . . . I unhesitatingly recommend."
—*All About Romance*

"Ms. Bradley has an effortless style to her prose."
—*The Romance Reader*

"A Top Pick . . . the best of [the Liar's Club] so far. Bless Celeste Bradley . . . She just seems to get better at it as she goes along."
—*Romance Reader at Heart*

THE IMPOSTOR

"Bradley carefully layers deception upon deception, keeping the intrigue level high and the tone bright . . . Readers will race through this delightful comedy of errors and eagerly anticipate the next installment."
—*Publishers Weekly*

"With delicious characters and a delectable plot, Bradley delivers another enticing read brimming with the mayhem and madness that come with falling in love when you least expect it. The devilishly funny double identities, witty dialogue and clever twists will captivate."
—*Romantic Times BOOKreviews* (Top Pick)

"Don't miss this second book of the Liar's Club series. With humor, passion and mystery, it's absolutely delightful in every way! I can't wait for the next one."
—*Old Book Barn Gazette*

THE PRETENDER

"Totally entertaining."
—*New York Times* bestselling author Julia Quinn

"An engaging, lusty tale, full of adventure and loaded with charm."
—Gaelen Foley, *USA Today* bestselling author of *Lord of Ice*

"Bradley certainly knows how to combine engaging characters with excitement, sensuality, and a strong plot."
—*Booklist* (starred)

"Bursting with adventure and sizzling passion to satisfy the most daring reader."
—*Romantic Times BOOKreviews*

"A charming heroine and a dashing spy hero make *The Pretender* a riveting read . . . [E]ntertained me thoroughly from beginning to end."
—Sabrina Jeffries, *USA Today* bestselling author of *After the Abduction*

Duke Most Wanted

Celeste Bradley

St. Martin's Paperbacks

This book is dedicated to my sister, Cindy. Through life and loves and kids and gardens, you are always there. I love you.

I'd like to acknowledge the fortitude and beyond-the-call patience of my wonderful editor and friend, Monique Patterson. Sorry about the stress, sweetie! I'd also like to thank my assistant, Darbi Gill, for pushing while Monique pulled. Somehow Pooh made it out of Rabbit's door.

Prologue

Once upon a time, on a lovely spring day in the English countryside, three tiny girls played side by side by side—cousins and future competitors.

The eldest, Sophie, watched an insect crawling across the path, squatting awkwardly so that her hem dragged in the dirt. The middle, Phoebe, sweet and unrestrained, chased a butterfly. The youngest, Deirdre, even then a stunningly beautiful infant, grabbed Sophie's bug and ate it, ignoring Sophie's howl of protest.

Their mothers, Sophie's a frustrated and resentful widow, Phoebe's a kindly but overworked vicar's wife and Deirdre's, an ethereal and unwell beauty, sat watching them from the shady blanket left over from their picnic.

Sophie's mother, who was cousin to the other two, not sisters as they were, slapped irritably at something with too many legs that encroached upon her skirts. "Disgusting idea," she muttered. "I abhor eating outside."

Phoebe's mother, the only woman whose hands showed the wear of actual toil, gently removed the offending creature and set it free in the grass. She smiled to see her daughter playing so joyously. "Insects or no, I think it's delightful to sit at all."

Deirdre's mother fanned her pale cheeks and smiled as well. "I don't get out enough these days. And it's lovely to see the girls play together."

Sophie's mother eyed her own daughter for a long moment, then let her eyes rest on the very pretty daughters of her cousins. No one had said a word so far, but it was obvious that Sophie wasn't going to be the beauty of the three.

No one had mentioned the Pickering trust, either. Yet how could they not be thinking, even now, that their daughters had a chance where they themselves had failed so miserably?

Oh, one sister had found a wealthy enough man, though not a duke by any means. The other had settled for a vicar! She herself had not done much better, for though her late husband had left her settled fairly if she pinched her coppers, she was no higher in life than she'd started!

No, it was up to the next generation. Sophie's mother frowned, gazing at her child's knobby knees and awkward movements. She'd even inherited the Pickering nose!

Was that the sort of girl a duke most wanted?

I, SIR HAMISH Pickering, being of sound mind but ailing body, do make my last will and testament.

I've climbed as high as a man can, despite having twice the brains, wisdom and fortitude of the layabout aristocracy. Yet, a woman can wed as high as her looks will let her, up to a duchess if she may.

There, my own daughters failed me miserably. Morag and Finella, I spent money on you so that you could marry higher but you weren't up to snuff. You expected the world to be handed it to you. If any female of this family wants another farthing of my money she'd best set herself to earn it.

Therefore, I declare that the entirety of my fortune be kept back from my useless daughters and be held in trust for the granddaughter or great-granddaughter who weds a duke of England or weds a man who then becomes a duke through inheritance, at which time the trust will be released to her and only her.

If she has any sisters or female cousins who fail, they may each have a lifetime income of fifteen pounds a year. If she has any brothers or male cousins, though the family does tend to run to daughters, more's the pity, they will receive five pounds apiece, for that's all I had in my pocket when I came to London. Any Scotsman worth his haggis can turn five pounds into five hundred in a few years' time.

A set amount will be given each girl as she makes her debut in Society, for gowns and whatnot.

Should three generations of Pickering girls fail, I wash me hands of the lot of you. The entire fifteen thousand pounds will go to pay the fines and hardships of those who defy the excise man to export that fine Scots whisky which has been my only solace in this family of dolts. If your poor sainted mother could only see you now.

Signed,
Sir Hamish Pickering
Witnesses,
B. R. Stickley, A. M. Wolfe
Solicitors' firm of Stickley & Wolfe

* * *

NEARLY TWENTY YEARS passed before three young ladies, chaperoned by Deirdre's stepmother, took up residence in London for their debut season.

At first, it seemed that pretty, openhearted Phoebe would be the one to land an almost-duke. When she ran away with his rakish half-brother instead, beautiful, willful Deirdre snatched him up, wedding him within weeks.

Deirdre may have loved her new husband desperately, but he wasn't nearly so pleased with her. Luckily, when she refused to mother his wildly out-of-control child, Meggie, sparks flew—and grew to white-hot flames.

With Deirdre's handsome lord about to inherit the title of Duke of Brookmoor, everyone assumed it was only a matter of time until Deirdre was handed an enormous amount of money she didn't especially need.

Sophie, tall, plain and socially awkward, had never nurtured any hope of winning the inheritance herself. After all, scholarly, reserved Sophie had never even met a duke!

Chapter One

England, 1815

If someone had told Sophie Blake one year ago that tonight she would find herself sprawled on the rug before the fire with one of the handsomest, most desirable men in London, she would have laughed outright in disbelief.

Yet here she was, stretching lazily in the warmth, gazing fondly at Lord Graham Cavendish, tall of form and dashing of countenance, as he stroked long capable fingers over her bare, sensitive palm—

"Ouch!" Sophie snatched her hand back.

"Got it!" Graham held his pinched fingers up high in triumph. Then he brought his hand down close to his face and peered at his quarry with his striking green eyes. "Blue glass? How in the world did you manage to get a sliver of blue glass in your hand?"

For Sophie, the question wasn't so much how it happened as why she didn't glow like a stained glass window after twenty-seven years of shattering delicate valuables with her clumsiness. She simply shrugged innocently at Graham. "Haven't the foggiest. But thank you. That has bothered me greatly."

He bowed his head facetiously. "All in a day's good works." Then he moved away from the fire, where he had towed her to get the benefit of better light.

They were in the front parlor of a rented house on Primrose Street, near the fashionable district of Mayfair but not quite in it. Sophie had no choice in the house, but she would have liked it well enough had her chaperone, Lady Tessa, not been in residence.

Not that the snide and insulting Tessa spent much time properly chaperoning Sophie—thank Heaven!— for she became easily bored and turned to her lovers for attention for weeks at a time.

Tessa believed that Sophie had come to London to find a husband—more precisely, to compete with her prettier cousins for the few unwed dukes in Society and win the Pickering fortune—so it might have a subtle form of strategy to abandon Sophie to a solitary life without benefit of a chaperone to accompany her to the many events and balls she had every right to attend.

What Tessa didn't know—nor did anyone else—was that Sophie had never intended to make a play for the fortune, nor even, in truth, to look for a man to make her own. This opportunity to escape the drudgery of her life in Acton had been seized and perpetrated almost before Sophie herself had been aware of what she was doing.

When the letter from Tessa had arrived, announcing the plan to take all three cousins to London to try their hand at winning the Pickering pounds, Sophie had packed within the hour and left within the day—without a word to anyone.

Here in London without permission or purpose, free for the first time in her life to please herself and not merely be the unappreciated handmaiden of a fretful and demanding woman who held her in no particular regard, Sophie told no one her true mission.

Sophie wanted to have fun. Unsurprisingly, Sophie's fun was not everyone's cup of tea, but she relished being free at last to pursue her own interests and her own pleasures—to read for hours, uninterrupted! Heaven!—and to speak to new and interesting people.

To be truthful, she wasn't very accomplished at that yet, but she had every intention of improving, someday, when there was nothing breakable in sight—and to see something of the world before she must return to a life of dreary servitude. Tessa's petty vengeance suited Sophie perfectly well.

When Sophie's cousins, Phoebe and Deirdre, had yet been unmarried, the three of them had spent many enjoyable hours avoiding Tessa's poisonous company, but now with her cousins away from London with their new husbands, Sophie had no one.

Except Graham.

Of course, Graham had his own house in London, or at least, his father, the Duke of Edencourt, did. It was surely much larger and grander than this simple house. Yet Graham avoided his home as much as possible. The stories Graham told of his three elder brothers made Sophie much happier about her own lack of siblings.

And the time that Graham spent with her made her much happier about her chosen solitude. He never made her feel odd about her extreme height—for his own quite surpassed hers—nor did he twit her about her lack of fashion or her penchant for scholarly pursuits. At least, he did so only in a fond and lazy way that made her feel as though he actually approved.

He was very intelligent himself, though he rarely exerted himself to show it, and his breezy insouciance was a welcome antidote to her own more thoughtful bent.

He was also extremely enjoyable to look at. He was tall and lean, but solid with muscle and more than enough shoulder to fill out his dandy's coat most appealingly. His fair hair curled back from a high brow, and sea green eyes gleamed over sculpted cheekbones and jaw. Most decorative indeed.

Sophie only wished she could return the favor. She was too aware of her not-quite-blond ginger hair and her spectacles and the nose that Tessa had pronounced "the Pickering Curse," with a decided bump where no bump should be.

She watched Graham as he stood brushing industriously at his trouser knees. As well he should, for Lady Tessa was not inclined to treat her servants well, either in manner or in pay, and therefore was picked up after accordingly. Sophie had given up on trying to keep tidy any but her own chamber and this parlor—where she spent these precious rare hours with Graham.

In any case, those he could spare from his busy calendar of gaming, carousing, wenching and generally living up to his reputation as the layabout youngest son of the Duke of Edencourt. As Graham himself said, with three elder brothers to stand between him and the title, such activities were practically his required duty to perform!

"After all, someone has to wear the wool of the black sheep." He'd sighed melodramatically, then grinned. "And I look very fine in black."

Now Sophie, still seated on the carpet with her outrageously and unfairly long legs tucked beneath her, rubbed absently at the sore spot on her palm and gazed up at the most intelligent, difficult, contradictory man she had ever had the pleasure to know.

Not that she'd known many men at all. Until she'd come to London, she'd managed to go years without speaking to anyone but the mistress and all-female servants at Acton Manor.

She'd come to be fairly comfortable with the two men the other cousins had married. At least she didn't break things when they were in the room. Yet it wasn't until she'd met Graham that she'd ever really come to know a man at all.

It was Graham himself who'd set her at ease. "I am not in the market for a wife—ever!" he'd told her. "Furthermore, I, handsome bloke that I am, am entirely out of your reach. So you see, we might as well be friends, for there isn't a chance in hell that we will ever be anything else."

Comforted by that, and won over by a mind that finally equaled her own, Sophie was quite satisfied with the friendship.

Mostly.

Graham was great company—when he remembered to call at all. He was too handsome for his own good with that chiseled jaw and, most detrimental to his character, a rakish smile that made any woman he met forgive him for everything. In advance.

It seemed she was no different. At the moment, he'd not made a move to return to his previous seat on the sofa. Sophie knew the signs.

He was becoming restless. It was always so. He'd tire of the games and petty machinations of Society and he'd seek her out. She'd watch the tension ease from his shoulders and his smile go from smooth to sincere.

Then would follow golden glowing evenings of conversation and cards—he cheated, but then, so did she, only better—and scandalous gossip—his, not hers, for she didn't know any, except about Lady Tessa, who was Graham's cousin so it wouldn't do to repeat it.

Then, usually just when she'd begun to hope it wouldn't happen again, he'd become twitchy with the need for action and diversion. Of course, she made no sign that she was sorry to see him go. The slightest hint that she was becoming too attached would send him fleeing, possibly forever.

And she wasn't attached. Not seriously, anyway. How could she be, when he was so very far out of her reach? Who was she but a woman here on false pretenses? When she'd left Acton in the middle of the night, without a word, taking the money Lady Tessa had sent according to the Pickering will, the only thing she was sure of was that she would die if she stayed any longer.

She was no one, a woman too unattractive to marry,

too unskilled to work. Only an idiot would allow herself to become too fond of a man she could never have.

Sophie was no idiot. Plain, poor "Sophie the Stick" knew that this time in London was stolen magic, that dreams ended on waking and that some girls had better learn never to dream at all.

So she sent Graham a glare of friendly contempt. "You're off to that slavering mistress of yours again, aren't you?" *Very good. It sounded as if you couldn't care less.*

He slanted her a reproving look as he tugged his weskit smooth. "You ought not to speak of such things. Furthermore, Lady Lilah Christie hardly drools at all—and then only in private."

Sophie narrowed her eyes. Lady Lilah Christie, social she-wolf, reportedly avid student of all things erotic and sensual, stunning beauty and recent widow, had been married to the only man in London rich enough to support her and enslaved enough to turn a blind eye to her extramarital adventures.

He could not have been actually ignorant of them, for Lilah's every move—and now Graham's as well, as her current paramour—was observed and ruthlessly masticated in print by the daily scribblings of that omnipresent tale-bearer, the Voice of Society.

Every night Sophie swore to herself that she would ignore the gossip sheet and every day she rushed to get her hands on it before it disappeared on Tessa's afternoon breakfast tray.

It was tawdry and inconsequential and beneath

her . . . but it was the only way for her to take part in the life Graham led outside the walls of this house.

Oh, she could attend all the same balls and events herself—for as the cousin of the new Marchioness of Brookhaven she would certainly be tolerated—and she sometimes did when forced to by Tessa's belated and half-hearted sense of duty to her charge.

Yet as the properly virginal lady appearing in her first (and last! God, how was she to ever go back to Acton now?) Season in London Society, Sophie was not privy to the other side of city life. It seemed there was another world, the world of gaming hells and sultry mistresses and whatever else it was that Graham did all the hours he was not with her.

So she waited for him to tire of the fast-paced underbelly and kept the parlor as inviting as possible. When allowed, she treasured these evenings when Graham would sprawl in the chair before the fire and tease her and make her laugh with outrageous stories of his hairy-chested brothers and their obsession with hunting, or play the pianoforte with absent-minded skill, ignorant of the way her heart soared on the music.

He smoked the tobacco she purchased with money she'd intended for more books and drank the brandy that she'd stolen from her cousin Deirdre's house while Deirdre and the Marquis of Brookhaven were on their honeymoon.

If someone had remarked upon the impropriety of a young lady spending such long hours unchaperoned with the likes of the notorious Lord Graham Cavendish, Sophie would have tartly retorted—if the speaker were female, of course; if it were a man, she would probably freeze in terror, then spasmodically break something!— that Graham, being Lady Tessa's own cousin, was practically family. Therefore such a thought was ridiculous and the thinker ought to be ashamed, etc.

It was a well-rehearsed speech and went on at length, but since no one in the world gave a fig about the virtue of one tall, plain girl with no expectations other than scholarly spinsterhood, Sophie had never had the opportunity to use it.

After all, she had no real future to lose and Graham, who took nothing and no one seriously, including Lilah, thank the gods, risked nothing by it either. Their clandestine friendship harmed no one and benefited them both greatly.

For one brief Season Sophie was determined to do precisely as she pleased—and she pleased to explore museums and libraries and play with Graham.

Matters might be different if she were serious in her search for a husband or if Graham would ever wish to marry and have an heir.

Fortunately, there was no reason why he should when his brothers intended to procreate often and well, as soon as they had slain one last elephant, bagged one final rhinoceros, taken down one more tiger—well, anyway, there was simply no reason why things could not go on forever precisely as they were.

AFTER LEAVING SOPHIE to her early bedtime in the house on Primrose Street, Lord Graham Cavendish strode whistling into Eden House, the London home of the Duke of Edencourt.

The Edencourt name was old and venerable and its estate vast and once beautiful, but the past few generations had failed to hold up their end of good taste and self-restraint. Now the name of Edencourt was equated with loud, boorish behavior and a predisposition for dying at the hands of liquor or firearms—sometimes both.

The house itself never changed, unless it was to gain a few more unfortunate trophies on its already cluttered walls, so Graham had long since stopped noticing the shabby conditions and the furnishings that had been elegant generations ago but now suffered mightily from the rough usage of its current residents.

The marble floors were scuffed beyond polishing and the dark wood panels and trim were gouged by things thrown or dragged against their damaged finish. The carpets were worn thin by heavy boots and the sofas were sprung by years of supporting great lounging louts who rarely bothered to sit up straight.

Graham, blinded by years of familiarity, merely came and went from the house and tried not to run into his brothers. Tonight, if he changed quickly enough, he could be at the tables within an hour. Still, as was his habit, he stopped in the entrance hall and listened for a long moment.

He heard no roaring laughter. He smelled no foul clouds of tobacco. He felt no thudding of wrestling bodies breaking the remaining furnishings into kindling.

No, the house was entirely empty except for the

skeletal staff of servants still employed. Ah yes, his family was still far, far away.

Thank God.

His father's butler came to take Graham's hat and gloves. Graham grinned at him. "The chest beaters are still absent, eh, Nichols?"

After forty years of service, Nichols was the duke's man, always and forever. His usual haughty expression soured further at Graham's impious words.

"Good evening, Lord Graham. His Grace and your elder brothers have not sent word as to their return from their hunt in Africa. However, there is a Mr. Abbott awaiting you in His Grace's study."

Graham blinked. "For me? Whatever for?"

"Indeed, my lord." Nichols looked as though he could not begin to imagine why anyone would want to speak to Graham. Ever. Graham didn't blame him for it, for the servant was only aping the attitude of the master. His own father hadn't said more than a dozen words to him this year.

Graham reluctantly made his way to his father's magnificently masculine study. It was a dismal place at any time, for every wall housed a menagerie of glassy-eyed, stuffed and mounted death.

During the day the room was depressing. At night Graham harkened back to his boyhood, when nothing but the threat of his father's heavy hand could make him step foot into the darkened, fire-lit hall of gleaming, vengeful gazes reflecting the flames of the hatred he'd imagined in their eyes.

Even now, a man grown, he hesitated outside the

door, then took a deep breath and pushed it open, smiling at the young, rather exhausted-looking man waiting within. After all, the duke was not there. There was no need to brace himself.

He couldn't have been more wrong.

Chapter Two

The tale went thusly—

On the edge of the veldt, on the dark continent of Africa, man was a soft, fragile creature out of place in a harsh, wild environment. Intelligent men moved carefully and usually lived. Stupid men, on the other hand, tended to die. Badly.

In a hunting camp in the African country of Kenya, a sun-darkened physician pushed open the canvas flap of the largest tent and stepped wearily into the circle of light created by a large central fire and several standing torches.

Three burly Englishmen awaited him outside. "How is the duke?" "Will he live?" "Bloody hell, man, speak up!"

The doctor sighed as he straightened. "I fear that the injuries His Grace suffered during the trampling by the bull elephant were too serious. He is no more."

After a moment of stunned silence—and it was a long moment, for the three eldest sons of the Duke of Edencourt were not the quickest of men—one of the younger ones looked to the eldest, awe in his face. "You're the duke now."

The eldest, but alas, least intelligent of the brothers drew slowly to his greatest height. "I am the duke now. I'll take on the estate and the title—but not until I've avenged my father and destroyed that killer elephant!" He raised his fist into the air. "That bull elephant must die!"

The second eldest brother, only slightly less thick-headed and nearly as drunk, nodded emphatically. "A battle to the death!"

The Kenyan guide, an experienced man of the savannah, moved to divert catastrophe. "Your Grace, my lords, this elephant is very dangerous. We should flee his territory and take your father's body back—"

"*Flee?*" The third brother, who had until now been fostering the glimmerings of a similar thought, raised his hackles at such cowardly phrasing. "By God, man, the sons of Edencourt flee nothing!" He joined his brothers, raising his rifle high. "To the death it is!"

Alas, and so it was.

BACK IN THE grim death-decorated study of the late Duke of Edencourt, his youngest son fancied that the eyes that surrounded him and the young, round-faced solicitor took on a feral gleam of satisfaction.

"All of them?" Graham leaned back in his chair— his father's chair, had he but noticed—and ran one hand weakly over his face. "But of course. They were indivisible to the end. Good God. Death by self-inflicted stupidity."

The man, Mr. Abbott, nodded. "Just so. The guide

tried to save them but only he and two of his men escaped with their lives."

"There was nothing he could have done." Graham waved his hand. "He couldn't have stopped them. No one ever has." He shook his head, still too shocked to feel anything like grief. At least, he hoped that was the case.

He'd never felt close to his father or brothers, for they were another breed of men entirely from him. Alternately ganged up on or ignored when he was young, he'd learned over time that the best way to deal with his family was to avoid them as much as possible.

When he'd gained something of reputation as a lady-killer in adulthood, he'd been offered a grudging sort of respect, for the chest beaters ever relished a hunt, any hunt. Still, the truce was always wary and short-lived on either side.

"Your Grace, I must inform you—"

Graham's world stopped abruptly, then began to spin again with a nauseating new tilt to its axis.

Your Grace.

He swallowed, but his throat was too dry. Reeling, he staggered to his feet and stumbled across the room where his father's—no, now his!—whiskey decanter glimmered like amber salvation.

Graham tossed back one for the dry throat and another one to take away the taste of the first one. He poured yet another, just to look at. Then he turned back to Abbott.

"I'm the Duke of Edencourt."

Abbott nodded. "Yes, Your Grace, you are."

Graham moved to reseat himself in his father's chair, then recoiled and found himself one with less weighty history. "I'm the Duke of Edencourt," he informed his glass of whiskey. Oh, hell, it was already empty.

Abbott took it away. "Your Grace—"

"Oy! I was drinking that!"

Abbott threw it across the room, where it shattered in the fireplace. Graham blinked, realizing for the first time that Abbott wasn't just weary. The man was tight-lipped with fury and disgust!

"Your Grace, my family has served yours as solicitors and men of business for five generations. Your grandfather never managed to pay us on time or completely, and your father never paid us at all. The advice I am about to offer you is the first and last you'll ever get from an Abbott, so listen closely."

Graham drew back, eyes focusing at last. "I'm listening."

Abbott straightened, his eyes snapping in his mild face. "Waste no time in assuming your responsibilities. Your estate is in ruins and your lands lie fallow. Your people are suffering and your debt is overwhelming. For God's sake, man, if there is not a great influx of cash to Edencourt as soon as possible, there won't be anything left to save! The only recourse left to you is to find a rich wife and find her quickly, before it is too late. There is less than a month left of the Season. I suggest you charm her quickly and well."

With that, Abbott turned on his heel and strode from the study and from Eden House. Graham watched him, dimly aware through his reverberating shock that with

Abbott went any hope he had of getting help with the vast and ailing estate of Edencourt.

Which he had never bothered to learn a single thing about.

He closed his eyes and rested his forehead against the cool glass of the window. "I'm so thoroughly buggered."

HOW COULD EDEN House, already empty, now seem emptier? Graham strolled the halls restlessly in the dark. Room after room, grandly shabby, had an eerie echo of desertion never noticed before. Had the mere expectation of its owner's return populated the rooms with life? Or had Graham's own distaste for his family kept him from feeling alone? Better alone than with them?

He was certainly alone now. The emptiness of the house, his house now, was merely a manifestation of the emptiness of his entire life. A man didn't become a duke every day. Yet here he was, promoted beyond the bounds of his wildest dreams, had he ever bothered to dream at all, and there was no one to tell.

Except Sophie, of course. The thought comforted him. Sophie would listen to the awful story of his father's and brothers' end and she would see the ludicrous waste of it. Sophie would say something tart and sensible and it would be just the thing he'd been thinking at that moment. As always, he would instantly feel less alone. However, she was the only one. An entire life spent in play and only one good playfellow to show for it.

He paused in his mother's room, a gracious chamber that had been spared the hard usage of a house full of men. The silk bed hangings were a deep rose beneath the dust, and the furniture was dainty and elegant, though Graham remembered that it had also belonged to his grandmother in her day.

Upon the dressing table was a box, an inlaid case that held a lady's small, daily jewelry. Graham doubted his mother had owned any other kind, for the coffers had been depleted years before she'd married into the Cavendish clan. He flipped open the lid with one finger, but the case was empty. Someone had emptied it of valuables long ago, he imagined. Just what his mother would have wanted, her little treasures pawned for more adventures in fatality.

It was a very nice room, but it was just a room. Once this room had meant something to him, as it had even to his father, he imagined, for though his father had never spoken of her, the duke had never married again either. That might have been because he already had his heir along with several spares, or it might have been something deeper. Graham would have liked to believe that his father had been capable of something deeper, once upon a time.

He snorted. Probably not. His father had been precisely what he'd seemed, aggressive and coarse.

Turning to go, he grazed the edge of the little dressing table with his hip. Being rather more elderly than stable, it teetered. Graham caught it with a quick motion, but the jewel case slipped off and fell to the floor. God, he was as bad as Sophie!

He bent to sweep up the case. It had cracked along one corner, the joined wood parting in a thick dark crevice. Graham frowned as he gazed at it. It wasn't of value to him particularly, but he hated to throw it out.

Then he saw a gleam of metal through the crack. Tilting the case, he shook it, but nothing fell. Looking more closely, he tugged at the ancient velvet lining in that corner, pulling it away to see that it had come unstuck long ago. Beneath it lay a ring of gold.

It wasn't an especially impressive ring. The stone was diamond but not overlarge, and the simple band and setting showed no particular finesse. For all that, it was very pretty. Merely a simple, unpretentious ring, the sort a lady might enjoy wearing simply because she liked it.

Graham barely remembered his mother. She was a whiff of perfume in his mind, a softer voice amid the manly roaring. Even so, he doubted his mother would have wished him to use this bauble for a betrothal ring. It wasn't nearly ostentatious enough to offer to a girl he hoped to make a duchess.

Still, he slipped it into his pocket. After all, he needed both a girl and a ring, didn't he? Perhaps the trick was to find a girl who would fit the ring he already had, not the other way around.

THERE WAS SELDOM a criminal disturbance on the sedate street where was situated the esteemed—even though no one of true importance had thought of them in years—firm of Sticklcy & Wolfe, Solicitors. The office itself was on an upper floor, above a glover's at street level and a servant-placement agency on the next. Wide windows looked down upon the street, but the noise, even during the day, rarely ascended so high.

If someone had strolled the street below late that night—for one could with little danger, even so deep in the night—they might have glanced up at just the right moment to see the flicker of candlelight where none should be.

Fortunately for the intruder in the offices above, there was no one on the street.

The tall, once-handsome, now dissipated-looking man standing in the silent office of Stickley & Wolfe, Solicitors, might not have seemed as though he belonged there. After all, he wore dark, common clothing and the secretive air of a thief. Of course, the impression wouldn't be helped by the fact that it was the middle of the night.

In point of fact, he had every right to be there. Wolfe wasn't much of a solicitor—in school he'd cheated more than studied and bribed his way more often than either, in addition to holding a tasty spot of blackmail over the dean —but what did his lack of competence matter when he and his very capable partner only had one client?

His partner, Stickley, wasn't someone he would have chosen himself, but their fathers had been partners before them and besides, Stickley was a genius at nurturing and growing the single trust left in their hands. Under Stickley's paternal supervision, the fifteen thousand pounds originally left by Sir Hamish Pickering had grown to nearly thirty thousand.

Some of which Wolfe would like to get his hands on. Now.

The safe wasn't hidden, for it was a great iron box large enough to hold every one of those thirty thousand pounds—at least, Wolfe assumed it did. He didn't bother his head with petty little details of the actual money. That was Stickley's job.

It was also Stickley's job to parcel out Wolfe's retainer in equal portions on a monthly basis. This month, the gold had lasted only three days. He'd then coaxed a bit extra out of Stickley, whose prim mouth had pursed at such irresponsibility, but that had only lasted another week.

Now he was down far more than that. He owed people, dangerous people—the sort of people who ran dark, dirty betting establishments full of dark, dirty customers. The thought of his fate if he didn't repay them spurred him to lift the tools he brought to bash the safe into submission instead of using the numerical combination.

He caught himself after a moment of disappointing exertion, for banging on the safe would do no good. He wasn't prepared to stage a robbery just yet. Right now all he wanted was enough to placate his debtors until he could get the rest of the money out of Stickley.

The trouble was, he couldn't remember the combination. He thought it had something to do with his father's birthday, which he couldn't remember either. He tentatively spun the dial for a few moments, but nothing came to mind but the memory of his father's disappointed eyes.

Leaving the safe itself for a moment, he went to his own desk, which faced Stickley's as if they actually worked together, and threw himself down onto his large richly padded chair. Tossing the tools down at his feet, he rubbed his face hard.

He'd given up drink for the moment, all the better to stay one step ahead of his pursuers, but his head pounded and he felt shaky and ill. He wanted nothing more than a fistful of whiskey or six, but he didn't dare. Nightmares of waking up dead haunted him.

Idly, he began to search his desk. There wasn't much in there but dried-up inkwells and quills left over from his father's time, although he did find a penny stuck in the back of a drawer. Tucking it into his waistcoat pocket, he then poised his elbows on the desk and stared across at Stickley's empty chair.

How he hated Stickley. From boyhood they'd been thrown together, expectations heavy on their shoulders. Stickley, adroit sycophant that he was, had studied hard and well. Wolfe had chafed at being forced into a profession, for wasn't there money enough to live a gentleman's life?

The Pickering trust—a great wad of money left by an uneducated Scotsman who'd overstepped himself, meant for some title-grubbing female descendant. Had there ever been a bigger waste of beautiful piles of gold in the history of mankind? Wolfe's fingers tingled with greed.

He rose and walked slowly over to Stickley's side of the great double desk. Stickley was annoying and fussy, but he was no fool. He wouldn't leave the safe combination lying about in his desk, would he?

What the hell? It wasn't as though Wolfe had anywhere else to be. His rooms were being watched, he was sure. Besides, he hadn't paid his landlord in weeks. He wasn't even sure his things weren't tossed in the street at this very moment.

So, out of idle curiosity, he pulled open the top drawer of Stickley's desk.

Precise piles of foolscap were divided by neat lines of pencils and rows of fresh ink bottles. Sickening.

The next drawer held stacks of stationery and envelopes—as if Stickley had anyone to write to!

The third and last drawer held one leather folder tied with cord. Interesting.

Wolfe pulled the folder out and seated himself in Stickley's chair. He wasn't much of a reader, but he knew Stickley's writing as well as his own.

Well, well. Another will. This time it was Stickley's will. There was a long list of scholarly groups that were to receive this piece or that piece of Stickley's collection—none of which sounded very interesting or valuable to Wolfe—but at the end, he read something that made him straighten off the base of his spine in surprise.

Stickley had left everything else—including a sizable pile of savings *and* all future shares of the Pickering retainer—to his father's partner's son. Wolfe. The man who'd tortured his boyhood and made his adulthood as miserable as possible.

"It is what my father would have expected of me."

Wolfe blinked in surprise for several long moments. Then a slow smile grew upon his handsome, haggard face. Stickley had left it all to him.

What an idiot!

When Stickley came in a few hours later, brisk and prim as only a virtuously early riser could be, he found Wolfe seated motionless on the proper side of the great desk, his elbows braced on the blotter, his chin resting on his folded hands.

"Heavens, you're up early!"

Wolfe only smiled. "Early. Yes."

Stickley blinked away his surprise and crossed to his own side of the desk, where he neatly stored away the case he carried to and from work every day. Wolfe idly wondered what sort of work Stickley needed to take home every night, when they only had the one account to worry over. Come to think of it, what did Stickley do during his properly structured work day?

Bored simply thinking about it, Wolfe didn't bother to ask.

"I've been wondering if I ought to send a message round to your rooms," Stickley said. "We received some wonderful news the other day. The Duke of Brookmoor is up and about! Isn't that marvelous? Why, he might go on for years yet. We'll have time to grow the account to a superior size now, won't we?"

Wolfe, who kept his ears close to mouths that tended toward gossip anyway, had already heard that the present Marquis of Brookhaven had gone to visit his uncle,

Brookmoor. He'd also heard that Brookmoor had turned to a new physician and had seemingly achieved a miraculous recovery. Therefore a certain upstart heiress wouldn't be spending her gold any time soon.

Wolfe didn't believe in miracles. One got what one wanted by taking it.

He leaned back in his chair, letting it creak as he relaxed into the tufted leather. "Stick, old boy . . . did you change the combination to the safe?"

Stickley nodded, eyes bright. "Oh, yes. Years ago. We had that assistant for a time, remember? Useless lad. After he drank your whiskey and made sick on my desk, I fired him. Then I changed the combination, just to be on the safe side."

Wolfe didn't remember the assistant, although he did remember making sick on Stickley's precisely arranged desk. Good day, that. He gazed down at his folded hands. "Don't you think I need to know the new combination?"

Stickley blinked. "Whyever for? I can always open it for you."

Wolfe raised his lidded gaze at last. "What if something happens to you, old friend? What if you step in front of a speeding cart? What if a street thief cuts your throat on your way into work one morning?" *What if I beat you to a pulp with your own blasted case?*

Stickley drew back at the flat stare emanating from Wolfe's eyes. "I . . . I made sure that you'd be given everything you need to run the firm, should something like that happen." He swallowed. "In my will. Would you . . . would you care to see it?"

Wolfe smiled then, a charming show of teeth that had disarmed many a man about to strike and many a woman about to call for help. "Don't be silly, Stick, old son. I don't need to see it. I trust you implicitly."

After all, he knew everything he needed to know.

Chapter Three

Late summer days in London looked much like any other day in London. Rain was wont to fall at any time, carrying with it a load of the soot that hung perpetually in the skies. Damp chill turned more to damp rot in the summer months, and by now it seemed that the smell of the sewers would never be erased from one's nostrils.

Still, flowers bloomed brightly in green gardens and birds chirped merrily in the trees carefully nurtured around the finer houses. Pretty girls in vivid bonnets strolled arm in arm with dandies, maids and footmen trailing behind, encumbered with parcels.

Even in this less than fashionable neighborhood just past the edge of Mayfair, the denizens of Primrose Street had sought to earn the name. Tending more toward window boxes than full gardens, the terraced houses still wore as many flowers as could decently be crammed in. It was rather shabbily charming if one bothered to notice.

Standing outside Lady Tessa's rented house at the ungodly early hour of noon, Graham could have cared less for flowers or bloody birds or even pretty girls. He hadn't slept all night, instead forcing himself to try to read through the piles of papers that Abbot had left behind.

Graham wasn't a stupid man, he knew that, but he felt like one this morning. How could he possibly inhale a lifetime of information and training in time to save Edencourt?

And do you even want to? Wouldn't it be easier just to let it lie?

His father had apparently thought so. Graham himself had been inclined to take after his father for the first time in his life—until he read about the conditions in which the few remaining cottagers lived.

His cottagers. His people.

Which was ridiculous, when one thought about it. What sort of idiot system of inheritance would leave *him* in charge of actual people? He'd never even kept a pet!

Yet the weight of his responsibility, once engaged, would not rest. He had stuffed as much information into his mind as it could handle at the moment, then he'd left Eden House and walked restlessly through Mayfair to this familiar address.

All he could think was that Sophie would know what to do. Which was more idiocy, of course. Sophie was a gently-reared young lady from a little manor house in the country. She was intelligent, that was true, but scholarly translations would not help him now.

Still, Sophie was the only person in London who actually gave a damn about him. This would change, he knew. Once his title was announced he'd be besieged by a sudden influx of "friends." Not as many as if he were rich, but enough to be very annoying.

Until then, he wanted one more day of being just Lord Graham Cavendish, younger son, a man of charm and leisure and little account. As he climbed the steps to the rented house, he didn't think to ask himself why he wanted to spend that last day with no one but Miss Sophie Blake.

Graham entered the music room. "Sophie?"

Her papers were everywhere, spread out in some chaotic version of order that only Sophie understood— and beware the person who moved a single sheet!

No Sophie. He was about to look elsewhere when he spotted one of her slippers on the floor next to the window embrasure. Then he saw the stocking-clad toes dangling just past the curtain. His lips twisted wearily. "Got you."

When he came closer, he realized that she wasn't hiding. She was asleep, shoes off, paper-covered knees curled up, spectacles awry and all. Graham's grim smile softened. Poor lass. She was working too hard on her blasted translations—and Tessa was likely making her life miserable, something that Tessa excelled at.

Carefully, Graham cleared the translations from Sophie's lap and set them aside—keeping them in precisely the same order, of course. Then, with gentle fingers, he removed the spectacles from her nose and from behind her ears.

Without the wire and glass, her familiar bony features seemed rather vulnerable and unknown. She was a true case, this one. Just look at her! Endless legs curled awkwardly beneath her like a newborn colt, ink-stained fingers and bitten nails, hair tumbling loose—

Her hair had given up the fight against pins and gravity and fallen to her bosom in a heavy twisted rope. Curious, Graham reached to ease the twist. Abruptly he found his hands full of amazing silken red-gold. The sensation of her warm hair in his fingers sent an unexpected jolt to his neglected male senses.

His eyelids slid nearly closed in drowsy sensuous pleasure. He let the rope of hair roll over his fist, winding the length until his hand rested just beside her chin. At the faint warmth from his fingers on her skin, she rolled her head until her cheek rested on his wrist and palm. A soft, sleepy sigh left her lips, wafting across the sensitive skin of his inner wrist.

In the warm, enclosed space behind the curtain, he became aware of her scent as he never had before. She smelled wonderful, really. She smelled like sensible soap and sun-warmed skin and something else, something girlish and sweet, as if incorruptibility had a perfume of its own.

Her eyelashes fluttered. Graham released her hair and straightened, closing his hand against the loss of that silken splendor. When she stretched and opened her eyes, he stood a proper distance away, grinning down at her in his usual affable way.

After all, it was only Sophie. He was simply overdue for a visit with Lilah, that was all.

"Gray? What are you doing here?"

He tilted his head instead of answering. "You've never cut your hair in your life, have you?"

Startled, she reached to feel that her hair had fallen. She reddened as if she had something to be ashamed of and sat up quickly. She seemed so discomfited that Graham politely pretended to be interested in the view from the window until she'd pulled herself together. Once her ginger-spiced locks were tightly wound onto her head, however, he had the inexplicable desire to pull it all down again.

He cleared his throat. *Don't be a cad. She'd die of shock if you so much as hinted at such a thing.* His Sophie was completely unaware of the world and all its evils. He meant to keep it that way, even if he himself was one of those evils.

Now she was looking at him expectantly. That's right, she'd asked him a question, hadn't she?

Abruptly, he didn't want to tell her about his family and the title. He wanted to pretend that nothing had changed, just for a few moments more. He'd been so very comfortable with Sophie just the way things were.

So instead of answering her—again—he reached for the first of the pages that rested on her lap. He blinked at the flowing, lovely script there. Had he expected something tight, cramped . . . repressed?

Before he had a chance to actually read what was written there in German, she'd snatched it back. "Don't look at that. It's only notes." She glared up at him. "I don't like my translations disordered. You'd know that if you ever did anything with your mind other than waste it."

She was fussing at him now. He smiled, comforted by the familiar testiness of her tone. Most people were charmed so effortlessly by his manner that he'd lost all faith in the world's acuity. Only Sophie bothered to look closely enough to be accurately displeased.

He smiled at her fondly, so happy to be "Gray, the useless layabout" again that he quite forgot to mask his grin with the usual layer of irony.

She blinked in surprise, her eyes widening in wonder. Graham recovered quickly. He plunked himself next to her on the window seat, intentionally crowding her papers until she fussed further, safely distracted from his aberrant sincerity.

"Go on, Sophie. What are you working on? Tell me a story."

She flicked him a suspicious glance while she rustled up her straying notes. "Are you serious or are you going to make fun?"

He leaned his head back against the window embrasure and closed his eyes wearily. "Lover, I'm too tired to make fun. I just want to sit here in your peaceful parlor and listen."

Sophie hated it when he called her "lover" or "darling"—hated it because her ignorant heart tended to leap a little every time. And because it came too easily to him. A multitude of women had probably been called so by Lord Graham Cavendish—either playfully on the ballroom floor or playfully in the bedchamber.

She hated being one of the multitude.

Yet there was something different about Graham today. He was truly weary, and not in a "had too much to drink and stayed up all night seducing" sort of way. Sick and weary, as if his mind was too worried to rest.

Which was ridiculous, because Graham worried about nothing. Worrying implied caring.

Nonetheless, he was here and he wanted to know what she was working on. She shuffled her papers one last time. "I haven't finished yet . . . but I think it's my favorite folktale to date."

He murmured something encouraging, so she took a breath and began to read to him. He listened silently, but she felt the tension easing from him with every breath.

"*. . . and the rich man took a second wife, who brought along her two daughters. They had beautiful and fair features but nasty and wicked hearts . . .*"

He snorted. She looked up. "What is so amusing?"

He didn't open his eyes. "Why, in your fairy stories, are the beautiful girls always cruel?"

Sophie grimaced slightly. "Oh, that part is the simple truth."

He opened his eyes. "Deirdre is beautiful, but she's very sweet."

Sophie shrugged. Her cousin Deirdre was a blond beauty of the goddess variety, statuesque without being overly tall and well versed in Society's little nuances by Tessa's sometimes cruel tutelage.

She was also willful, seditious and more than a little outrageous. Only a man as strong and self-assured as Lord Brookhaven could ever have tamed headstrong Deirdre. Sophie had become fond of Deirdre eventually, for her cousin's heart was as warm as it was determined, but Dee wasn't precisely "sweet." Sophie certainly wasn't going to argue about it, however. "Deirdre is merely the exception that proves the rule," she said primly.

He rolled his eyes. "I hate it when people say that. What does it mean? Either something is a rule or it isn't—exceptions don't prove anything."

Sophie opened her mouth to cast some aspersion on his reasoning ability, but then stopped. "I—I never considered that before."

Having won his point, he then graciously demurred. "Then again, Tessa proves the rule enough for anyone."

They both snickered at that. Tessa, being of venomous personality by sheer will and selfishness, was easy but satisfying game. As lovely as Deirdre but well-known for her spite, Tessa provided endless opportunity for derision simply by being herself.

Sophie found it doubly tempting to tell Graham of Tessa's latest sexual exploits, but refrained. Tessa was rather disgusting, but she was also the only chaperone Sophie had. Without her, Sophie would be expected to return to Acton forthwith—and that could not be allowed.

Sophie changed the subject. "There are many truths to be found in these stories. I have learned a great deal about life in general."

He uttered a disbelieving laugh at that. "Truths? They're entertaining, to be sure, and it is reassuring to hear that the virtuous usually win the day, but they are nothing like real life."

But I want the virtuous to win the day.

No, Graham was right. Sophie put down her papers. "I am not so naive as that, Gray," she said sternly. "I know perfectly well that the Tessas and the Lilahs will usually triumph." Damn the Lilahs anyway. "But that point doesn't detract from my conviction that they ought not to."

She expected him to laugh that argument off, as he usually might. Instead, he seemed to grow almost angry.

"Sophie, nothing really turns out the way we expect." He stood, suddenly too agitated to sit. "You ought to expect nothing, from anyone!"

Even you?

Especially not from him. Ah, but she knew that already, didn't she? Dented a bit by the reminder, she stiffened. "I see no reason to allow the grimness of the real world to interfere with a desire to make things as they should be."

Graham was returned to the moment by the husky hurt in her voice. Damn it, he'd gotten lost in his own predicament there for a moment.

Tell her. She'll understand.

Telling Sophie would make it real. He didn't want to make it real, not quite yet.

Desperation welled up in him—the need to escape like a surging tide. He retreated into old habits.

"That's because I live in the real world and you live in your mind, Sophie."

"I hardly think there is more than one world, Graham. I particularly find it hard to believe that a world of gambling and overindulgence could be classified as the 'real' world."

He waved a hand. "I'm not talking about those. Those are only how I pass the time."

Until when? she wanted to ask, but he went on.

"I'm talking about the physical world. You spend all

your time in this house, or in some bookshop, and you never notice what is right in front of you."

That was going a bit far, coming from Graham! She folded her arms and glared. "What am I missing? The bad London air? The stench of horse manure in the streets?"

"Yes, London can be a filthy pit sometimes." Then he tilted his head as he gazed at her. "Yet . . . tell me, Sophie, what did you do in Acton? The air is good there, is it not?"

She'd spent all her time in the house, with her nose in her books, at least when her duties had allowed it. If she'd ventured out, she might have encountered someone of the male species. The need to converse might have arisen and then chaos would have ensued.

Still, there was no need to admit that to Graham. She lifted her chin. "I was the toast of the village. I had no end of callers."

He smiled fondly. "Liar." Then he leaned closer, his nearness and his urgency taking her breath away. "Sophie, there's so much more to life! There's beauty and passion and fire!"

"Oh." She leaned back and gave a knowing scoff. "You're talking about overindulging in spirits and coitus, aren't you?"

His jaw dropped. "What?" Then he shook off his surprise. "Sophie, I'm talking about *living*." He gazed at her for a long moment. "You really don't understand, do you?"

Discomforted, she glanced away. "I like my life as it is." *I hate my life as it is, but what am I to do about it?*

She'd already risked everything to come to London in the first place, but the adventure had only exposed what would never be hers, in full color and graphic detail.

Graham's brows drew together in thought. "All right," he said slowly, "then close your eyes."

She drew back. "No." Then, "Why?"

He laughed softly. "Sophie, shut up and close your eyes."

Chapter Four

The room was still but for the breeze wafting through the partially open window sash. Sophie could hear wheels on the cobbles, and distant voices, but with her eyes closed, the noise blurred into the awareness of Graham near her—near but unobserved.

At that thought she opened her eyes again to see him reaching for her hand. "What are you doing?"

He sat back, clearly exasperated. "Can you not relax for a single moment?"

She scowled. "Not when I don't know what you're going to do."

"Stubborn Sophie. I can see we're going to have to start at the beginning." He pulled out his handkerchief and rolled it quickly. She drew back when he started to put it over her eyes. He challenged her movement with an I-dare-you glint in his eyes. She gave a grumpy twist to her lips but complied.

"This is silly . . . a child's game."

She could almost hear him smile. "Precisely." He took her hand—his skin seemed shockingly warm when she was in the dark—and put something in it. It was cool and hard and circular.

"It's a coin."

"Ah, but what coin?"

She ran her fingers over the relief, then weighed it in one hand. "A guinea."

He took it away and replaced it with something spherical and hard. His fingers were gentle and quick on her wrist, on her fingers. She could feel the faint horseman's calluses—

"Sophie, what is in your hand?"

Brought back to the moment, Sophie cleared her throat. "Oh . . . an apple." She took a bite, then grinned. "Most of an apple."

He took it from her. She heard the crisp sound of his teeth biting into it—did his lips touch where hers had? When he put something else into her hand, she let it sit in her lax fingers for a moment, half-hoping he would close her fingers about it for her. When he did, she savored the touch, then scolded herself for such thoughts. Really, it was a silly game!

Then she realized that she could not tell what she held, not even when she used both hands, running her fingers over it again and again. "A . . . stick?" It was smooth but hard and branched twice. "Some sort of carving?"

"Hah," he said, so close that his breath puffed on her cheek. "Sophie doesn't know everything."

She grimaced. "Neither does Graham." Yet she couldn't help rising to the bait. She concentrated, running her fingertips over the pointed tips of the thing—not sharp, not really. She brought it to her cheek and ran it over her skin. "Polished . . ." She realized that it had warmed in her hand, the way wood might. It was lighter though, like . . . "Bone?"

He chuckled. She felt it all the way through her body, the deep masculine sound of it shivering through her belly, making her thighs press closer beneath her skirts.

"Close," he said. "But no."

She forced herself to concentrate on the piece and not on the fact that she could now feel the heat of his body on her skin, just where he leaned close to her side, not quite touching . . .

Then she had it. "Horn!" She brandished it blindly. "It's a horn!"

He laughed aloud, though she felt him duck. "Indeed, although technically I think it's an antler." He took it from her. "I put in it my pocket last night at the house and forgot about it."

"Ah. A trophy from the mighty hunters?" She waited, for Graham never let pass an opportunity to make jest of his brothers or father.

Another object, small and circular, warm from his hand or perhaps his pocket, landed in her palm. She closed her hand over it. A ring? She absently slipped it onto her finger. It fit.

She wriggled her fingers and laughed. "How does it look?"

Silently, his warm fingers took possession of her hand and slipped the ring off. Sophie had the feeling

she'd said or done something wrong. "Is it meaningful?" She hadn't meant to make light, but then again, it
was a game. Wasn't it?

"Just something old," he said slowly. Then, "Give
me your hand again."

His touch felt different this time. Less playful,
more . . . forceful? Then he brought their hands up and
lay her palm on his face.

She drew her breath in slowly. For all their hours of
intimacy, they'd never touched more than hand to hand.
Now her hand cupped his sculpted jaw, her fingers tentative on the unshaven stubble there. The bristly texture
surprised her. She'd thought beards would be soft, like
animal fur. Then she realized that his jaw worked beneath her hand.

She pulled it away slowly. Something serious was
afoot. "Graham, are you all right?" She started to lift
the blindfold. "What is it?"

"Nothing . . . nothing at all." Graham pulled her fingers away from the blindfold and returned her hand to
his cheek and held it there. *Not yet. It is not real yet.*
Closing his own eyes, he concentrated on the feel of
Sophie's cool hand on his cheek.

Sophie lived so safely, so sheltered. So much unknown. Did she even know the difference between a
man's skin and a woman's? Had she ever felt a cool-
running stream against her bare, summer-heated skin?
That was only the innocent sensuality of childhood.
What of the satin slickness of hot skin, open lips, the
volcanic heat of flesh on flesh?

His trousers tightened at such thoughts—damn, it had

been weeks!—and without realizing it, his fingertips changed their intent from innocent demonstration to practiced seduction. His hand slid down her wrist to the sensitive inner elbow, his touch slow and purposeful.

Sophie couldn't breathe. His hands were all she could feel. One pressed her palm to his cheek, tugging slightly but implacably. She gave in instantly, eagerly, unable to do anything else. The other hand was flame on her skin, leaving trails of shimmering embers behind it as it moved higher, until the back of his hand brushed the side of her small breast.

Her lungs might not be in service but her heart was racing. She felt her skin wrapped about her as she'd never known it before. She could feel the throb of her own heartbeat in her ears, in her throat, in the pulse that fluttered beneath his exploring fingers.

Wild, furious desire swept her, making her belly tremble and her toes curl inside her slippers. Flesh tightened and throbbed and dampened in ways new and exciting—and frightening, too, for she never wanted it to end. Dreams never dared, wants never acknowledged, longings she had choked and imprisoned burst free, vengeful in their intensity. She couldn't breathe, she couldn't think—

With a flailing motion of her other hand, she pulled the blindfold off. Her eyes flew open, locking gazes with his. Her dry mouth worked to unstick her tongue. *"Please . . ."*

The shock of intensity in Sophie's eyes reverberated through Graham. *All right. Yes.*

Then . . . *What are you doing, you rotter? Why*

are you seducing this girl—to take your mind off your debt?

Oh God, he was a bounder, through and through. Too many hours closeted with her, too many evenings of freedom and casual intimacy. He drew back, shutting away his reaction to her plea, revising it, deliberately misinterpreting it. "Yes, of course. I'm stopping. My apologies."

He stood slowly, willing his near-erection to subside before he made it all the way upright. He needn't have worried, for Sophie's gaze was now locked on her hands, tightly twined in her lap.

Fool! Silly, stupid, unrealistic fool! Thank heaven he'd misunderstood her patent begging. She was obviously not as immune as she'd thought, but she hadn't realized that she would spread herself on the carpet for him at the slightest touch!

Why worry about such a thing happening? He was bored—playing a child's game. He doesn't want you.

Graham turned away, ashamed of himself and worse, reminded of what he'd been trying so hard to forget. The brief moment of respite had only made matters worse, for the totality of his situation came crashing down on him like the crumbling stones of Edencourt itself.

He rubbed both hands over his face. "Ah, Sophie. I'm sorry. I'm . . . I'm not myself today, I fear."

She cleared her throat behind him. "Why . . ." He heard her move, the rustle of her plain muslin gown moving away from him. As she should, after that display of selfishness on his part.

She continued. "Why aren't you yourself?"

He laughed shortly. "A funny thing happened after I left here last night . . ." He didn't want to say it out loud. Telling Sophie had a way of making things real—but perhaps it was time to do so. "My father is dead."

"Oh, how terrible!" Her voice warmed again, which only made him feel worse. "No wonder you're not being the Graham I know."

That made him laugh out loud, a sharp bark of near hysteria, if she knew the truth of it. "My eldest brother died with him."

Now she moved before him, putting a hand on his arm. "Oh, Graham!"

He covered his mouth with one hand, pressing back more hysteria that pressed upward. Now she was gazing at him in wary confusion. "A double tragedy," she said. "How sad."

Laughter, desperate and panicked, began to fight its way free. "There's more—!"

Sophie drew back and folded her arms, staring at him. "Gray, just spit it out."

"They're all gone." His voice, strained already from resisting the laughter, broke oddly on the word "gone." He rubbed at his face again. His hand came away wet. He inhaled deeply, alarmed by his own lack of balance.

And then Sophie was there, taking his hand in hers, leading him to a seat—nearly shoving him, actually— and kneeling at his feet.

He was about to thank her for staying close when he realized that he had her hand tightly in his. His knuckles were white with force but she made no sign of pain. He eased his grip. "I'm sorry."

She reached toward him. He leaned closer. *Yes*. She placed one hand on his chest—and pulled his handkerchief free of his breast pocket. "Here," she said calmly. "You're dripping."

He was dripping. It didn't seem right to use the word "weeping," for he felt calm enough except for the remaining unbalanced laughter and the tendency for his eyes to leak.

He looked at Sophie. "You know what this means, don't you?"

She nodded in unruffled sympathy. "Yes. You're all alone now."

He tamped down on more wild hysteria. "No. I mean . . . yes, I'm alone. But more importantly, for I've virtually been alone all along . . . I'm the new Duke of Edencourt."

Sophie had always wondered why people used the word "heartbreak." Hearts raced and sometimes stopped, but how could a muscle break?

Completely without effort, it seemed.

She'd thought herself immune. She'd arrogantly assumed that because she didn't have a lover that she wouldn't feel love.

What an idiot she was.

Through the pounding in her head and the roaring in her ears, she heard Graham say her name. He sounded so far away.

He is, farther than he's ever been.

And he's not coming back.

Chapter Five

The room that had once seemed a refuge against a hostile world now surrounded Sophie in all its tawdry dilapidation and deceit. Her sanctuary was only a room in a cheap, rented house and her prince was simply a man she couldn't have.

"Of course, there isn't a penny to be had," Graham was saying lightly, as if it were of no consequence. "All that land and not a bit of it offering up my just deserts as duke."

Money. He was talking about money—when he ought to have heard the crystalline shattering of her heart from across the room?

What did you expect of a man like him and a woman like you?

"So it seems," he went on to say, "that I must marry immediately and marry rich, if I please to continue living in the manner to which I am accustomed."

Well. Thrice an idiot in a single afternoon. She'd thought her heart could break no more. She was truly going to have to learn not to make such naive assumptions.

"Marry," she repeated flatly.

"Yes." His gaze was on the view through the window—or perhaps much farther than that. All the way to Lady Lilah Christie's house?

"Who?"

He blinked, his surprise bringing him back to the parlor, back to her. He grinned crookedly and shrugged, his hands held wide. "I haven't the foggiest notion, I fear." He tried to bring back his former teasing tone. "Why don't you pick for me, lover? Preferably someone I can stand for more than an hour at a time."

He didn't mean to be cruel. She had to believe that. If she'd needed further illustration of just how far out of her reach he was, all she had to do was look in a mirror!

Enough!

She stood abruptly. When had she seated herself? She couldn't remember. "I'm sorry, Graham—ah—Your Grace. I just realized the time. I hope you'll forgive me, but I've so much to do today . . ."

Ridiculous excuse, when he'd caught her napping on the windowseat not an hour past. He was too polite to say so, but only bowed and made the proper apologies for keeping her. She nodded, trying to keep the frantic need to flee from her manner.

"If you don't mind showing yourself out—?" A swing of her arm toward the door and the porcelain vase—which had never been in any danger in all the hours they'd spent together in this room—sailed several feet to shatter against the wall.

Sophie jerked away from the crash. No. Not now. *Please not now.*

It was no use. In her hasty withdrawal, she sent the small side table toppling, the crystal inhabitants of its top smashing themselves on the floor as well.

"Sophie—"

She felt his hand warm on her arm, the concern in his voice—or the pity?

Unbearable.

She jerked away from him, sending the embroidered footstool shooting across the room with a random spasm of her ankle, then tripping over the edge of the carpet to nearly plant her face in the wood of the parlor door.

"So sorry, must be off—" She had to get out get out get out—

Then she was on the stairs, skirts held high in one hand, feet mercifully sure on the narrow treads. Her chamber, as bare as a cell in a convent, was blessedly empty of breakables.

Good-bye, Graham.

She wished she was the sort of female who could throw herself across the bed and weep copiously. Alas, she could only sit, cold hands twisting in her lap, as she faced the end of a dream she hadn't even realized she had.

She'd thought herself adjusted to the idea that he would never be more than a lovely fancy and she'd determined to enjoy it for as long as she could, then walk away with no regrets. She'd thought herself realistic, yet though she'd known he would never want her, she hadn't a clue how devastated she would be when he chose someone else.

Good-bye forever.

He would find someone soon, for what more did any rich family want but to use their money to purchase a title?

Just like Sir Hamish Pickering.

Sophie paused as it dawned on her. *No.* She couldn't do it. There was no possibility that she could convince Graham to marry her without breaking the conditions of the will by telling him—which would cost Deirdre her chance as well.

No, the money was Deirdre's, not hers. It was as good as decided, for Deirdre's husband would be duke soon enough, and Deirdre had won him without cheating in the slightest. For Sophie to now steal it away with tricks would be too unfair.

The quiet of the room pressed down on her. Silence. Isolation. She ought to be accustomed to it by now.

She'd best become so, for she wouldn't have much of a future if the world found out how she'd taken the money sent by Tessa to come to London without telling a soul, unaccompanied and unallowed. Unwanted.

The future of a woman alone in England was an uncertain and dangerous one. Sophie had seen how the orphanage near Acton had turned its grown girls out with nothing but a dress, a meal tied in a handkerchief and barely enough reading ability to follow signs on the road.

Some found work in the fields or even in Acton's kitchens, and some disappeared entirely. Some traveled to find work in the factories—hard, filthy work that left young women old before their time. Some reemerged later as victims of violence and murder and some became pale faces in the windows of bordellos in the city.

She had a few more advantages than that. She had a lady's education and a lady's standing. That standing actually worked against her, however, for a relative of the Duke of Brookmoor would hardly make an acceptable governess. She might secure a place as a lady's companion, but that too closely resembled what she'd run away from in Acton.

She could sponge off Deirdre or Phoebe, be their household fixture as she aged and stultified. She could just see herself now, her spectacles thick from too much reading, her curling hair gone grizzled, her mind frayed from a lifetime of not mattering to anyone, lurking in unused portions of the great house, mumbling translations to herself.

Mad Cousin Sophie, the Wicked Witch of the West Wing. After all, the nobility wouldn't be the nobility without the required mad relative or two, would it?

Unless she did something about it first. . . .

After all, there was no reason she shouldn't take advantage of her final weeks here to find a husband of her own. Not love, certainly, but she couldn't stay here and she couldn't return to Acton.

There were men . . . out there. Men who might not mind a hardworking, plain sort of woman who wasn't too good to step foot in a kitchen.

"You could wipe them all from the minds of Society if you wished it, my darling. All you need do is say the word and I will make you my muse, my pièce de résistance, *my masterpiece!"*

A wild recklessness rose in her as she remembered
the words of the premier dressmaker in all of London.
She'd had that feeling once before, when she'd opened
the first letter from Tessa proposing the Season and secretly arranged her own future.

All you need do is say the word . . .

He was mad, of course, a master of exaggeration at
least. Lementeur's very name translated from French
to "the Liar."

Tessa had sniffed and said that no one had ever heard
of the man a few short years ago—he'd simply *appeared,* creating gowns for some of the most influential
women in London. A poseur, she had put forward, convincing all that he was the best in the business when he
was probably just some tailor who'd lifted himself up
from the gutter.

Naturally, Tessa had been quick enough to take the
gowns when offered. How could he be a fraud when
his gowns were so very beautiful and had made Phoebe
look like a princess and made Deirdre look like a
goddess?

Perhaps . . . just perhaps . . . he could work a bit of
his magic on her and transform her into a normal
woman?

She must take charge of her own destiny yet again.
It wasn't enough this time to simply be Sophie Blake.
She must become someone else.

Someone who will attract Graham?

She suppressed that hope hurriedly. She was done
dreaming such impossible fantasies. No, all she needed
was a practical arrangement and a home of her own.

For that, she would throw herself into the world with a vengeance.

DESPITE THE FACT that Sophie had only been there once, she had no trouble finding the entrance to the grand salon of Lementeur—so much more than an ordinary dress shop. There were no wares on display in great glass windows for passersby to gawk at, for one. Neither was there a sign of any sort, but for the unique knocker in the shape of an exotic bird on the substantial oak door. One could have driven right by without noticing, were one not a woman in London with her wits about her.

Even as Sophie approached, and even through the murmuring chaos of her thoughts, she could feel the tendrils of expensive luxury reaching for her. Normally, she would have cast a longing glance and walked on by, for gowns such as those created by Lementeur were not to be dreamed of by girls like her.

She actually owned two—simple white muslin day gowns which could have been produced by any competent dressmaker, if one gave no account to perfection of fit and attention to creating the most flattering silhouette.

However, those had been gifts from Deirdre's magnanimous husband, Lord Brookhaven. Even Tessa had benefited that day. Lementeur had appeared briefly, sized up all four women with a glance and then, inexplicably, had focused all of his intense energy upon Sophie. It had only been for a moment, indignantly interrupted by Tessa, of course, but for that single moment, Sophie had seen herself as possibly, someday . . . someone else altogether.

At this moment, someone else altogether was precisely what was needed.

At the door, her knock was answered swiftly and she was ushered into the rarified air within by the rather decorative young man she'd seen here before, Cabot.

"Is he here? I must see him." Her words came out in a rush. She would plead if she had to, beg if she must.

Cabot indicated the double doors down the hall. "He is in his office—"

Sophie moved at a near run, before her nerve could desert her. With a single push, she was through the doors and standing before the great designer himself. A little man behind a very large desk, cleared of everything but strewn sketches and pencils.

Sophie emptied her reticule on the desk, her hands shaking as the last coin hit the blotter.

"It is everything I have. You have to take it. You said—you said—" She couldn't breathe, for what if it had all been empty promises, a cruel joke at her expense? What if there was no chance that she could ever—

Nevertheless she could not go on without knowing for sure. She took a shattered breath and stiffened her spine. Then she gazed at the small, dapper man behind the desk, who was still frozen in surprise. "You said you could make me beautiful."

He shook his head slowly. "No, I didn't. No one can make you beautiful."

The disappointment hit deep beneath her heart, dizzying her with its profundity. No breath—no hope—

A hand gripped hers, tightening until she was forced to blink back the water swimming in her eyes and meet Lementeur's intense gaze. "I did not promise beauty," he said. "I said I could make you outshine every other woman in Society."

Sophie gasped a sob. "So you admit you lied."

He shook his head slowly, a smile forming on his lips. "My darling, beauty is something you are born with, or not. Pretty girls abound, like dandelions in the field. Pretty is common, simple, easily enjoyed and just as easily forgotten. Style, now—elegance, presence, being completely *unforgettable*—that is what I promised you. With your bones and my gowns—and a few lessons in deportment, for you slouch abominably—you will take London by storm."

Sweet relief—was that hope?—began to trickle through her. "Gr—men will like me?"

"Men will duel to the death for you. They will long. They will ache. They will pine. There will be so many sonnets written in your honor you'll be sick of them. I will turn your height into superiority, your thinness into elegance, your shyness and clumsiness into hauteur and languid grace!"

She could only laugh damply at such ridiculousness. It was all so impossible—but perhaps, just perhaps, with his help she just might become attractive enough—

"Is that enough money?" It must be, for there was no more.

Lementeur huffed and swept the money to the floor with his other hand. "Did Leonardo da Vinci charge his Mona Lisa?"

Sophie sniffled and swiped at her eyes. "Well, actually, it was a commissioned portrait, so—" Then she realized what he was saying. "Why—why would you do this for nothing?" She drew back. "What do you expect of me?"

He patted her hand. "I know you don't trust anyone, pet. No reason why you should, eh?" Then he gazed into her face with sudden intensity. "We recognize each other, I think. The outcasts always do."

Sophie blinked. The man before her, the successful, sought-after mantua-maker faded away for a moment, revealing someone who had once been just a boy . . . a boy perhaps unlike other boys.

He saw the enlightenment enter her eyes and smiled. "I should think that being too tall and too thin and too plain—and perhaps unwanted in the first place, eh?— might be a little bit like being a poor Cockney lad who dreamed only of beautiful fabrics and fine lace. Understanding was as hard to come by for you as it was for me."

Then his smile widened. "However, someone helped me. A costume-maker for a theater troupe, who saw me fondling the silks at a market stall. He took me in and taught me to sew. I tried to repay him once, as if I ever could, but he told me to find another lost soul and save it instead. 'You cannot pay it back,' he told me. 'You can only pay it on.' "

Sophie shook her head. "But . . . you helped Phoebe and Deirdre already!"

He leaned one hip back on his desk and folded his arms. "And I charged them very well for it, too!" He smiled confidently. "It was worth every penny." Then he tilted his head. "Furthermore, I thought perhaps if you saw what I could do for them that someday you might come to ask what I could do for you."

She smiled. "And perhaps you overcharged Lord Brookhaven just a tad, just in case?"

Lementeur laughed and kissed her hand. "Sofia, you are priceless."

"Oh, no." She shook her head. "I am just Sophie."

He caught her chin in his fingers, his gaze suddenly serious and just a bit too intense for comfort. Who was this man, really? "My love, my muse, my darling," he said softly and sternly. "If you ever call yourself 'just Sophie' again, I will wash my hands of you, do you understand? That and only that will send me packing forever."

She blinked wide eyes at him. He was mad. Then hope tingled anew. "Mad" might be precisely what was required.

He released her and straightened. "You are, from this moment forward, to be known far and wide as 'that stunning Miss Sofia Blake.' Now, we will need some time, and an invitation of appropriate weight and countenance—which I can easily arrange—and you must be completely available to me for . . ." He eyed her slumping posture. "A while."

Sophie straightened self-consciously. "I haven't al-

ways done so," she mumbled. "I simply felt so tall
around—around London ladies."

Lementeur pursed his lips. "You are rather too polite,
my dear. Let me be clear. Lady Tessa is a well-known
shrew. No one likes her, not even her alleged friends.
Besides, I know for a fact that she has always longed for
some height. I might venture a guess that she is actually
jealous of your stature."

Tessa jealous? Of *her?* How very . . .

Delightful.

Sophie allowed her lips to curve in a slow, unfamil-
iar smile of satisfaction as she straightened to her full
inches and gazed serenely down at the top of Lementeur's head. "Is that better?"

He matched her cat-who-swallowed-the-cream gaze
and doubled it, approval shining from his face. "That is
perfect."

Chapter Six

John Herbert Fortescue was a free man, servant to no master . . . at least temporarily. His employers, the Marquis of Brookhaven and his bride, were attending the elderly Duke of Brookmoor. For the moment, Fortescue, butler to Brookhaven, could pretend to be an ordinary fellow, spending an evening with an extraordinary girl.

If the atmosphere of his office in great Brook House was rather more that of a classroom, that was because he'd taken on the task of teaching Miss Patricia O'Malley to read. The fact that, as butler and head of staff of Brook House, he had not a moment to spare had been dismissed without a thought.

He caught a glimpse of himself in the gleaming silver vase on the mantel—and quickly wiped away the besotted smile that kept crossing his face when he forgot to pay attention to his usual dignified demeanor. He was one of the highest of the high, by God, of the vast servant class of England. He had best retain his somber demeanor or he'd soon lose his post!

With an effort, he returned his reflection to its normal haughty, chiseled state and quickly smoothed the silver streaks at his temples that gave people such a top-drawer impression. He'd earned every one of them through hard work and years of service—years that he sometimes wished he hadn't wasted so.

There. Back to normal. He glanced down to see if Patricia had noticed his distraction with his own reflection, but she was bent studiously over her work on the desk, pencil scratching steadily. Such a lovely girl. Such a pity no one had thought to educate her before now. Still she was young—*too young for you and you know it!*—and she'd shown a remarkable aptitude for her work, so her ladyship had asked Fortescue to see to her further education.

Now, normally a lady traveling would take her lady's maid along, but Fortescue had mildly suggested that Patricia might be the appropriate person to keep a special eye on young Lady Margaret.

Since Lady Margaret, although much improved since the arrival of her new mother, had something of a reputation as a . . . well . . . whirling catastrophic disaster on skinny little legs, milady had hurriedly agreed with Fortescue and arranged to take along another maid instead.

Fortescue had also been prepared to point out that her ladyship wouldn't want to interrupt Patricia's education, now that real progress was being made there, but it hadn't been necessary. There was simply no one else in the world who could handle Lady Margaret.

Hence, matters had worked out very much to Fortescue's satisfaction. With the reduced duties during his lordship's absence, Fortescue had even more time to devote himself to Patricia—er, that is, to Patricia's education.

At the moment, he was leaning over her shoulder to examine the sums that she'd completed for him. She learned quickly—a bit too quickly, one might think if one were a rotter with designs on a sweet redheaded maid fresh from the shores of Ireland, which of course Fortescue was trying very hard not to be—so he knew the sums would be correct.

The reason why he hung there, suspended above her, his silence growing in length was simply that she smelled so good he'd quite forgotten what he was going to say.

And his reason for being there.

And his name.

She twisted about to gaze up at him worriedly. "Is it wrong, then?" The sweet lilt of her voice tugged at his gut.

So wrong. So very wrong, my darling. You simply have no idea.

He was her superior. He was nearly old enough to be her . . . uncle. He could not risk his integrity, his reputation and his career on a pert, outspoken Irish maid with a freckled nose and leaf green eyes and a figure that would tempt a saint into sin. . . .

Damn, again he'd forgotten what he was saying.

So he repeated what she'd said back to her. "Now say it again. Leave off the last word."

She smiled slightly. "Is it wrong?"

"Actually, it is 'Are my mathematics correct?' "

Her eyes narrowed slightly, but she dutifully repeated it.

He shook his head. "Patricia, I've told you before that if you're going to serve in a great house, you need to sound less . . ." There was no help for it. He must say it. He loved the Irish lilt of her voice, but if she were to have a successful career in service, she needed to dispense with it. "Less Irish."

She turned away, looking down at her paper for a long moment. Then she put both hands upon it and pushed it away. She stood slowly and straightened. Then her emerald gaze rose to meet his.

"Mr. Fortescue, I thank you for all your efforts, but I fear I must get back to my duties. I'll not return to this. I've told *you* before that I've no objection to better grammar, but I will no more hide my birth than I would paint myself blue!"

Fortescue had been so distracted by the glow of distant lands in her eyes that he took a bit too long to understand her words.

Oh no.

"Patricia—" She was already turning away. He couldn't bear it. These hours teaching her were the only reason he rose each morning, that and the possibility of a few words passed in the hallway during the day.

"I apologize," he said.

Since Fortescue was the master of all who served in this house, such an utterance was quite enough to stop Patricia in her tracks. She blinked. "You're apologizing . . . to me?"

God, she was beautiful. Fortescue smiled then without

realizing it. All he knew was that Patricia's gaze widened in shock and her breath left her.

"What is it?" The way she was looking at him, as if . . .

He felt himself move closer—she swayed toward him—

A hearty knock made them spring apart, though they'd not yet touched.

A footman stuck his head into the office. "Mr. Fortescue, there's a guest come. Miss Blake is here and she says it's for a long stay."

'TIS EASIER TO *beg pardon than to beg permission.*

As Sophie stepped from Lementeur's ridiculously elegant carriage—really, it was like a cake iced in cream and gold!—and was handed down to the walk in front of Brook House, she held Lementeur's admonition close.

The fine day notwithstanding, she quaked just a bit inside. She was not accustomed to simply taking possession of anything, much less something she had no right to.

And yet you're making quite a habit of it.

She had no right to invade Deirdre's house this way, especially with her cousin gone. But Lementeur was right when he said that her new persona, Sofia, needed every advantage of status and address.

This address had status enough to share. The wealthy Lord Brookhaven, soon to be Duke of Brookmoor, was a good master and had a keen business sense, so his fortunes had never suffered like so many of the aristocracy. Brook House gleamed, the marble steps scrubbed thrice daily, the trees shading the circular drive trimmed neatly and the great brass door knocker . . . gone.

Ah, yes. Well, it would be, when his lordship wasn't in residence. Sophie lifted her chin, feeling all the more like an intruder. The Brook House footmen moved forward instantly, their expressions devoid of surprise, when her luggage was handed down as well.

She'd stayed here for a few months until Deirdre and Brookhaven had wed, so they knew her well enough to smile slightly. She did catch a few of them casting worried glances into the empty carriage. Making sure Lady Tessa wasn't accompanying her? Sophie could have reassured them that Tessa had no inkling of the move, but she didn't think it advisable to call attention to her lack of chaperone.

"No one will dare to whisper a word against you," Lementeur had assured her. "Between my powers of transformation and Brookhaven's wealth and imminent rank, there isn't a soul in London who would doubt you."

Grand words. Sophie, for she was still Sophie and not yet the promised Sofia, was going to reserve judgment thank you very much. No one had ever hesitated to abuse her in the past. She was having trouble believing any future changes would be that dramatic.

Fortescue met her in the front hall, looking oddly flushed for such a paragon of dignity and restraint. Her unannounced visit must have put him out more than she'd thought it might.

Behind him, Sophie spotted Deirdre's maid, Patricia.

She blinked in surprise. "Is her ladyship at home already?"

Patricia smiled and shook her head. "No, miss. I stayed behind to watch over Lady—"

"Sophieee!"

Sophie braced herself for impact, luckily, for Lady Margaret was running so fast that the slick marble of the entrance hall did not allow for braking. After Sophie caught her breath and untangled herself from pointy knees and elbows, she stood Meggie on her feet and gazed at her in mock severity. "Nutmeg, don't you understand the science of friction and momentum?"

Meggie grinned up at her. "Sure. When I'm in stocking feet I can slide from the back stairs to the front door, if Graham is here to throw me."

The mention of Graham stole away some of Sophie's pleasure at seeing her new little cousin, but she lifted her chin to gaze evenly at the butler, one of the few men she tolerated well.

"I've come to stay, Fortescue."

Fortescue seemed to have recovered himself as well. "Indeed, miss, you're very welcome. How long will you be with us?"

For as long as it takes. She smiled noncommittally. "I can't say. I simply felt like a change."

A sparkle of wry sympathy shone in Fortescue's eyes. "And how is Lady Tessa?"

Sophie shook her head ruefully. "In for a surprise, I fear, if she ever bothers to notice I've escaped."

Fortescue made no response, but his brisk orders to the footmen concerning her baggage made his welcome clear. As he moved off, Sophie smiled at Patricia. "I'm very glad you're here. If you don't mind, I'd like your help."

Patricia tilted her head. "I'm happy to, miss, but you've never let me do your hair before."

Sophie looked down at her gloved hands. "Things change."

Patricia let out a breath. "Indeed, miss."

Sophie glanced up to see the pretty maid's gaze following the male servants up the stairs. Did Patricia fancy one of the handsome young footmen? If so, Deirdre probably wouldn't stand in her way like most mistresses would.

Lucky girl—a romance without obstruction.

Envy became no one, however. Sophie had come here to accomplish something and there was no time to spare on might-have-beens.

Meggie tugged at her hand. "Sophie, Papa and Dee are at Brookmoor visiting Great-Uncle. I couldn't go. I'm not a soothing visitor for an elderly gentleman," she stated matter-of-factly.

Sophie knelt fluidly, putting her at eye level with the child. "You know, Nutmeg, I don't think I am either."

Meggie grinned. "Want to play cards after dinner?"

Sophie squashed the pert little nose gently between her knuckles. "You cheat, you little beast."

Meggie's smile widened. "So do you. I just do it better."

Sophie laughed and stood. "You're on, beastie." Then she turned to Patricia. "Lementeur will be arriving shortly. I— "

Patricia blinked in shock. "Mary, Jesus and Joseph," she breathed. "*Here?*"

"Yes." Sophie knew that the ladies in London admired Lementeur's designs, but apparently she lacked the full truth of his importance. "He is helping me . . . improve my style."

Patricia's jaw dropped. Then shut. Then a slow, eager smile bloomed. "Oh, miss. You're goin' to look like a princess!"

Sophie grimaced. "Pity the kingdom." Reaching down, she took Meggie's hand. "Lady Nutmeg, why don't you help me unpack?"

Meggie gazed up at her with narrowed eyes. "You're not as pretty as Dee, Sophie."

Sophie nodded calmly. It was only the truth, and Meggie's loyalty to her new mother was understandable.

"Except when you smile."

As she walked up the stairs with Meggie in tow, Sophie wondered if Meggie had meant to say that she *was* as pretty as Deirdre when she smiled?

Not possible.

On the way to her room, Sophie paused in the gallery, noticing several new canvases hanging in the long Marbrook family line. Where once the row of paintings had ended with very young Raphael and Calder portraits and one of Calder's deceased first wife, there now extended an entirely new sequence.

First, a portrait of Calder, the elder and the current Marquis of Brookhaven, and his bride. He was a big man, broad-shouldered and dark-haired, with brown eyes glowering out of chiseled features. His expression made Sophie smile, for she could just imagine his impatience with the process of sitting for a portrait. Calder was a man of action, not of leisure.

Standing next to him was an exquisite rendition of Deirdre. She was a regal, golden-haired beauty with eyes like sapphires. The smile she wore was cool and haughty, but her gaze snapped with humor and a trace of impatience of her own. If Sophie was not mistaken, her cousin's hand on Calder's shoulder was quite literally pinning him in place!

Theirs had not been an easy courtship, especially considering that most of it had taken place after their marriage of convenience, yet even in the portrait Sophie could see the way that Calder's entire being gravitated toward Deirdre's as if she were the earth and he was the smitten moon. Every day was a battle of wills, yet it seemed that the prize was nothing less than complete devotion.

In the next portrait stood Lord Raphael Marbrook, the illegitimate but recognized second son. The resemblance between the half-brothers was astonishing if one only looked at hair and eye color and general bone structure. The difference between them lay entirely in attitude. Rafe's brown gaze was lighter, nearly laughing, and the faintly besotted smile on his lips was a permanent one.

Seated in a chair slightly before him, with her honey-gold hair down over one shoulder, Phoebe gazed out of the painting with a love-light in her summer-sky eyes that made Sophie's heart thump just a little in envy. Rafe's hand on her shoulder was a benediction and a caress, his fingers ever so slightly buried in his wife's silken hair.

Love at first sight, despite the fact that Phoebe had agreed to wed Calder and very nearly gone through with the wedding. Love forever, Sophie thought as she gazed at the tenderly lingering hand on Phoebe's shoulder.

"Papa gave me Mama's portrait to hang in my room," Meggie stated calmly. "I like it there and so does Dee." The little girl gazed fondly up at her new mother's face. "I used to wish that Mama had taken me with her, but now I'm glad she didn't."

Sophie closed her eyes against the tragedy that Meggie had narrowly escaped. Calder's first wife had died in a carriage accident while fleeing with her lover. Thank God the woman had had the sense to leave Calder's two-year-old daughter behind! "I'm glad, too, Nutmeg."

"I'm going to sit for a portrait, too, Papa said." Meggie scratched her nose. "As soon as I learn how to sit."

Sophie smiled down at her. "I'd practice, if I were you. It looks like the Nameless One has it down to an art."

Meggie looked down at the leggy kitten dangling limply from her arms like a boneless cat suit. "Mortimer the Mighty." She scowled. "No, that won't do." She heaved a great sigh and shrugged. The kitten drooped blissfully. A loud rasping purr rose on the air. "I don't know what to call him."

Sophie stroked the girl's hair with one hand. "That's all right, my sweet. As long as he comes when you call."

Meggie looked up at Sophie and blinked. "Like Gray does with you?"

Sophie glanced away casually. "Hmm." It wasn't until the girl had walked on ahead of her that Sophie wondered if Meggie had meant that Sophie came when Graham called—or the other way around?

Which was ridiculous, of course. Graham didn't need anyone. Ever.

Chapter Seven

If a man's status could be measured by the number of eyes upon him, then Graham should have been a king.

Of course, the aforementioned eyes were but glass, gleaming lifelessly from the stuffed and mounted heads of the late duke's victims—er, hunting trophies—so perhaps it was appropriate that Graham's status was equally fragile.

The study decor was an oppressive combination of dark wood, dark paper and dark death. Graham fancied that the glossy gazes followed him as he paced, their glinting opacity a plea for final release. The smell, unfortunately, was not born of imagination.

Had this room always smelled of musty tobacco and dry, fusty decay? It was a scent that Graham permanently associated with his father. Add freshly fired gunpowder and whiskey and one would expect the old duke himself to stride in at any moment.

The duke is dead.

Long live the duke.

Graham turned and snarled back at the giant brown bear looming in the corner. "I am duke now."

An hour later, Graham toasted his back-garden bon-fire with his fourth . . . fifth? . . . whiskey. Antlers burned like dry wood, he'd found, and if one stood carefully upwind, one could even enjoy the fiery glow of relief in the glass eyes before they were lost in the flames.

Graham raised his glass. "To my fallen comrades." He staggered only a little, considering he'd drunk a lot. "You have been avenged. All hail the mighty phele-mant . . ." Wait. That wasn't right. "Ephalent." Close enough.

He tossed his whiskey back and wiped his arm across his face, for the heat from the fire made his eyes water. Or perhaps it was the smoke . . . except he stood upwind . . .

Now the study was silent and, better yet, uncrowded. The bear was the only remaining corpse left to gaze at him with reproving eyes. Graham decided to leave the fourteen-and-a-quarter–stone trophy where it loomed. However, the creature's mood required lightening, forthwith.

The addition of the old duke's stained floppy safari hat to its head, and one of the elderly flintlocks from over the mantel laid across its menacingly raised forelegs, gave it a jaunty air.

Graham stood back and regarded it critically. "It's missing a little something." He shrugged, then saluted his furry companion. "Sorry, Sir Fangsalot, I'm fresh out of wit." He staggered to the thronelike chair by the fire and collapsed into it. Staring mournfully at the tro-phy, he hiccupped. "And out of whiskey, as well."

He leaned his head back on the padded chair and finally closed out the reproving gaze . . . and slept at last.

THE NEXT MORNING, Graham made his way to Primrose Street, ready to pin Sophie down on her sudden coolness toward him.

She wasn't there.

Graham didn't know who was more surprised to learn that Sophie had decamped, him or the promptly awakened Tessa. Since Tessa's role as chaperone was to keep track of the whereabouts of defenseless maidens, etc., Graham did not approve of the shoddy job she was making of it.

"She isn't my daughter, you know," snarled his cousin, tightening her wrapper and pushing her disheveled hair back from her forehead with the back of her hand. "I'm only here as a favor to her mother."

Graham frowned. "You're only here to make sure that your stepdaughter marries a duke. Now that you've accomplished that, more or less, you think you can toss Sophie to the wolves."

"Don't worry, she is in no danger from wolves." Tessa's laugh was mocking. "Dogs, now . . . they chase sticks, don't they?"

Graham turned away from the only family he had left in the world, realizing that he had nothing to gain there. Evidently she hadn't yet heard of his advancement or she would have played the encounter with more fawning and flattery. He shuddered at the thought. Let her remain in the dark a little longer.

A quick question to Tessa's long-suffering maid, Nan, gave Graham the information he needed. She also added, *sotto voce*, that Lady Tessa's latest lover had just jilted her, striding out that morning under an avalanche of abuse screamed from an upstairs window. Classic Tessa.

Upon arrival at Brook House—and really, he ought to have figured that one out by himself and probably would have if he hadn't been so overwhelmed by his own troubles—he was greeted at the door by Fortescue and shown to the family parlor.

"I shall tell Miss Blake that you're here."

There was already a young lady waiting there. Graham leaned both hands on the back of the sofa and grinned down at the child playing on the floor. Little Lady Margaret was a skinny brat with big feet and too much hair. In a few years she was going to be a right stunner, and Graham for one was looking forward to seeing her flay the young sods of Society to bits.

"Hullo, evil mastermind. What's on the agenda for the day—world domination?"

Meggie spared him a smile. "Hullo, Gray. Sir Mittens is going to chase string."

Graham eyed the scrawny black-and-white kitten in her lap. Every time he saw it he found it more unattractive than before. The black-and-white markings were striking, but its enormous ears, crossed eyes and quirked whip of a tail formed a feline nightmare.

When the beast had been younger, its tininess had been somewhat appealing, but now the baby charm was lost in lanky, wild-eyed youth. Deirdre had rescued it from a tree not long ago. Graham rather thought it might have been the tree that needed rescuing. "Is that the final name, then?"

"No. I'm just trying it out. What do you think?"

"Er . . . is that it? Sir Mittens?"

She blinked at him. "Too boring? I thought about Sir Snow Mittens." The kitten reached higher during her distraction, snagging her finger with one needle sharp claw. "Ouch!"

Graham smiled, remembering the bear. "What about Sir Clawsalot?"

Meggie smirked. "I don't want him to think he's too dangerous. It might give him ideas. Dee says he's going to be a very large gentleman cat someday."

Graham considered the current ferocity of the scrawny beastie and his smile slipped. "Perhaps not, then."

Meggie sighed, then picked up the kitten and cradled it in her arms. It hung its head upside down and glared at Graham. "I have to put him in my room now. Patricia is taking me on an outing."

The cat, now at liberty from the need to stand on any of the aforementioned claws, was free to snarl all four paws viciously into the tangle of string. Just to ensure its complete destruction, he gnashed the wad repeatedly with his tiny baby teeth, purring raspily all the while.

Graham would have offered to kitten-sit, but honestly, the creature's maddened attack on the innocent string quashed any thought of such charity. He'd freely pay for the exorcism, though. "You do that."

And lock the door on the barmy little thing. He ought to let it loose on the old duke's bear. That would fix them both.

Fortescue appeared in the doorway of the parlor. "I'm sorry, Your Grace, but Miss Blake is not available this morning. She asks if you will please call again another time."

Graham blinked. Not available?

But . . . Sophie was *always* available!

Not today, apparently, at least, not to him. Damn it, didn't she realize he needed her? Well, not *needed* of course, but it would have been very *useful* to talk to her just now. Vastly irritated and more hurt than he was really willing to admit to, Graham stalked out past a bowing Fortescue, twitching his gloves back on so violently that he pulled a seam.

Blast it, he wasn't going to be able to buy gloves for a very long time, if ever.

Far better to be angry at his gloves, his circumstances and his friend than to spend too much time wondering why her refusal to see him upset him so.

Instead, he decided to ride out to Sussex. It was high time he took a look at Edencourt for himself. One could only learn so much from a report, after all.

If Sophie wondered why he didn't call back . . . well, she could just go on and wonder.

At the top step, however, he halted. Some impulse caused him to turn about, stride back to the parlor and lay the polished bit of antler from his pocket on the side table like an offering. No, not an offering. A gift.

Damn it.

*   *   *

FOR THE NEXT two days, Sophie learned that not only did she not know how to dress or do her hair, but she apparently lacked the ability to stand, sit, walk, nod, carry a fan or hold a glass.

In the great dining room of Brook House, where a table that could comfortably seat thirty people stretched nearly the length of the room, Sophie was so exhausted and furious that the grandeur and intimidation inspired by the luxurious setting had finally worn off. She plopped down into one of the dining chairs with no respect for its rarity or value.

"Thank heaven you came along," she finally barked at her small but terrifying nemesis. "I don't know how I ever managed to survive!"

Lementeur, still crisp and dapper, none the worse for wear though the work had been grueling, folded his arms and lifted a brow. "Oh, you survived, but I doubt that you *lived*. What's more, there's no excuse for it! You've a natural grace—of a coltish sort, at any rate—and if you'd simply get over your silly fears, you wouldn't have a bit of trouble!" He threw up his hands again.

Sophie decided then and there that if he made that gesture one more time, she was going to make monkey noises through her nose. There might also be some banging of her skull against the nearest wall.

She was exhausted, her spine ached, her neck pinched, her feet throbbed, and she was fairly sure she had blisters on her fingers from trying to flick her fan!

She gazed across the table at her torturer with unconcealed loathing. "You are a . . . a . . ."

His eyes narrowed. "A what, pray tell?" He'd begun patiently enough, but somewhere around her ninth sprawl on the floor he'd turned pitiless.

"A tyrant!" It was the best word she had. Her brain ached and her eyes burned and she longed to lie down. Anywhere. The middle of the street would do.

Her persecutor smiled thinly. "Tyrant will do for now. Stand, if you please." She obeyed, lifting her chin, throwing her shoulders back and down, firming her aching spine with stomach muscles that threatened to tremble.

With an effortless flair, he snapped open his own demonstration fan and sneered. "Now do it again."

"But . . ." For the first time in her life, Sophie detected the possibility of a whine rising in her throat. Oh no. Not *that.* Startled, she barely paid attention when she flicked open her fan yet again.

Out of habit, she waited for Lementeur's usual rebuke. When it didn't come, she lifted her gaze to him.

He was smiling.

"Absolute perfection!" His hands clasped as if in prayer—and who knew, for it had been a very long two days—his puckish face creased in smile lines, he bowed deeply to her.

"Miss Sofia Blake, how lovely to meet you at last."

Sophie blinked, then looked down at the hand that held the fan.

The fan . . . the lovely, graceful, perfectly poised fan! She laughed aloud, her relief overwhelming. She closed the fan and did it again . . . and again . . . and again!

Lementeur stepped forward and swept her in a joyous circle, his hand on her waist, his other holding the one with her fan. Sophie laughed again, whirling with him, her exhaustion and her tiny, hard-won accomplishment making her dizzy with glee.

Then she realized—

"I'm dancing!"

Lementeur nodded. "And very nicely, too."

He let her go, spinning her out of his arms and into the upholstered chair by the fire. Sophie sat, still dizzy from the motion, her movements still very nearly set to music, her limbs posed with gangling grace.

Lementeur bowed again, then he lifted her hand and kissed it, pride shining from his bright eyes. "Miss Blake, you are a very good student—once you stop thinking so bloody hard!"

Sophie blinked to make the room stay still. "So that's the secret to the delicate grace of Society women—empty heads!"

Lementeur laughed with glee. "Oh, that you must never change, my sweet! Your wit will carry you through any encounter. Now remember, stand as tall as you can, never move quickly, only smile at those who deserve it and if anyone, anyone at all, gives offense, you must never blush or shy away or let them see even the tiniest hurt. You must stare them down until *they* shy away from *you*."

That sounded easier than it likely was. "What will I say to people? How will I know what to talk about?"

He shook his head. "Never ask. Only answer, and only after the briefest, bored pause. *Ennui* is very stylish at the moment. Don't worry, you'll soon see—it's all quite boring in its way."

She frowned. "It is? I've always been too terrified to notice that. If it's so boring, then why go? Why spend night after night dressing and primping and dancing?"

He grinned. "The players might be boring, but the game is not!"

With that, he bowed again. "I take my leave now, Miss Blake. I shall return in the morning with everything you'll need for Lord and Lady Waverly's masked ball tomorrow night."

Oh no. "A masque?" She swallowed. "Already? I'm not—we haven't—"

He grinned over his shoulder as he exited. "Miss Blake, have I ever let you down?"

Sophie looked down at her hands, twisting tightly in her lap. Tomorrow? She could never be elegant, languid Sofia by tomorrow! Did he expect her to work magic?

She closed her eyes and forced the tempest in her gut to settle. She might not be a magician, but Lementeur was. In one of his gowns, a woman could stand in a corner all night and still shine.

A normal woman, anyway.

Well, at least she'd be wearing a mask.

GRAHAM SAT HIS horse with the ease of long practice. A good thing, too, for if he wasn't an accomplished horseman he might slither off onto his head at this very moment.

The great manor of the Edencourt estate lay before him. It was huge, grand, imposing—and in ruins. From where he sat his horse on the low hill just above the house, he could see that the stables had fallen in, the servants' wing was crumbling and the vast gardens were a tangle of noxious weeds and rubble. The main part of the house seemed intact, but Graham made no move to ride down the hill to enter it.

How could it be so bad? He'd visited here only . . .

By God, it had been nearly fifteen years! It had been shabby and unkempt then, and yes, a bit creaky and neglected. Yet, it now looked as though no one had spared a nail or a bucket of mortar for more than fifty years.

Houses, it seemed, deteriorated quickly once the process began.

Graham closed his eyes against it. Abbott's reports had not exaggerated as he'd hoped. In fact, it looked to Graham as though the man had actually been conservative in his estimates. Abbott still believed the estate could be saved. Graham was not so sure.

As he'd ridden the last several miles on Edencourt lands, the state of the fields and orchards had been very disheartening. Family history held that this had once been one of the most beautiful, productive estates in England. What could have happened to it?

Graham gazed at the house he'd hated all his life, not for the stones and the windows and the gracefully angled roof, but for the people who dwelt within it . . . people it seemed he was more like than he'd realized.

He had happened to this place—he and his brothers and his father, and his grandfather and great-grandfather before. Cavendish men liked to play, not work.

Cavendish men were no better than parasites.

Graham turned his horse about and urged it into a gallop. Just as in his youth, he could not put enough distance between himself and Edencourt. However, instead of oppression and resentment nipping at his heels, this time it was nothing but the blackest shame.

Chapter Eight

Late that evening, back in his father's study at Eden House, Graham closed his eyes against the papers spread everywhere over the surface of the giant desk. Bafflingly, he'd never seen his father read or write anything on this great barge of a desk.

Too bad. Perhaps if his father had ever used this room for anything other than smoking and drinking, the Edencourt estate wouldn't be in its current condition.

His closed lids couldn't keep the words from playing across his mind.

Flooding. Crop failure. Fire.

Famine.

That was the worst. The few loyal or helpless cottagers remaining were literally starving. He'd ridden past the cottages on his fine horse, in his fine clothes, sickened by the poverty and squalor he saw. Every time Graham thought about the money he'd carelessly lost at the tables or squandered on wine and women, his stomach turned. In the past, whenever he'd found his pockets empty and his lenders unavailable, he'd cajoled more out his brothers or father, never thinking about where it came from.

He had avoided Edencourt for years. Even when he had visited, he'd paid no notice to the conditions except to disdain the place for its shabbiness. Selfish idiot that he'd been, he'd only sighed with relief when he'd ridden away from it.

Edencourt had been his father's responsibility—but he ought to have known his father too well to think that responsibility had been met with action. *I didn't want to know. I only wanted to amuse myself.*

Which made him just as bad as the old duke—or worse, since he was a smarter and more able man.

Sophie, you were so right about me.

Regret ate at him, but he knew he couldn't take too much time for self-flagellation. After all, wasn't that just another form of selfishness, wasting his energies on himself yet again?

He lifted his head from his hands when Nichols announced a visitor. "At this hour?"

Nichols cast him a sour glance, implying that if Nichols had to be up and about to tend his thoughtless master, everyone in the world might as well be up and about.

Poor old Nichols hadn't taken the passing of the Edencourt torch well at all. Graham had hoped the man would take his retirement—though he had nothing to pension him off with—but Nichols doggedly continued to serve, albeit with many a disdainful sniff for punctuation.

The true test had come when Graham would not

schedule a grand lying-in-state for when the old duke and his sons arrived back in England after their three-week voyage by ship.

Graham didn't think that the bodies would be viewable after the elephant and the long voyage. Nor had his father so many friends that might merit a great funeral. Graham planned on slipping them quietly into the family cemetery on Edencourt lands the moment the ship made port. The less fuss the better, although Nichols might never bring him hot bathwater again.

The caller was a stout man whom Graham had never met. The fellow's name escaped Graham's memory immediately, for introductions were followed by the presentation of the late duke's IOUs.

Graham flipped through the signed sheets, hoping to see some sign of fraud, but it was evident from the scrawling signature that his father had borrowed against the estates profits several years in advance—profits that would never arise if considerable funds were not pumped into the lands at once! It was so much worse than he'd feared! Where was he ever going to find a bride whose family would not only shore up Edencourt, but pay back bloody decades of debt!

"Are you sure . . ." Graham rubbed at his face. "I mean . . . isn't there some way we can come to some sort of agreement?"

His caller leaned forward and tapped at the documents. "Your Grace, these are the agreements! I've made concession after concession for your family. I have no choice but to call these due at once."

Graham took a breath. "I have a lot of numbers to

tally before I can come up with any sort of . . . Well, there is a solution of sorts in the works—" Would the fellow take a possibility of a wealthy marriage as assurance enough? It sounded pretty damned weak to Graham.

The man gazed at him pityingly. "Your Grace, I'm not the worst of what's coming. I know the men your family went to in the end when no honest man would extend them further credit. That's why I came quickly while you're still . . . here."

Graham looked up at that hesitation. *While you're still alive.* Was that what the fellow meant to say? Surely not. Surely his father had had better sense than to sink to dangerous levels?

Yet where would this better sense have suddenly appeared from, when the old duke had never exhibited a bit of it before?

Graham spread his hands helplessly. "I fully intend to meet all my family's debts. How can I assure you of that fact?"

The fellow cast a glance about him, his eyes greedily taking in the art, the hangings, the fine if dented furniture. "Well, I've a cart outside, by chance—"

Chance. Right. Graham gazed at him with sour resignation. His heritage was going to be peeled right down to the walls before all this was done, wasn't it?

An hour later, the fellow left with a cart full of valuables—including the silver, the loss of which had sent Nichols into fits of dour agony—and a satisfied look. In return, Graham had kept back several of the IOUs.

Now he knelt before the fire, tossing them slowly in, one by one.

Trying to make them last—make it seem like more? That's pathetic.

Ah, but pathetic he was, or at least that's how he felt at the moment.

Right now, Edencourt's people needed him. And he needed a rich bride. There wasn't a moment to spare, for with the span of courtship and engagement, it might be months before he had anything to put into the estate.

There were only a few weeks left of the Season as well. All the charm in the world wouldn't get his people through another winter. The weight of his situation threatened to bow him to the ground.

Returning to the desk, he rubbed at his face, forcing his eyes to focus on the reports spread before him. He took the chair again without a thought, settling unconsciously and easily into its size and grandeur.

Acres, groves, woods—the bared bones of Edencourt. Crumbling mills, decrepit stables, rotted silos—the tatty garments of the dying estate. The cottagers—the beating heart that slowed with every passing moment.

To save them he would marry a horse, provided it was a very wealthy one. If his bride merely looked and neighed like a horse, he would consider himself a lucky man.

The words and figures before him began to swim in his vision. Shaking his head, he pushed back from the desk. It wasn't possible to learn in days what he ought to have spent a lifetime studying. The best he could do for Edencourt now was to get some rest and be bright-eyed and ready to sell himself body, soul and title on the auction block of Society tomorrow night.

He glanced at the hour. Rather, tonight. It was surprising how much it bothered him to contemplate a loveless marriage of convenience. Odd, he'd never even realized he was such a romantic.

The sky outside the arched window had brightened. Another night without rest. He really ought to go to bed before he frightened off any potential heiresses. Instead, he pushed himself to his feet and left the study, grabbed his hat and gloves from the table in the entrance hall and strode out into the early morning light.

Without thinking, Graham allowed his feet to turn in the direction of Brook House.

GRAHAM WASN'T THE only one who had a sleepless night.

In her bedchamber at Brook House, Sophie leaned forward to peer at herself in the vanity mirror. She was going to pay when Lementeur saw the circles beneath her eyes, but she simply hadn't been able to close them all night!

Behind her, Patricia nearly danced with excitement as she brought in the gown for "Sofia's" debut. "Oh, miss, it's so elegant. You'll look a treat, you will!"

Sophie stood, dying to see what had come this morning but hardly daring to look. If it was only an ordinary gown, if the result weren't truly magical—if she

really was beyond hope—well, she simply wasn't prepared to learn that.

Taking a deep breath, she turned—

A brisk knock on her bedchamber door interrupted
her. Patricia, not realizing that Sophie hadn't seen it,
continued over to the wardrobe to hang the gown inside. Torn, Sophie hesitated. Patricia hurried to answer
the door.

Fortescue stood outside, politely staring into space,
not into the room. "Excuse me, Miss Blake, but the
Duke of Edencourt is here to see you."

Duke of—? Oh, of course. Graham.

Her stomach did a little flip. Now that she realized the
depth of her attachment, she knew it was a very bad idea
to spend more time with Graham. She'd had no intention of seeing him today, but now that he was here . . .

Well, it would be rude to refuse to see him, wouldn't
it? After all, she hadn't actually told him not to come.
He wouldn't understand if she turned him away.

*He's not an infant. Let Fortescue do it. Your heart is
too foolish.*

*No, go see him. Soon he'll have a wife and then
you'll be sorry you lost these last weeks with him.*

Well, she would see him, but she wouldn't expend a
moment of effort to make him comfortable. Or to look
her best. Although her hair was sadly awry—she noticed things like that now, thanks to Lementeur—and it
would be good practice to take such matters more seriously, wouldn't it?

Something inside her threw up its hands. *Oh, go
ahead. But don't say I didn't warn you.*

Her better judgment faded, neatly silenced by the silly excitement she felt knowing Graham wanted to see her. "Patricia, my hair!"

Downstairs in the parlor, Graham stood with his back to the room, gazing out onto the grand square with unseeing eyes. He was thinking of Lady Lilah Christie, beautiful, greedy, immoral and very, very rich. The daughter of an earl, she'd married the richest man she could find, then—some said—killed him with disappointment. She had enough money to save Edencourt, not to mention the valuable resource of an elite family.

He hadn't sought her out since gaining the title. He told himself it was because he was too busy assessing the needs of the estate, but the truth was that he was no longer a harmless toy to divert the she-wolf. He was afraid she was going to come after him in earnest now.

Lilah was looking for another husband, though hers had passed quite recently. And this time, he knew, she was looking for a title.

Graham suppressed an inexplicable shudder. Or perhaps not so inexplicable, after all. Though he'd left her bed only weeks ago, that didn't mean he could conceive of taking her home to Edencourt to be mother of his brood. Not that he would have any assurance that said brood would actually be his.

God, Lilah was no answer. He probably ought not allow his aversion to taking a stranger to wed to convince him to inflict Lilah on Edencourt. His family's legacy was stained enough, thank you.

No, he would find a bland and proper young maiden,

possibly from one of the wealthy shipping families who were panting to be let into Society, who at least would come to him grateful for his rank. Heirs would happen—he'd prefer not to picture how—and his people would be saved, at least for one generation.

It might not be a bad idea to breed some business sense into the line, seeing how his father and grandfather had carried on.

His mind spun in circles. Brides, babies and business—three things he would have wagered he'd never have to concern himself with just a week ago!

Outside the parlor door, Sophie hesitated, her hand on the latch. Graham awaited her inside. She was dying to see him . . . but wouldn't it be better for him to see her when the final transformation was complete? Wouldn't it be better—wouldn't it be marvelous!—if Graham were to see her for the first time as the grandly dressed Sofia?

She backed away a step, her palms pressing to her midriff, her fingers atwitch with longing. Yet wouldn't it be perfect if the first time he saw her, she was wearing a mask? What things might she learn about him, about herself, if she could meet him again . . . for the first time?

As a beauty.

Her breath left her at the thought. Not that all this was for Graham's benefit, of course. She had every intention of finding herself a suitable, stable, hopefully not-too-dull position as some man's wife— -some *other* man's wife.

Turning away swiftly, she nearly stumbled into Fortescue. "Oh! Fortescue, will you please tell Gr . . .

His Grace that I'm not available at the moment—but ask him if he plans to go to the Waverly's masque this evening. Only don't let him know that I asked. And if he isn't, try to get him to go. But don't tell him I'm going. Simply be . . . casual, do you see?"

Fortescue gazed at her evenly despite every indication that she was stark, staring mad. "Yes, miss. Is there anything else you wish me to pass on to His Grace?"

Ask him if he'll be wearing blue.

No. That was silly. Only . . .

"Point out that he looks very fine in blue!"

For the first time in Sophie's experience, she saw a flash of rebellion in the butler's gaze. "Ah, yes, well." She shrugged in apology. "I suppose there's simply no way to make that sound appropriate, is there?"

"I will do so if you insist, miss, but I think if I drop a word to his valet in secret . . ."

Sophie smiled. "That would be perfect!"

Fortescue gazed at her in unconcealed surprise for a long moment. Then he shook off his inexplicable moment. "Ah . . . yes, miss. I can also confirm his plans this evening with his valet, who, I'm sure can be counted on to pass along a recommendation to attend the masque."

"My goodness, that's a useful channel of communication!" Sophie nearly danced to the stairs. "Tell him to be on time," she sang. "And tell him not to bring Lady Lilah Christie!"

Chapter Nine

Graham stalked out of Brook House, furious and frustrated once again, and strode unseeing down the gracious streets of Mayfair. What the blazes was Sophie up to? Did she think he had nothing better to do than to wait on her whims? Didn't she know that he—enjoyed her? Enjoyed her company, yes. She was quite entertaining underneath that drab, bluestocking exterior. Damn it, he missed—

He missed the company, that was all. Cards and conversation and . . .

Snapping gray eyes, seeing him for the fool he was. The soft rope of her marmalade hair tight in his fist. Easy laughter, bright warmth, drawling irony that never ceased to surprise him into laughter . . .

Bloody hell.

THE GOWN FROM Lementeur wasn't lovely. It wasn't stunning.

It was *magical*.

Lementeur had told her that he'd been inspired by

Titania, Queen of the fairies—and Sophie wondered if Titania herself had waved her wand and bestowed the dressmaker with powers beyond the rule!

It was truly a miraculous creation, an enchanted gown, a shimmering, graceful fantasy of silk of the palest green somehow shot with tints of shimmering lavender.

The tiny sleeves, dropped off her shoulders, were really nothing more than loops of pearly beads. She strongly suspected that they were real, not glass, but dared not ask for fear she might be right—and then she would not have the nerve to wear it!

Also, Lementeur had done something suspicious to her corset, for surely she'd not been so endowed by nature! Yet the burgeoning creamy flesh that swelled above her neckline was all her own—a mystery indeed! Twisted strands of the pearls crisscrossed over and between her small high breasts, outlining and emphasizing them.

The bodice was high and tight, but just below it the skirts were draped and slung in a fashion reminiscent of a toga worn by a Grecian goddess. Sophie wasn't quite sure why but the entire effect gave her curves where she'd thought she had none, and lent statuesque grandeur to her height. Fortunately for Lementeur's persistent lessons, there was no possibility of slumping in the gown. The merest sag of her shoulders caused the bodice to simply cut off her breath. She wondered if he'd done it on purpose.

Probably.

The muted iridescent colors made her skin gleam like polished ivory and her hair glow with brighter fire than if she'd worn more brilliant shades. And Patricia had washed something into her hair—it had smelled green and herbal—that put a cinnamon blaze into the reddish blond. What had once fallen unmanageable and untrimmed about her face was now cropped into dainty bangs that coiled all on their own, with the rest piled high and smooth to give her even more elegant height. Inches of hair had come off, but Patricia had assured her she could spare it.

She turned to look at herself over her shoulder. From beneath each exposed shoulder blade fell a frothing swath of silvery-white organza so fine one could read through it. When she moved even the slightest bit, they sailed lightly out behind her like a pair of gossamer wings.

Patricia was working more strands of the pearls into the woven pile of her hair.

"Are you sure we ought to have cut it?"

Patricia grinned at her in the mirror. "Bit late to doubt it, miss!"

Then the maid came down off her tiptoes and stepped back. With a sigh of dreamy satisfaction, she clasped her hands before her. "The fairy king himself will come to steal you away tonight, see if he doesn't."

Sophie gazed into the mirror. She looked completely unlike herself—in other words, she looked beautiful. It felt like a lie . . . yet, were those not her eyes? Was that not her natural height, her hair, her bare arms, her long neck? How could it be dishonesty when it was only a change of dress and a bit of powder and rouge?

And a mask.

Patricia handed her the outrageous mask, a white owl-feathered, pearl-bedecked creation that ought to have been hung on a wall as art, not hung on her face. Still, it covered her nose admirably, yet left her eyes exposed in a way that made them large and fathomless. Now she truly was someone else entirely. Now she truly was Sofia.

Sophie was no more.

You have nothing to be ashamed of. You are just as you are meant to be, a sylph, a reed in the water, a slender flame!

Lementeur's words rang tinny and weak, barely present through the pounding fear and insecurity that robbed her of her breath.

If this was a mask, then she could be unmasked. If this was a lie, she could be found out. Plain, bookish, socially awkward Sophie Blake could never become Sofia. Never, it was impossible, it was all some horrible trick—she would never, ever be able to pull this off!

Why not? You've done worse!

Yes, and look where that got her! She forced herself to inhale slowly. One lie was much like another, it was true. If she could make her way here to London under false pretenses, surely she could make her way onto the ballroom floor.

Sophie had been able to do only so much. Now Sofia must finish the job, or all the deception would have accomplished nothing. That would be the worst thing, to go back to having nothing at all.

*   *   *

GRAHAM HAD TAKEN his valet's advice and endeavored to begin his search at Lord and Lady Waverly's masque. He didn't have a costume, so he chose to go as a duke. He wore his usual evening attire and simply added a plain, black silk mask. He was not the only fellow who opted out of the sumptuous madness.

It wouldn't have done him any good to hide behind a King Henry VIII doublet, for all eyes were upon him the minute he stepped into the ballroom.

Only that morning had his advancement been announced by the ubiquitous yet invisible Voice of Society. By the time he'd returned to Eden House from his aborted attempt to see Sophie there had been a pile of invitations so high they slithered over each other to fall from the silver salver.

Now the Society mamas would have him pinned in their tenacious sights as never before. A poor fourth son was a long way from a man who could make their daughter a duchess!

Very well. He would do his duty and pursue an heiress. Luckily there were several at the masque. Graham knew the mamas by sight. All the young and titled did—although usually for the purpose of avoidance.

This evening Graham made himself available. Papas came to him to idly chat about the weather, the best tobacco, the races and oh-have-you-met-my-lovely-daughter?

Graham smiled. He bowed. He danced like the performing bear he was. Throw him some coin and see him stand on his head for an heiress! There were tall ones and short ones and thin ones and a few astonishingly curvaceous ones.

"So how are you enjoying your first Season, Miss Millionpound?" He could hardly keep his gaze properly on her face. She was full-bodied and fair-haired and wore a grandiose version of farmgirl attire, sky blue silk with rows of old-fashioned white ruffles about her considerable decolletage and a ribbon in her hair.

She had possibilities, for he did think it rather audacious of her to wear a milkmaid costume when sporting those . . . assets.

"Season?" Blue eyes blinked at him. "Oh, I like summer all right but I much prefer winter. More time to sit."

"Er. Yes." Another turn about the floor before he could try again. "I like your costume. Very . . . mischievous."

Another slow blink. "I'm not wearing a costume, Your Grace."

Yes. Well. Perhaps the sloe-eyed brunette, Miss Richpapa, would be more to his taste.

"Oh, Your Grace, you're sooo humorous!" Titter-titter.

He'd asked her if she was having a nice evening.

"Oh, Your Grace, you're sooo strong!" Titter-titter.

His biceps would be bruised tomorrow.

Perhaps she was nervous. Perhaps she was doing what her mother told her to do.

Or perhaps she was doing these things only when the dance took them past a certain brooding young fellow who lurked next to a potted palm, glaring at them with hot eyes.

Graham bowed out of the dance halfway through. He had no time to play out her game. On his way around the dancers, he passed the scowling boy once more.

"Do you truly want to endure that sort of thing for the rest of your days, lad?"

He moved on, but not before he saw a gleam of enlightenment in the young man's eyes.

Then there was Miss Catriona Shippinggold. She was an utterly charming pixie of a girl. As he danced, Graham felt himself relaxing and even laughing at her saucy manner.

Perhaps . . . just perhaps. She was actually rather adorable and they seemed to get on famously. He took a closer look. Pity she was so tiny, for he felt a bit as though he were dancing with Meggie—

Bloody hell.

"Catriona," he asked sternly, "how old are you?"

She chewed her lip for a moment, precisely like Meggie when she was contemplating a lie. Then she leaned close and whispered, "Fifteen, Your Grace."

He stopped in his tracks and removed his hand from her waist as if she were molten metal.

"Mummy told me not to tell," she confided, "unless you seemed the type to like that sort of thing."

"How . . . flattering." Firmly he took her arm and steered her back to her procuring mother. "Madam, you should be ashamed of yourself." He bowed to little Catriona. "I shall see you again, I hope—in several years."

She twinkled a smile at him. "Will you wait for me?"

He bowed again. "Alas, I cannot. But I wish you all the best, little one."

Fifteen? Gah!

Yet, eighteen, nineteen, even twenty seemed just as unrisen and unbaked to him. How could a girl that young even know what she truly wanted? What might she say in years to come when the naiveté wore off and she realized she'd been traded for a title and connections?

No, he was abruptly certain. He didn't want a girl. He wanted a woman, an equal, someone with her eyes fully open.

So, was it to be rich widows then? Because unfortunately, the richest widow in London at the moment was none other than Lady Lilah Christie.

SOPHIE STOOD AT the entrance to the ballroom, her mouth dry and her heart pounding, her silk shawl clutched over the gown beneath. The masque was another world.

Sophie had been to a few balls this season, though she'd never danced. At other times, she'd thought the array of pale gowns and dark surcoats a pretty picture, gently lighted by gracious chandeliers of sparkling crystal—all very civilized and restrained.

It was nothing compared to the riot of opulence and excess unleashed by the lax rules of the masque.

Lementeur had warned her. "In costume, a virtuous woman can be a whore and a whore can be a princess."

It seemed as though there were a lot of virtuous women here tonight. Bodices were tighter, necklines lower, ankles—clad in stockings so fine as to be barely there—flashed coquettishly from beneath gowns that clung damply to curves rather than concealed them.

A wave of heat struck Sophie's face as she stood in the shadows just outside the doors. The clashing brilliance and gasping riot was already in full force. How was she supposed to make any sort of impression in this room full of luxury and vibrance?

Then she recalled that she was not supposed to be seeing any of this. Turning to one side, she slipped her spectacles off her nose and donned her mask. Then, taking a breath, she willed her feet to move forward. One step, then another. She longed for the concealing cloak she'd relinquished to a footman. She would rather yet have been back in Lementeur's confection of a carriage, speeding off into the night.

You asked for this. To be perfectly accurate, you begged for it.

Recalling that, she felt her heart slow its fleeing-deer pace a bit. This was not something that was being forced upon her—she had made this night happen out of sheer will.

A new sense of power and purpose infused her. She wasn't here to shy away—to hide—to be plain Sophie the Stick anymore.

She'd come here tonight to be Sofia.

Slowly her right hand lifted and with a precise flick of her wrist, she opened her fan with one graceful motion. *There.*

A secret smile grew on her lips. Sofia had arrived.

Chin high, stomach trembling, shawl draping artfully off her bare shoulders, she glided down the stairs into the grand ballroom. If anyone were to ask, Tessa would have conveniently stepped out for some air.

According to Lementeur's instructions, she avoided furniture and pillars and potted palms. One could not trip over something if it wasn't there, after all.

She kept to the open for all to see—thank heaven that the world blurred to insignificance without her spectacles, so that she could not see except for the few faces closest to her. Actually, it was rather comforting.

Just as instructed, she made one languid meandering circle through the ballroom, her expression conveying the very height of haughty boredom.

Then she chose a spot well lighted and very public to hold court. For a long moment, her will wavered. Why should anyone speak to her? She would be thrown into the street and declared a fraud!

However, Lementeur had powerful friends, just as he'd promised. Gentleman after gentleman came to her, their deliciously gowned ladies in tow, to greet her as if they'd known her for years. Trying valiantly not to squint, she played along, greeting each memorized face with the proper memorized name, fighting back the trembling in her voice.

Important names, some so high that she'd suspected Lementeur of teasing her. Yet here they were—Reardon, Wyndham, Etheridge, Greenleigh—the count went on, each man handsomer than the last, each lady more gracious and beautiful.

If Sophie hadn't known what a mummery it all was, she would have been mightily impressed with her own importance! The exalted names passed through the queue, then returned moments later accompanied by eager young aristocrats who had begged introductions.

It was all a ridiculous lie and yet so easy. Sophie wondered why someone hadn't done this years ago. Then it struck her that people might be doing it all around her. Why, half the people in this room might have entered Society as frauds!

Of course, there was nothing new about her connection to the name of Brookhaven, but her presentation suddenly *sounded* more impressive.

So she accepted introduction after introduction, not really caring if she remembered most of them, for they were a lot of silly boys for the most part. Lementeur had told her not to show interest in anyone at all, for it would reveal her to be susceptible.

"Tonight is simply the first call of the hunt, my dear," he'd impressed upon her. "You must be the fleetest, most difficult doe to ever lead the hounds. Remember, easily caught, easily forgotten."

Lementeur had kept his promise. She appeared to be an arresting beauty, she was surrounded by admiring men and Society was eagerly agog.

He'd been right about one other thing as well.

Once her grand entrance had been accomplished, Sophie found that she wasn't just pretending *ennui*— she truly was bored out of her tiny little mind.

Chapter Ten

At the far end of the ballroom, where the unattached gentlemen tended to congregate near the smoking and card rooms, Graham tossed back another glass of Lord Waverly's flat, warm champagne. It tasted like hell, but if he drank enough of it, perhaps he could find his old self floating in it.

What was the matter with him? For the first time in his life, he had nothing to say to the group of rowdies he'd once called his friends.

He had nothing to say to any of the insipid, empty-headed women in the room either. His golden tongue had deserted him, his charm had fled. He was . . . he was . . . he was *brooding!*

God, why now? Why did he have to become an adult now, when he needed his boyish glibness the most?

Beside him, though he'd intentionally put a few steps of distance between, one of his former friends guffawed, spraying another with a mouthful of champagne. Once upon a time, Graham would have laughed, or at least dryly ribbed the dripping man.

Now he only wanted to grab the both of them by the collar and shake some sense into them.

Stop wasting time! Stop abandoning the people who need you!

Stop behaving like me!

However, he was here for another purpose. Dutifully, Graham took another glass of champagne from the tray of a passing servant. If he had to be drunk to find a bride, then he would get drunk and stay that way until his wedding day!

A third fellow joined them. Graham barely noticed, except that the man's excitement made his voice louder than the others'.

"Lads, I'm in love!"

Since said former friend fell in love on a monthly basis, Graham ignored him. The champagne lay flat and nasty in his gut. Perhaps he ought to find something to eat.

Muttering escalated into arguing. "Edencourt could do it, couldn't he?"

Hearing his new name startled him out of the contemplation of his nausea and he found his attention reluctantly drawn. "Could do what?"

"He can't. No one can. She's as cool as a winter lake."

"Edencourt, you have to see her. She's a lovely creature, like a gazelle. So refined. I hear she hasn't smiled once all evening."

Graham grimaced, already sorry he'd joined in. "Perhaps she's simply too dim to see the joke."

The three of them stared at him without comprehension. Right.

He sighed. They wanted him to go forth and conquer, as in the old days, so they could live vicariously through his success.

He opened his mouth to refuse the challenge. Instead, he heard himself ask, "Is she rich?"

The others smirked. "She's well connected and superbly dressed. I heard one of the ladies say it was the finest Lementeur gown she'd ever seen."

So she was wealthy. With a sigh, Graham disposed of his revolting champagne into a palm and dusted off his hands.

"I suppose I'll go beg an introduction, then."

The group parted to let him through, admiring acolytes ready to learn from the master.

Graham couldn't believe that he'd actually cultivated such a group of useless people. Had they no pride? No dreams? No ambitions?

Sophie had been so right about him. *You'd know that if you ever did anything with your mind other than waste it.*

Thinking about Sophie only worsened his mood. She was acting strangely, always off busy doing something, making him wait on her.

He missed the days when she'd been simply there, when he'd turned toward Primrose Street after becoming jaded with the *ton*, knowing that when he walked into that parlor he would find a cheery fire and cigars and brandy, and Sophie to listen and ask all the right questions and pierce his meandering thoughts with a pointed barb of perfect sense.

Thinking of Sophie, he almost didn't see the new

femme fatale. Then he realized that it was because she was surrounded. God, the blokes were three deep and more were on their way! All Graham could see from where he stood was a long, elegant neck, bare white shoulders and a shimmering fringe of red-gold curls, topped with intricately twisted tresses set with pearls.

She was a tall one, that was for sure. Graham did prefer a taller sort, for he always felt ridiculous dancing with someone who was forced to stare at his waistcoat buttons.

The crowd was thicker before her, so Graham sidled up to the rear guard. With a stomp on an instep—"Oh, dear, was that me?"—and an elbow in some ribs—"So sorry, bit too much champagne, I think"—he was behind the woman, nearly close enough to kiss the back of that stunning neck.

In her astonishing gown, she gleamed like a pearl from the sea, simply lovely amidst the clashing riot of color adorning everyone else. Like a chilled sip of wine after being trapped in a crowded, sweaty, smoky ballroom . . . like this one.

Her head was tilted slightly, so he could see the turn of her high cheekbone and long, auburn lashes. She seemed to be listening to some stout fellow who burbled outlandish praise. "And the moon'th light will catht a fainter glow now that thuch an ekthquithite creature hath joined our fine athemblage—"

"Superb prose." Graham laughed softly. "Or should I say, 'thuperb'?"

Graham. When Sophie heard the voice, felt the warm whisper on the back of her neck—where no gentleman should feel free to be—her knees weakened. With fear, or anticipation?

A bit of both. Wild thoughts chased through her mind. Should she run away? Did he already know it was her? He was flirting, but then, Graham would flirt with a lamppost if he was bored enough.

Should she spin about and shout "Surprise!"?

Frozen with indecision, she did nothing. Before her, several young men were talking, all vying for her attention, but their combined chatter faded to a cricket's chirp while Graham stood behind her, so close she could feel the heat of him against her bare upper back.

Still, what was he thinking? It was rude of him to crowd a lady so, rude and bold and undeniably charming—if one were here to be charmed by rogues.

Which she was not.

Graham was quick, but even he nearly lost an eye when the lady's fan was flicked over her shoulder. Ducking the lethal thing lost him his place in the crowd, but it forced a smile and a spark of interest from him as well. This one was no cringing flower! Nor was she one to tolerate his admittedly discourteous behavior. With a grin, he dove back into the fray, this time in a frontal attack that left him with sore ribs and a place facing her. He bowed playfully. "Pray, my lady, tell me where a knight might win the favor of an introduction?"

She wore a half-mask, a thing of fantasy and dreams that left her enormous eyes free to send scathing sparks in his direction. "I thought I'd left you wounded in my dust." Her voice was low and husky, yet tantalizingly . . . familiar? Her lips pursed. "How disappointing."

With another deadly flick of her fan between them, she turned away to speak to a fellow at her side. Graham found that the circle turned with her, leaving him to the rear once again.

So that's the way she wanted to play it, hmm? Graham let the crowd slide around him, leaving him standing alone, his brow creased in thought over his own brief domino mask. A woman like that, clever and proud, required that he adhere to all the proprieties.

He smiled slightly, anticipating her reaction when she heard his title announced. He hurried off, not realizing that this was the first time he was happy about the legacy he'd been left with.

Following the throng, he grabbed one of the trailing, kowtowing suitors by the arm and pulled him away from the throng.

"Oy!" The fellow, whose name, if Graham recalled correctly, was Somers Boothe-Jamison and who wore the garb of a harlequin, gave Graham a protesting push. "You've made me lose my place!" Then he realized who he was shoving. "Oh. Hello, Lord Edencourt. I beg your pardon, Your Grace."

"Somers, you sat on me and shoved sand up my nose first year. I think we're beyond 'Your Grace,' don't you?"

Boothe-Jamison, who was actually an all-right fellow, just not inclined toward interesting and imaginative trouble-making, gave a rueful grin. "Well, you know how some fellows can get, once the title lands on them."

Graham tilted his head toward the mob behind them. "Are you officially acquainted with the new temptation?"

Boothe-Jamison drew himself up. "I am. In fact, I'm an old friend of the family. Remember Lord Raphael Marbrook? She's related."

Graham frowned. "What? I've never heard they had any more cousins." And he would know. Good God, he'd spent half the Season hanging about Brook House! Sophie would have told him if there were any more family visiting—

An eerie feeling started on the back of Graham's neck. He passed his palm over his nape. No. That was ridiculous. He looked over his shoulder at the girl in the midst of the crowd.

And remembered that when he'd stood behind her, she'd smelled surprisingly good. Like sensible soap and warm skin and incorruptibility . . .

He grabbed Somers by the arm. "Introduce me," he said through a hardened jaw.

This time—perhaps it was his rank or perhaps it was the homicidal glint in his eye—the sea of backs clad in all the colors of the rainbow parted before him, no stomping or elbowing needed. Somers took him right up to the girl, who was turned away, listening to another round of shameless flattery.

Somers started in with the usual forms of address, all very correct, but Graham wasn't listening. He was looking at her delicate collarbones, the turn of her jaw, the pile of silken hair that needed no feathered ornament or grand turban to be luxurious.

No.

"—may I present Miss Sofia Blake, Your Grace?"

It can't be.

She turned slowly. He watched every movement, for time had slowed madly. He saw the way she drew a deep breath, he saw her swallow, her elegant throat betraying her nervousness. He saw her straighten so that when she raised her gaze to his at last, her eyes were nearly on a level with his own. *Her eyes . . .*

"Hello, Graham."

Graham felt as though he'd been kicked by a horse somewhere in the vicinity of his heart. The breath left his lungs and he felt his thoughts slow, able only to gaze helplessly at her.

Sophie. His Sophie. His funny, awkward companion and friend—transformed to the ethereal beauty who stood before him?

Sophie waited, unable to breathe, unable to do anything but wait for her heart to start beating again.

Would he see her now? Would he think she was beautiful? Would he laugh at her, ask her what the hell she thought she was playing at? Would he care at all?

He was staring at her, his expression still frozen in shock, his eyes fiercely green and bright—but with what? Humor? Disdain? Something else that she'd sworn she wasn't going to hope for?

"Oh, you two have already met?" The fellow who'd introduced Graham was talking. She didn't care. But then the jostling admirers began to close in, some protesting Graham's advantage, some clamoring for her attention.

Graham blinked. Then he glanced around at the throng around them. His gaze returned to hers and he tilted his head toward the dance floor with one brow raised.

Waltz?

She heard it as clearly as if he'd shouted it. Not the most elegant of requests, but she was dying to get away from the cursed admirers anyway. She quirked her lips.

About bloody time.

He bowed deeply, a dashing figure who suddenly looked every inch the Duke of Edencourt. Sophie curtseyed effortlessly, suddenly wondering why she'd had so much trouble with the gesture just days ago.

Then she laid her gloved hand on his arm and glided through the wide-eyed suitors—for she'd refused to dance with any of them, no matter how prettily they begged—and into the waltz as if they'd begun dancing before they'd even come through the door.

Graham's warm hand on her waist. His eyes gleaming at her with what looked—yes, definitely!—like approval.

For one delicious sweep around the floor they did not speak. Graham could not take his eyes off her face. Had her eyes always been so large and beguiling behind her spectacles? How could he—who could spot a pretty girl from a half-mile away!—spent so many hours with Sophie and never seen this woman?

"Sofia?"

She smiled slightly. Had her lips always been so sweetly curved? "Lementeur's idea. I think it worked on me as least as well as it did on the slavering pack."

Graham returned the smile, his tinged with wonder. "A new name, a new woman?" Still, he frowned slightly. "All this to gain Society's attention?"

Her chin lifted. "Why not? Don't you think I can accomplish it?"

He smiled at her appreciatively, his teeth flashing in his tanned face. "I think you can do anything you wish. If you decided to become queen, I'd simply cheer you on—and warn everyone else to get out of your way!" He shook his head. "I'll admit, I'm relieved to find that this is what you've been up to. How long has this been going on?"

She hesitated. "Oh, well . . . I've been a bit at loose ends since Phoebe and Deirdre left London."

He laughed, shaking his head again. "At loose ends? Heaven help us if you're ever really bored! And you never said a word to me."

Her lids dropped, hiding her eyes from him. "Wasn't it more fun to be surprised?"

He grinned. "You look—"

Her gaze flew up, locking on his. "I look what?"

His smile softened. "You look like Sofia, who is about to take the city by storm."

A slow smile curved her lips and then continued, the first bright carefree smile he'd ever seen from his dear Sophie.

Dazzled, his breath caught in his throat, he could

only continue to sweep her around the grand ballroom, not even realizing that the other dancers had dropped back to watch the tallest, most graceful, most beautiful couple in the room waltz while gazing deeply into each other's eyes.

Chapter Eleven

Stickley and Wolfe had never shared a meal voluntarily, so it was with some surprise that Stickley opened his front door at breakfast time to find Wolfe standing outside, twitching with impatience and wielding a number of newssheets rolled into a club.

Stickley fought the urge to duck. It had never served him well with Wolfe to show any sign of intimidation. That only brought on jeering and a tendency to leave large insects in his unmentionables drawer.

"Good morning, Wolfe. Won't you join me for eggs?"

At the mention of food, Wolfe looked a bit green. Stickley repressed a smile. "I've a wonderful batch of kippers as well. Or would you prefer bacon?"

Wolfe swallowed harshly. "Shut up, Stick." He pushed past him into the house.

Stickley was rather proud of his little corner of England. He'd put a lot of thought into the address, neither too showy a location, nor too shoddy a one. He knew Wolfe had lost his father's house in a card game years before and now moved from rooming house to rooming house, when he couldn't cadge free board from his diminishing circle of friends. Wolfe made them easily enough. It simply seemed to be a problem in keeping them.

Stickley had not bothered to accumulate people, but he'd spent years on his collections. In every room of this house were displayed all the various interests he had, from butterflies pinned with precise labels, to paintings by obscure but someday sure to be famous artists, to fine china and precious Egyptian artifacts.

Wolfe stumbled past them all without seeing, thank heaven. One wouldn't want a man like Wolfe to *appreciate* one's possessions. One might end up with less of them after Wolfe left!

With a sigh, Stickley passed by his breakfast room, set for one with piping hot eggs and fine tea, and followed Wolfe down the hall to his study. Once there, Wolfe threw himself into the single large chair and let the newssheets drop to the desktop. They unfurled in a rustle of paper, revealing a drawing that made Stickley twist his head sideways to get a better look.

"Is that . . . is that *Miss Blake*?"

Wolfe groaned. "Yes. With *Edencourt*!"

Blinking in surprise, Stickley used one finger to spin the top sheet to its proper alignment and read. "The Fairy Queen takes Waverly's masque by storm! Miss Sofia Blake rose to the top of the crème de la crème last evening as she swept up the hearts of a hundred gentlemen and trod them beneath her dainty heels. The Voice of Society wonders . . . if only one man caught the eye of Titania, could the Duke of Edencourt be her Oberon?"

Stickley flipped through the other sheets, but it was as if there had been only one event last evening and only one couple in the world. There were sketches aplenty and Stickley had to admit that Miss Blake seemed much improved since the last he'd seen her. Of course, he'd always rather liked her. Such a sensible, diffident young lady. If only she weren't so unfortunately tall . . .

Yet the Duke of Edencourt didn't seem to mind. There were at least three sketches of Miss Blake and Edencourt dancing, gazing at each other in dreamy ignorance of the fires they lighted under spying eyes.

"Er, well, good for her, I suppose. I shouldn't have thought she'd be the sort of girl a duke would want, but—"

Wolfe groaned again. "Stickley, why must I always spell these things out for you! If she weds Edencourt, we'll lose everything!"

Stickley didn't appreciate having his nose rubbed in the fact that he wasn't up on the latest gossip—as if that constituted a true intellectual pursuit!—so it took him a long moment to realize Wolfe's point.

"But why? When Miss Cantor became Lady Brookhaven, you seemed resigned enough that she might soon be a duchess."

"That's because she won't touch the Pickering trust. She mentioned leaving it intact to pass on to her own children. Brookhaven doesn't need our money—"

"It isn't *our* money, Wolfe," Stickley interjected primly. "We are only its custodians and protectors."

"Well, we ought to be concerned about protecting it

from Edencourt, by God! You've never met any of that lot, but they are the most profligate men in England! They never had a penny to their name that didn't have thrice its own weight in debt attached! He'll run through our . . . through Miss Blake's fortune in a heartbeat!" He rubbed his head and muttered on. "I wonder how he learned of it—surely she wouldn't have told him."

"Why do you think he knows of it? Perhaps he likes her." Stickley tapped the top sketch with one finger. "It certainly looks like that here."

Wolfe rolled his eyes. "Stick, old son, have you seen this girl? She looks like a cross between a horse and fencepost!"

Stickley drew back, offended. "I found her to be a sensible, intelligent girl—"

"Precisely!" Wolfe threw his hands wide. "No one ever says that about a pretty girl!" He flung himself to his feet and began to pace. Stickley quickly took possession of *his* chair. Wolfe ran hands through hair that needed cutting—and washing, for that matter.

"No, Edencourt knows all right, and he's trying to cut us out! If he gets his hands on the money, he'll piss it away like his father and brothers before him and we'll all be broke—" Wolfe grabbed up the newssheet in his fist. "Including your precious Miss Blake!" He balled the sheet up and threw it into a corner. Stickley pondered the unwanted, ruined wad worriedly.

"I shouldn't like anything to happen to Miss Blake," he said slowly. "Perhaps she doesn't realize Edencourt's true character?"

Wolfe had stopped pacing and was now eyeing Stickley narrowly. "She can't possibly know the danger she's in," he agreed. "A handsome duke—girls don't have much sense about those. She's a babe in the woods, poor thing." He sighed craftily. "If only there was some way to stop that nefarious gold-digger . . ."

Oh, no. Not again. Not after the last two debacles, the fumbled kidnapping of Lord Brookhaven—who could have known his brother and he would look so much alike in the dark?—and then that even more badly managed attempt to get one of Lady Brookhaven's suitors to steal her away so that Brookhaven would dissolve the marriage! Stickley took a breath and firmed his backbone. "Don't you dare try to stop Miss Blake from catching Edencourt."

"It's too dangerous to leave alone!" Yet Wolfe seemed unwilling to push Stickley.

That was fortunate for Wolfe, for after his partner's scheming had put Lord Brookhaven's child in danger by inciting a madman's obsession with Lady Brookhaven, Stickley had decided that he would no longer permit— or by God *join*!—Wolfe's rather criminal solutions to their problems.

If that meant that he himself must pay for his past participation . . . well, he'd rather not, of course, but he would choose that over any further unlawful meddling! "If you believe that warning Miss Blake will help our cause, then by all means do so." He narrowed his eyes. "But do not cross that line, Wolfe."

Wolfe snarled, but glanced aside. That surprised Stickley. Was Wolfe mellowing with age? It didn't occur to him to ask himself if it was perhaps he who was the changed man.

Wolfe lifted a shoulder in half-hearted agreement. "Whatever you think best," he muttered. Then he brightened. "I can court her myself, can't I? Try to turn her attentions away from Edencourt?"

"With honorable intentions?" Stickley eyed him closely. "I thought she was a fencepost."

Wolfe spread his hands wide to the side. "She's not pretty enough for a duke, but she might do me nicely indeed. I've been meaning to settle down for a while. I've simply not met the right woman—" He snickered. "At least, not in the circles where I travel."

Stickley snorted. "Oh, please, by all means. She's far too sensible to fall for the likes of you."

"Oh, you think you could do better?"

Pursing his lips primly, Stickley smirked. "I would be quite a catch for someone like Miss Sophie Blake, and I daresay we'd get on famously. She is a very learned young woman."

Wolfe nodded amiably and wandered to the front door. On the way, he ducked into the breakfast room and swallowed Stickley's cold eggs in one bite. He wasn't the breakfasting sort, but he was bit short at the moment . . . and this way he'd have money for ale.

Whistling as he ambled down Stickley's obnoxiously boring street, Wolfe pondered the idea which had struck him in the very middle of his despair. If he courted Sophie Blake, he'd skirt the danger of losing the income of the Pickering trust's healthy retainer— but if he married her, he'd be permanently attached to

Brookmoor and Brookhaven, whose riches far out-matched Pickering's pot of gold. The pockets of wealthy relatives could be tapped endlessly.

It would be worth it, scrawny nothing that she was—and besides, she could always meet with an accident. Wives died every day, after all. Falls down stairs, house fires—the possibilities were endless. Things were looking up. Old Brookmoor was up and about and might last for years and Sophie Blake was all but taken care of. No danger, no danger at all.

All he needed was a little time to figure out how to bleed Stickley of more money.

Chapter Twelve

Though the noise of London's morning did not breach the thick walls of Brook House, something awoke Sophie from her exhausted sleep. She flopped over onto her stomach with a groan. She hadn't touched the champagne last night, but she'd not been able to eat all the previous day in anticipation of the ball. Now her stomach hurt, her head pounded and she felt quite wobbly.

Food.

At the smell of toast and steaming, fragrant tea, she lifted her head and peered blearily at the sitting area in her bedchamber. Who—?

She fumbled for her spectacles, then blinked in surprise.

"You didn't follow orders," Lementeur said sternly. Then he nibbled delicately at a piece of Sophie's toast.

He was altogether awake and dapper in an interesting combination of purple silk waistcoat and lemon yellow surcoat. Sophie shut her eyes against his chipper brightness and rubbed them, pushing the spectacles up onto her forehead. "I'm usually an early riser," she mumbled.

"Welcome to the life of the *ton*. You thought everyone slept late because they were lazy." He waved the toast, conceding the possibility. "It takes a certain amount of fortitude to be an entirely unproductive consumer."

She fell back onto her pillow, whimpering. "Throw me toast."

A slice plopped next to her on the bed. She reached for it without opening her eyes and began to nibble.

"You'll have to get up to have tea," Lementeur told her. "You don't deserve to have breakfast in bed."

Feeling better with half a slice of toast in her, Sophie opened her eyes to glare at the demon dressmaker from hell. "I was superb. I had everyone's eye!"

He snorted. "Indeed. So much so that your appearance was well documented in this morning's tattle sheets."

He pulled a folded newssheet from his breast pocket and opened it with a snap. " 'Waverly hosted the emergence of a bright new star in the firmament last evening when Miss Sofia Blake took the dance floor with the Duke of Edencourt for a waltz so romantic that it brought some of the more delicate ladies to tears.' "

Thinking of that waltz, Sophie dreamily closed her eyes. Whirling about the floor in Graham's arms, his dazzled approval apparent in his eyes, the world fading away about them . . .

"It was divine," she whispered.

Lementeur sniffed. "And then you left."

She shrugged, still dreaming. "I could hardly dance with anyone else after that—but I couldn't decently refuse either. Besides, you were right. It was boring."

"Sophie, my pet?"

At the gentle sadness in Lementeur's voice, Sophie lifted her head to gaze at him in surprise. He'd been such a stern taskmaster for the last week that she'd quite forgotten that he was really a very kind man. Now, he was looking at her with sympathy and pity.

"What is it?"

He shook his head slowly. "Everyone knows that Edencourt will marry money."

Right. Of course. Spurred by her own idiocy— again!—Sophie slid out of bed and began to pace before the fire. Was there no end to her stupidity? She pressed her fingertips over her aching eyes. "Why is it that man always makes me forget what I'm about?"

Lementeur tsked. "We are all, at times, subject to weakness for a fine set of shoulders and a firm derriere. The point is that although you certainly made a splash last evening, you forgot your intention. I thought you were in search of a husband, not a lover."

Lover. What a marvelous thought. For a moment Sophie found herself actually tempted to become Graham's lover, his mistress even after his cold-blooded Society marriage. He wouldn't be hers in name, but he might be hers in truth—

And you think you could bear that, to have him leave you cold in your lonely bed while he went home to his wife and children?

Pain sliced at her. *Ah. Perhaps not.*

No. Much as she longed for Graham, she could not allow an impossible infatuation to keep her from securing her own future. She was a poor, plain woman with no saleable skills. She must marry for security or she must starve. She'd left Acton forever, and frankly, she wouldn't go back even if she could.

I think I'd rather starve after all.

She must find someone not too stupid, though. If she was forced to spend the rest of her life with her own cold-blooded match, let it at least be someone who she wouldn't be tempted to kill after six months.

Unfortunately, most of the unmarried men she'd met last night fell well into the stupid category. She sighed heartily, then flopped into the chair opposite Lementeur. He glared at her ungainly motion. She crossed her eyes at him. "I'll be a lady after I have my tea."

Lementeur gazed at her with narrowed eyes for a long moment. Then he raised his own teacup in salute. "You'll do, Miss Blake. A week ago you wouldn't have dared be disrespectful to me."

Feeling guilty, she was about to apologize, but he waved it away. "You misunderstand. I'm glad you found the fight in you. I think you've been simply surviving for far too long. Now you can begin living in truth." Leaning back in his chair he sipped at his tea, then smirked. "Yet perhaps more important—by all accounts you made my gown look entirely delicious."

Sophie smiled ruefully. "Thank you, but I'm certain it was the other way around."

He waved his hand. "You'll learn, my sweet. There is a vast difference between a woman wearing a gown and it wearing her." Then he leaned forward to regard her with his head tilted slightly. "Miss Blake, whomsoever you choose, do make sure he's ardent about you."

Sophie stared at him with a slight crease in her brow, her chewing slowed.

He continued, his voice entirely serious. "A man will do astonishing things for a woman he is ardent about."

Sophie swallowed, but before she could question him on his meaning he stood and bowed. "I shall let myself out," he announced. "And you will eat a proper breakfast. Your maid will bring you eggs. Then, you will entertain callers this afternoon for precisely fifteen minutes and no longer. You are not to linger, or engage anyone in conversation for more than a few moments."

He tsked again. "At least you had the sense to leave immediately after dancing the waltz. It added quite the air of mystery, I must say."

Sophie was nodding, for she felt too raw from the previous night's adventure to be ready for prolonged entertaining.

"Then you must prepare to attend Lady Peabody's musicale this evening. I'll instruct Patricia on what you must wear."

Sophie's brows rose pleadingly. "May I stay for only fifteen minutes?" Lady Peabody only held musicales so that she could show off the dubious talents of her two tone-deaf daughters. "I'll not be able to hide the fact that I have no chaperone."

Lementeur's eyes snapped. "Mutiny! Sedition! Disrespect!" Then he grinned, his eyes bright once more. "She always has her daughters perform first. Time your arrival a bit late. All the better to command a stunning entrance.

As for chaperonage, I'll have a word with Lady Peabody. She'll jump at an opportunity for a discount."

Then he was gone and Patricia arrived with eggs and more tea on a tray. Sophie ate slowly, trying to ignore the one thought circling in her mind.

Would Graham be there tonight?

Her lips twitching in mischievous intent, she rang the cord hanging on the wall. Fortescue would know.

IT WAS AFTERNOON before Graham's valet, Peabody, bothered to bring tea to his bedchamber. Graham knew that Peabody disapproved of the fact that Graham had yet to move into the duke's grand suite, but the thought of waltzing into that stifling domain—where lurked even more defenseless trophies!—and tossing out all his father's things and treasures . . .

No thank you.

If he had a butler like Fortescue, he could request it done for him and know that when he strode through the door the rooms would be a marvel of perfection. Unfortunately, Nichols was not proving to be so amenable to the change of order.

He couldn't keep the man, yet he could hardly fire him, not after so many years of service. What would Calder, Marquis of Brookhaven do with a butler like Nichols?

Graham could almost hear Sophie's tart tone if he were to ask her. "He'd send him off to Edencourt with a skeleton staff to start putting that house in order!"

Laughing softly, Graham rubbed the weariness from

his eyes and found the wherewithal to put his feet on the chilly floor. Coal was at a premium at the moment and Graham meant to save every penny he could. If that meant he had to tolerate a cold floor and extra blankets, then he would. Sophie would approve.

Where had she gotten that luxurious gown? It had obviously been created just for her, for there were few women in England who could have pulled it off so elegantly. A gift from her new cousin, Brookhaven?

Probably, and it was none of Graham's business anyway. Deirdre was just the impulsively generous sort to give Sophie an impossible gift like that.

Impossible? Seemed rather possible last night, didn't it?

Which was odd, really. After all, this was *Sophie.* Sophie was the sort of friend one laughed with and talked to and played cards with—but not the waltz-until-the-world-fell-away sort, not at all!

Yet there you were, as smitten as all the rest.

Uncomfortable with that knowledge, he banished it thoroughly. That lasted until Peabody finished shaving him. He wiped his face with a steaming towel and then—

"Such marvelous sketches of you and Miss Blake in the gossip sheets this morning, Your Grace," Peabody commented as he cleared away the shaving implements. "It was very kind of you to help her make such a splash. She's sure to find a good match now."

Match? As in, *husband?* Graham felt his jaw drop, then shut it hurriedly. "Do you think she's angling to get married?"

Peabody gazed at Graham as if he weren't very

bright in the mornings. "Of course, Your Grace. Ladies do like to get married. Why else go to all the trouble of making such a display of themselves?"

Sophie, married to one of those sniveling idiots? Sophie running the idiot's household? Sophie, buttering the idiot's morning toast? Sophie, going to the idiot's bed?

Over my dead body.

Which was ridiculous. Of course Sophie should get married. She'd make a marvelous wife—well, if a fellow was discerning enough to desire clever conversation over deference and obedience. It would help if he was a well-read man, with educated opinions and the backbone to voice them. And there was no helping the fact that Sophie wasn't in the least bit social, so she'd be a terrible hostess. A bloke would have to be tolerant and generous enough to compensate for that, as well.

Yet in return, the aforementioned paragon of husbandly virtues would receive a lifetime of fierce loyalty, razor wit, open warmth and, rather surprisingly still to Graham, considerable beauty.

No. That wasn't quite right. Even with all the trappings and bits, Sophie hadn't been beautiful last night. Not beautiful, or pretty, or any other faint praise would do.

Last night, Sophie had been quite simply . . .

Magnificent.

Lucky idiot.

She only danced once, they all said so. She liked you best.

Well, that might be because he was the only one

there who could form a complete sentence without lisping or guffawing or uttering something completely banal. Sophie wasn't very tolerant of the less-than-sharp. He smiled thinking of the way she'd flicked him away with her fan—twice!—when he'd been rude. Fatal flirtation. Death by Fanning.

Buttoning his waistcoat, he wandered to the tall window in his dressing room. He gazed unseeing outside as his mind traveled back to the way she'd looked in that gown.

Magnificent.

Graham felt a familiar stirring within—familiar, but not something he'd ever experienced in regard to his plain, innocent friend Sophie!

Oh, really? What about when you woke her in the window? What about when you played that thrice-damned game?

No. He didn't want Sophie.

A boy crying for a lost puppy. *Please, Papa, please go look for him!*

Shut that racket! A man doesn't weep!

A sharp backhand blow, a round of vicious jeering, but worse was the loss. Nothing was to be loved. Nothing was to be treasured, for it would surely be mocked and derided. Don't dare care about anything because he wouldn't get to keep it.

Nor would he get to keep Sophie. He needed an heiress. Last night was . . . simply an aberration. He'd been supportive of a friend who was making a change, helping her along socially, dancing with her to show all of London how special she was.

The way he'd felt—as if he was floating above the crowd, as if a wall of mist had lingered between them and the rest of the world, surrounding them, containing the magic—was ridiculous.

There was no such thing as magic. Only too much bad champagne.

Still, he wondered if he ought to call on her today— just to see how she was doing in her new persona. Last night the throng had been bewitched. They'd be all over her today. She'd never had a great many callers before. How was she to know who was worth her time? He'd hate to see her waste herself on those panting puppies.

Somers Boothe-Jamison, now, he was all right. Solid. Not one to be swept up in fashionable passions, only to lose interest when something brighter and shinier came down the river. A man like that might be just the ticket for Sophie.

So why did the thought make Graham's fists clench?

Chapter Thirteen

The formal parlor at Brook House was *inundated*. It was horrifying, like contemplating throwing oneself into a pack of snapping hounds. Tall men, short men, thin men, fat men. Some so young that shaving was a hobby, some so old that Sophie could be sure they'd be blind to her faults.

Outside the door, Fortescue and Patricia took point, readying Sophie for the encounter. According to Lementeur's instructions, she was to stay no longer than fifteen minutes.

"It will be a speedy maneuver, miss," Fortescue assured her. "In, out, then I'll show them the door."

"Won't they think it's odd that Tessa isn't here?" Sophie plucked nervously at the lace on the sleeves of her day gown. Another of Lementeur's miracles of simplicity, the deceptively plain muslin was cut to play off Sophie's length of limb. Layered ruching at the bodice provided a bit of feminine trickery and long, fitted sleeves gave her arms a dancer's grace. Patricia gently took Sophie's hands away and deftly repaired the worried threads. Then she removed Sophie's spectacles and tucked them into her lace sleeve.

Fortescue made a noise. No one could make noises like Fortescue. He had an entire vocabulary of "disdainful," "contemptuous" and, for the truly reprehensible, "disgust."

"This is Brook House, miss," he intoned grandly. "No one would dare hint at such an impropriety."

Sophie swallowed, then nodded. "Open the door."

She swept into the parlor, her Sofia hauteur in place. She accepted the greetings as if she was one breath away from a yawn, moved carefully around the furniture, then settled herself languidly in the chair by the fire. She'd intended to allow no one to sit at her side, but it had the added effect of serving as throne.

Quelling the always-nervous trembling in her belly, she waved an indolent hand. "I may only stay a few moments, as my chaperone is indisposed."

Somers Boothe-Jamison, one of the only men who wasn't completely dim, leaned forward. "Ah, how is Lady Tessa?"

Suppressing her alarm—if everyone knew Tessa, how was she to pull this off? Tessa would ruin it for her in a moment!—she turned to Boothe-Jamison. "*Indisposed.*" As if to an idiot.

Yet no sooner had she established that her chaperone was at death's door, but Tessa herself floated in, smiling and lovely. How had she made it past the butler's watchful eye?

Over Tessa's shoulder Sophie could see a blurred

Fortescue, his handsome face entirely devoid of expression, although one got the distinct impression that he'd just smelled something foul. Well, he could hardly refuse her entrance. Blast it.

Somers Boothe-Jamison was delighted. "Now you may stay as long as you like, Miss Blake!"

"Oh, dread," Sophie muttered. The gentleman who was currently boring her with tales of his sporting exploits gave her a startled look. Sophie, who had already crossed him off her list of potential husbands—she refused to spend the rest of her life listening to that idiot blathering about cricket!—merely gazed back at him with one brow raised.

Then matters worsened still. A few steps behind Tessa came Lady Lilah Christie herself. Sophie's hackles rose at the sight of Society's most beautiful widow. Black haired and silver eyed, rich, high-born, elegant and completely immoral, Lilah was everything that Sophie was not.

Blast it.

Tessa smiled and leaned over Sophie's shoulder. "I hope you don't mind, Sophie dear, but poor Lilah's been so blue lately. Her husband died recently, you know." Tessa's stage whisper carried clearly through the room. Lilah obviously tried to look appropriately mournful, but she was practically slavering over the roomful of men.

As for Tessa, it seemed she had seen this morning's newssheets as well. She was never one to pass up a chance to advance herself socially.

She was at her most adorable, her tinkling laugh chiming out over the room, drawing everyone's eye. Sophie knew perfectly well what Tessa was doing. After all, a beauty like Tessa would hardly have to exert herself to steal Sophie's triumph.

Lilah's mourning garb was black, but it was more revealing than concealing. The bodice of the gown was as tight as anything Sophie had seen at the masque the night before, and Lilah had more than enough bosom to make that a riveting sight. Of course, with her hair and eyes and moon-pale skin, the black only made Lilah more striking.

Her very permissive husband had recently died as quietly as he lived. For her to be out making calls was scandalous to be sure, yet when laid against Lilah's varied and sinful past, such a thing scarcely cast a shadow. Furthermore, Lilah seemed to feel she had a bone to pick with the great-granddaughters of Sir Hamish Pickering. It might have something to do with losing her former lover, Rafe, to Phoebe—or it might simply be that Lilah couldn't bear to share Society's attentions.

"But Sophie, where is Graham?" Tessa trilled. "Lilah's so very fond of Graham. They're old, *dear* friends."

Old, dear lovers, she meant. Everyone knew it. Suddenly, the whispers and gazes that had been trained on her were shifted to Lilah. Sophie gritted her teeth and prayed for a sudden breakout of locusts. Tessa was most certainly not going to behave herself. Sophie's venture was headed for the rubbish bin, only a day after it had begun.

BROOK HOUSE WAS one of the few grand houses in London that Wolfe had never managed to force, fool or finagle his way into, probably because the Marbrook brothers hadn't run in the same coarse, gutter-minded circles as Wolfe and his friends.

Ah, such good times . . .

Yet now, standing on the marble steps that invited even as they intimidated, Wolfe felt an unaccustomed twinge of nerves. It was possible that he would not be allowed in, if the houseman had any inkling of his past exploits. He was counting on the fact that the staff of such a house also ran in different circles than the staff of houses he knew well.

When the tall, striking butler opened the door to him, Wolfe did his best to project benign intentions. "Good morning. I am Mr. Wolfe, of Stickley and Wolfe, Solicitors."

The man's face did not change, but the respectability of Stickley had apparently paved his way, for he was allowed in.

"Are you here on business, sir? Her ladyship is not at home."

Wolfe remembered not to smile. Respectable people seemed to shrink back a bit when he showed his teeth. He shook his head. "I did not mean to misrepresent myself. I am here to call on Miss Blake . . . er, socially."

The butler reassessed him with cool precision. The man was good, Wolfe had to give him that. He felt as though his faults were written in ink on his forehead.

Fortunately, he'd planned for just such a barrier. He leaned forward. "Is she working on her translations? I so wanted to see them. Mr. Stickley knew I'd be intrigued. I'm a collector of folklore, you see. A little side interest of mine."

Actually, it was true—if one considered a vast assortment of pornographic pamphlets from all over Europe to be "folklore."

The butler's faintly furrowed brow cleared. "I see, sir. Miss Blake is in the parlor, entertaining callers."

Following him, Wolfe caught his image in the mirror hanging in the entrance hall. Wolfe's own mother, had she lived past his birth, wouldn't have recognized him. Without his luxurious mustache and dashing clothing, he looked entirely—well, perhaps not entirely— average.

He was still tall and broad shouldered and still had all his teeth and hair, which alone set him above most of the men his age, but more than this, he had the air of a man who'd seen more than his share of bedchambers— not to mention linen closets, carriages and dark, sticky alleys.

That simply wouldn't do. With one deep breath, he exhaled all that he was, collapsing his chest into a bookish slump, dropping his chiseled jaw into his neck and fixing his blinking, vague gaze upon the floor. One quick glance into the shimmering mirror told him that he'd done it. He was, for all intents and purposes, no more than a taller version of Stickley himself. It infuri-ated him, however, to see that he suddenly looked every one of his forty-mumble years.

From where he stood in the doorway, he could see Miss Sophie Blake, or Sofia, as she now pretended, conversing with a crowd of young pups who couldn't take their eyes off her.

Someone had done their best to make a silk purse out of a sow's ear. To Wolfe, she looked like nothing more than an overdressed scarecrow. A woman wasn't a woman without possessing enough bosom to suffo-cate a man. This creature might have cleaned up better than he would have suspected, but her new airs only in-furiated Wolfe further.

Snob. She wasn't born so far out of some Scottish hovel that she deserved to lift her chin so haughtily. Just looking at her made Wolfe's fists clench. She was just the sort of woman he hated most—and the kind he most enjoyed destroying.

For just a moment, he allowed his natural predatory smile to cross his lips. All this and the money as well. Breaking Miss Blake was going to be fun.

Chapter Fourteen

Wolfe only had one bad moment in the parlor of suitors and alleged ladies. A harlot of the highest order—who passed herself off as a proper lady, but whom he'd seen in some very compromising positions in some very illegal but treasured moments—spotted him through his Stickley disguise.

"Wolfe?" A look of amused derision crossed Lady Lilah Christie's face. "Aren't you looking dapper this afternoon?" Her tone dripped with irony. Wolfe saw indignation and sympathy cross Miss Blake's expression and pressed his suit with downcast eyes and a pained flush, which he accomplished by surreptitiously holding his breath.

"I'll leave you to your courtship, then, Wolfe." Lilah turned away with a snort of derisive laughter. "Take care, little girl. He's badder than he looks."

With his gaze downcast, Wolfe saw that Miss Blake's fists were clenched. She felt sorry for him! He hurriedly smothered his laughter with his handkerchief, then proceeded to dab at his brow. "So sorry, miss— Oh, dear, so embarrassing—"

"Nonsense," Sophie said sharply. "She is the one who ought to be embarrassed, mocking a respectable gentleman so!"

Wolfe sighed. "I fear I am easily mocked, for I've never quite been able to—to be—" He shrugged helplessly. "I'm not—"

Sophie patted his arm, feeling more warmth for him now than ever before. "I know precisely what you mean, sir. This world requires a bit of a roadmap, I fear."

Wolfe gusted a self-deprecating laugh. "Well, it seems I've misplaced mine!"

His plan seemed to be working. He played along with her when she offered advice in dealing with critics—so naive!—and nodded gratefully when she spoke of sending business his way.

"I'm so indebted, Miss Blake, truly. I only hope I can repay you in kind." He leaned closer. Now was the time to begin his sortie on Edencourt's good name—though in truth it was little better than Wolfe's own!

He really needn't lie at all, come to think of it. . . .

"Miss Blake, I've heard that you've taken an interest in the Duke of Edencourt."

She shot him a hot, embarrassed glance, then looked away. "I think 'interest' might be too strong a word."

Wolfe refrained from rolling his eyes. Spare him the lovelorn! "I hate to be the one to tell you this, but—"

Tessa's tinkling laugh rang out above the general hubbub. "Oh, I have the most amusing story. It concerns our own dear Sofia!" She sent Sophie a pretty smile beneath a vicious, triumphant glare.

Oh no. Alarm swirled through Sophie. She began to shrink into her chair—an impossible feat for a girl her height.

Most of the group turned their attention politely Tessa's way. *No, don't!* Sophie wanted to scream at them to turn away. *Don't listen to her!*

Tessa preened before the group. "First, I must tell you that although I had invited Sophie to share our little sojourn in London, I'd heard nothing from her mother, not even a note! Then, a week after we have settled into that dear little house, she arrives unannounced on our doorstep—I could hardly contain myself!—dripping wet, with nothing but a satchel of old gowns and a trunk of books! She was such a sight in an ancient cape that was six inches too short! I thought we'd opened the door on a skeletal specter!" She laughed musically and looked around for everyone to share in her little joke.

Sophie was completely speechless, gazing down at her hands. As always, the right retort did not occur to her until too late. What did it matter, when she was too tongue-tied to utter it anyway? If she could only maintain the icy calm that Lementeur had tried to teach her, if she could only lift her chin and portray an air of boredom—but still her belly writhed and her limbs tended to twitch from the sheer pressure of her boiling embarrassment.

She would never be that paragon of elegance that Lementeur had worked so hard to create. She would never actually master that fashionable ennui. Too many things mattered to her, her emotions were too deep and too entangled. Injustice angered her, unwarranted scorn offended her, the snobbery of the *ton* caused her heart to pound with fury.

The languid and the elegant had no such strong feelings, no such burning desire to right the wrongs of Society, no doubts and fears because they simply didn't care enough to do so. Such a life would be death to her soul, yet she—in a contrary impulse that confounded even her—still longed for a bit of the cool detachment, of that easy unconcern.

Yet, evidently her new coterie was a better class of friends than Tessa was accustomed to, for her chaperone's remarks were met with silence and uncomfortable averting of gazes. Tessa, unfortunately, seemed immune to such subtle disapproval. She only became more strident in her attempt to become more entertaining.

"Did I mention that Sophie traveled all the way from Acton by herself? She actually rode the coach *alone*. Of course, no one would interfere with a girl who looks like she does, but still—"

As always, Sophie felt muzzled by a lifetime of bashful withdrawal. She wanted to shout Tessa down, to say something cutting and devastating and permanently stifling—but her writhing was all internal. She simply couldn't open her mouth in front of all these people.

Succor came from somewhere entirely unexpected— although perhaps she ought to have expected it.

"Oh, I don't know, Tessa. I've always favored the independent sort." Graham leaned indolently in the doorway and sent an easy smile of approval in Sophie's direction. "And we all admire a woman who reads a great deal, do we not?"

His words sent a ripple of relieved agreement through the guests and sparked a discussion of the latest novels. Completely excluded and finally aware of general disapproval, Tessa fumed but thankfully did so silently.

Slowly the hot humiliation ebbed from Sophie's pale cheeks. She even managed to offer an opinion or two to the topic of conversation, but she had eyes only for Graham, who had moved around the outside of the group to take up a watchful station with one elbow on the mantel.

His expression was one of amused commiseration. *Do you really want to be here?*

She smiled slightly, meeting his eyes warmly. *I do now.*

"Hello, my love," purred a voice in Graham's ear.

Graham watched as Sophie's expression went from wry welcome to icy disinterest when she realized that Lilah had accosted him. Then Sophie looked away altogether, casting her attention upon the rabble instead.

As much as he might want to slither out of Lilah's grasp—for she'd wrapped both taloned hands about his biceps—he forced himself to turn and smile down at her. "Good afternoon, my lady." It wasn't a very good smile, more of a grimace, really, but Lilah didn't seem to be keeping a scorecard at the moment. That meant he was in serious danger, for Lilah never gave anyone an advantage—not for free, anyway.

This time, however, Lilah only gazed with infatu-
ated silver eyes at him and surreptitiously rubbed her
breast against his arm. "I've missed you, Grammie,"
she whispered. "Won't you come back to see Lillie
soon?"

"Er—" Graham slid his gaze helplessly toward Sophie. He knew if she heard Lilah call him "Grammie"
like that, he'd never hear the end of it! At least Sophie
had given him a decently manly pet name of "Gray,"
which he rather liked.

But Sophie wasn't paying a bit of attention. She was,
in fact, leaning toward some older fellow that Graham
hadn't noticed before. Then he felt Lilah's nails bite
into his arm and remembered the value stamped firmly
on his arse. *One ancient title, only slightly tarnished,
for sale to highest bidder.*

And Lilah had coin to spare. Graham tried not very
successfully to repress a sigh. "What will you bid, my
lady?"

"I beg your pardon?" Her eyes snapped, ever wary
of mockery, probably because it was a bit easy to do.

Graham thought of crumbling cottages and starving
dependents and added several candlepower to his
smile. "What is your bidding, my lady?"

Lilah purred. Literally. He'd once thought it highly
arousing. Now he only hoped Sophie didn't hear the
ludicrous affectation from where she sat. He could just
imagine the incoming sarcasm. *Keeping pets now,
Gray? Don't forget to dust the cat hair from your arse
before you leave.*

"Come to me tonight, my sweet," she urged, her

husky whisper almost an orgasmic sigh. "Come to my bed and let me console you . . . just the way you like best!"

Knowing he'd never get rid of her if he didn't agree— not that he wanted to get rid of her, of course, not when he was seriously contemplating marrying her, but she really couldn't be allowed to continue so or she'd embarrass them both—he patted her hand and whispered back.

"Yes, of course. Whatever you say, Lilah."

"Don't be late," she said crisply, releasing his arm at last. Graham secretly flexed his hand, for he'd lost some sensation there while she had clung.

Lilah retreated at once, just as he'd known she would. Having had her way, she would expend not a moment's more effort on the matter. With a flourish of her hand and a toss of her head, she collected Tessa on her way out the door.

Now free of her, Graham turned back to Sophie— who ignored him completely. She was surrounded again, nearly invisible behind a row of attentive men. Graham fought down irritation that she was not simply waiting here alone for him, as she once had. He'd suspected the throng would descend, but somewhere inside him he'd still expected her to be clad in some old rag, spectacles slipping down her nose, engrossed in something that left ink on her fingers and made her blink with annoyance when interrupted.

The way she used to be.

Yet at the same time, just look at her! He didn't know what that dressmaker had done to his Sophie, but she sat erect and composed, cool and serene in a room full of idiots that he knew she must want to flee at top speed. Possessive pride warred with ordinary possessiveness until he pushed off from his watchful perch, determined to leave this mess behind. He had a great deal to attend to.

On his way to take his leave, he brushed by a couple of the less worthwhile pups in the room.

"I'll take her to the opera on Wednesday, see if I don't!"

"Well, I'm going to ask to escort her to Lady Peabody's musicale tonight and—"

A snarl rose in Graham's throat. Before he knew what he was about, he turned it on the two young men. "*I'm* escorting her to Lady Peabody's musicale tonight!" He turned to the other one. It didn't matter if he had the right fellow, for they were surely interchangeable parts. "And I'll be sitting with her in Brookhaven's box at the opera on Wednesday!"

Leaving the pups near whimpering in his wake, Graham turned eyes sparked with murderous glee on the rest of the crowd. It began to thin at once. A few hardier souls thought to defy his claim, including Somers Boothe-Jamison, but Graham stalked them down one by one and made it quite clear that their presence was not welcome.

"Your presence is not welcome," he told Somers sharply.

Somers lifted his chin. "I say, Edencourt—you're being a right bully. I don't see that you've any more rights here than the rest of us!"

Graham growled—actually, physically *growled.* Somewhere in the back of his mind a saner voice wondered if there was perhaps more of his father in him than he'd previously thought, for even Somers drew back, a flicker of uncertainty in his gaze.

"Well, I suppose I've overstayed at that . . ."

Chapter Fifteen

Then nearly all the snapping hounds were gone, leaving only one man still in attendance. He seemed vaguely familiar to Graham, although by his dress and manner he was not someone of the *ton*. A man of business perhaps? Did he think he had an actual chance with a girl like Sophie?

Maybe Sophie likes him.

She certainly seemed intimate, at that. She was leaning forward to hear what he said and bestowing upon him the smile she ought to be saving for Graham.

Furthermore, for all his mundane appearance, the bloke was a good-looking lout—tall and powerful, if a bit drawn and creased.

The thought that Sophie might actually prefer that . . . that *clerk* . . . to *him* . . .

The fellow looked up then to meet Graham's gaze. Like measured like. This man was no stammering clerk. No, this was a different sort altogether. Instant distrust flared in Graham, to be matched by an answering flash of amused assessment in the other man's cycs.

*   *   *

SOPHIE WISHED MR. WOLFE would leave. At first she'd been intrigued by his interest in her translations and further distracted by his maturity and trusted connection to the family. Then, as their perfectly innocuous conversation turned to the current gossip, which seemed to center on Graham's exploits in particular, Sophie began to feel rather hunted in his company.

There was dark urgency in Mr. Wolfe's reddened eyes, as if he could scarcely keep from reaching for her with his hands, which kept opening and closing in nervous distraction. Mr. Wolfe *wanted* something.

Perhaps this was what Lementeur had meant when he'd said "ardent"?

It must be only that she was unaccustomed to such regard that his gaze made her feel like a steak on a plate. After all, ardent was what she was looking for, was she not? And unlike the simpering boys around her, Mr. Wolfe was a man of accomplishments. As a solicitor, he was an educated man, one who had learned the value of working for his place in the world.

He also seemed genuinely interested in *her,* not caught up in the glamour of Sofia. He was old enough to know what he wanted and not be swept up in the winds of the latest craze.

His abruptness and his awkwardness might be a bit jarring, but who was she to judge someone for not moving smoothly through Society? Yes, Mr. Wolfe ought to be quite high on her list of possible husbands.

It wasn't his fault that she simply couldn't imagine

any such thing. Ashamed of her reaction, Sophie made sure to bestow a little extra attention on the man. She wouldn't want him to detect her inexplicable aversion and have his feelings damaged in any way.

At last, the throng of younger men left and Sophie began to hope for eventual escape. Then she realized that it was Graham who was herding her admirers from the room, like a sheep dog cutting a ewe from the flock.

GRAHAM STARTED FORWARD, furious in his intent to separate this . . . this predator from his Sophie. By the time he reached her, however, the fellow had bowed a quick farewell and slithered out the door, following the rest of the pack, leaving Sophie alone with Graham, just the way he'd wanted.

When he reached her, however, he wasn't expecting the flare of fury in her eyes. He halted, startled.

She stood and advanced on him. "Just what, pray tell, was that all about?"

Ah, well, perhaps he'd not been precisely subtle. He cleared his throat and gave her his best charming grin. "You didn't want to spend all afternoon with that keg full of idiots, did you?"

She folded her arms and pursed her lips. "Oh, were they your callers to dismiss then? If so, then you've been keeping tawdry secrets from me indeed!"

He gaped. "My callers?" Tawdry secrets? What had that hairy fellow been filling her head with? Not sure he wanted to know—for what if he couldn't honestly deny them?—he backpedaled quickly. "I'm not the only one with secrets here!"

She drew back and paled. Why? He'd only been referring to her surprise transformation last night at the masque. Then, as quick as a blink, she was back in form. "I might have been enjoying myself. You'll never know for sure." She poked him in the chest with one finger. Hard. "We're friends and I've appreciated that, but you've no call to wax territorial. You don't own me, Gray!"

Territorial? Alarms began to ring back in that tiny sane portion of his mind. He ignored them. Instead, he scoffed, folding his arms. "That wasn't territorial! It was . . . it was protective! You're naive and barely chaperoned. You've no idea what wolves some of these blokes are!"

"You have no room to speak. You've taken advantage of my lack of duenna. You tell me—am I ruined because I spent a few hours playing cards with a rogue?"

He blustered at that, for he had indeed gone beyond the bounds of propriety—at least that once. The memory of her scent and the feel of her hair trapped in his fist slapped him nearly senseless with a sudden surge of longing.

He'd been a fool, he saw now. He'd thought himself the victim of a random urge to touch her that day, an impulse born of a need for distraction . . .

Not for diversion had it been, but for solace. For comfort. Not an impulse, but a yearning.

A strand of her red-gold hair had come undone in

her fury. It drifted down to coil next to a high, elegant cheekbone, framing one furious, dark gray eye. "You know what, Graham? I think you're a wee bit jealous."

He had a sudden vision of what she would look like sleeping, half her face buried in his pillow, her hair drifting over both their naked bodies, clinging to skin dampened by satisfied lust . . .

Bloody hell.

What had he become? What had he done to her—to himself?

Just look at him! He was becoming a chest-beater! He had no right to snort and stomp and scare away her suitors!

She fumbled in her sleeve and drew out her spectacles, all the better to glare at him through. She was a soldier dressing for battle. The gesture touched him in the oddest way.

The spectacles and the way her eyes peered through them belonged to him and him alone. The others might think they knew who they courted, might even believe they felt something real for her, but he was the only one she trusted enough to don her spectacles around.

What was so wrong with them, anyway? They were naught but a bit of wire and glass. He detested that she didn't feel as though she could be herself with that crowd.

"I can't believe you're looking for a husband among that lot! Why?"

She pushed her spectacles up with the tips of her fingers and glared at him furiously. "Why not? You're the jealous one. Tell me! Give me one reason why I shouldn't!"

What could he tell her? *I ruined everything.*

How had he let something so innocent and easy come to this—and why now, when he was no longer free to act on it? He'd dug his own grave, by God—dug it deep and wide with the sharp blades of loneliness and good intentions!

Through a throat tight with longing and lust, he pounded the last nail into his own coffin. "Don't be ridiculous!" he snapped at her. "I took pity on a poor, plain girl from the country! There's nothing to be jealous of!"

The flash of startled pain in her eyes made his gut ache. He didn't want her pain. He didn't want the responsibility of yet another soul on his shoulders. He turned away, unable to face her pallor and stunned silence.

Then, at the door, he glanced back to see that she had not moved, had apparently not even breathed. The pain forced him to continue. He needed to make sure she understood. It might not be a bad idea to remind himself as well.

"I have decided to ask Lady Lilah Christie for her hand in marriage."

Then he left like the coward he was, walking away from the damage he'd caused.

IN THE OFFICES of Stickley & Wolfe, Solicitors, there was, as usual, only Stickley. He wrapped up another

day of totting up the interest earned in various accounts by the Pickering trust and mused over his current
plan to put some of the money into shipping. It could be
very lucrative, but required a large initial investment. If
Miss Blake did wed the Duke of Edencourt, then she
might wonder where such a large amount of her money
went. Even the merest thought that something could cast
a shadow of doubt upon his ethical management of Sir
Hamish's fortune would not do.

He sighed. Such a pity to pass up a golden opportunity. Perhaps if he had approval beforehand—of course,
that would require signatures from all three of the
ladies, even though Lady Marbrook was already dis-
qualified . . .

Soothed by thoughts of money and putting matters
in neat and lovely order, Stickley had almost completed his weekly foray into the safe before he noticed
the marks on the door.

Scratches? Nay, gouges! What on earth—?

Then, as if he'd seen it with his own eyes, he knew.
That day Wolfe had come in early, he'd actually come
to try to crack open the safe!

But why? Surely Wolfe knew that Stickley only kept
their own personal retainers there, and only a month at
a time, with, of course, a second month's worth as mar-
gin against emergencies, of which Wolfe had constantly and Stickley never . . . or perhaps Wolfe didn't
know that.

Did the idiot think that the entire balance of the trust
lay within this iron box? Did the fool know nothing of
banking and investment?

Then again, it *was* Wolfe. With a sigh and a shake of his head, Stickley shut the safe box and dialed the lock shut. His partner was becoming more and more of a liability every day. Stickley hoped that Miss Blake would marry the duke—providing that the duke understood his proper responsibilities concerning the inheritance— because when that day came, Stickley would be free!

He closed his eyes for a long moment, savoring the pretty picture that thought made. Free of Wolfe's face, his foul habits, his tendency toward distressingly illegal acts—and, admittedly, his mysterious ability to make those acts seem like the most logical course of action!—free to invest his own money, or even to spend it, though he couldn't imagine needing anything he did not already have.

Real work.

Oh, yes. True work, work of meaning and progress and . . .

And nonsense, as long as he was tied to the trust and to Wolfe. Eyeing the disfigured door of the safe, Stickley pursed his lips once more.

He only hoped he could get out before he discovered what depths Wolfe was truly willing to sink to.

TESSA SAT DOWN at her feminine little escritoire and brought out the ink and pen and paper. She hated to sink to this level, really she did, but there was no denying that Sophie had gone too far.

Imagine, that horse-faced stick of a creature, creating such a stir in Society! And Graham, idiot boy, was being the most oblivious fool. Tessa remembered him as a mostly silent boy, skulking about trying to stay out of sight of his brutish brothers. Not that Tessa blamed him for that, for her elder cousins had been disgusting indeed, much like her own father. Good riddance to the lot of them.

Yet for Graham to dangle after *Sophie?* It was embarrassing!

And dangerous. The Pickering fortune was meant for Deirdre, not her horse-faced cousin. Only Deirdre would know the proper gratitude to pay her very own loving stepmother, once the checks were cashed.

Furthermore, if sweet Deirdre forgot her duty, Tessa had some nasty threats she could make against fat, moon-faced little Phoebe. Not everyone in Society would be as forgiving of Phoebe's wicked past as was her equally wicked husband! Deirdre doted on her stupid cousins. It shouldn't be too hard to exact a nice lifelong income from her.

All that would come to naught, of course, if Sophie won the day. The stupid girl would never recall that it was Tessa who allowed her to be here in the first place. She would only remember the few, paltry occasions where Tessa had lost her temper and called her a few harmless names.

All of which had been richly deserved. Why the creature was ridiculous! It was very alarming how no one in Society seemed to see that anymore.

With a slight smile, Tessa set to her work.

"Dear Mrs. Blake . . ."

Chapter Sixteen

After Graham left her, Sophie sat in the empty parlor, gazing unseeing at the trays with the remains of tea and cakes.

Crumbs. She was left with crumbs.

I took pity on a poor, plain girl from the country.

The heat was still in her face, she knew, and likely would be for days whenever she thought of that moment. She'd forgotten herself, so impressed had she been by her new popularity. She'd forgotten that all she was to the people who knew her was a "poor, plain girl."

What had she thought would happen when Graham saw the new "Sofia"? Had she thought he would drop to his knees and declare his undying love?

Apparently, some little part of her—likely the part that believed those fairy stories—had actually thought he might.

Fortescue entered with a footman. The room was cleared in an instant, polished and perfect in only a few moments more. Sophie stayed where she was, quite oddly comfortable with her misery. If she'd ever needed a clearer picture of her place on earth, she'd just been handed it—bound in silver paper with a ribbon on top.

Yet, apparently even "poor, plain" girls received mail. Fortescue brought her a thick ivory-colored envelope on a silver tray. "My lady has sent you a letter, miss."

Deirdre's handwriting was quick and careless, much like Deirdre herself. "Lementeur wrote me that you'd moved into Brook House," she'd written. "Bravo. Phoebe says to tell you to tell Fortescue to have all the locks changed against Tessa. I told her I already have."

Sophie blinked. She'd not thought to write to Deirdre to gain official permission to use the house. That was thoughtful of Lementeur . . . and a little managing, as well. Sophie smiled wearily at the thought.

The letter went on. The recovering duke had taken another turn for the worse.

"It looks as though I might be a duchess soon after all—so very sad, for we've all become very fond of His Grace. He's a kind old gentleman, and looks just like Calder and Rafe will in fifty years—I shall have to work hard to be so well-preserved myself, if only in order to match.

"All my love, and we cannot wait to see you in your new gowns. Tell Tessa to go take a dip in the Thames.

"And kiss my Meggie for me. And the kitten. Has she named it yet?

"D."

Sophie felt a flash of guilt then, for she'd quite ignored Meggie today. There was a bit of time before she
must dress for tonight's musicale.

Rousing at last from her gloom, she turned her back
on the scene of her great social triumph and headed up
the stairs to give, and hopefully get, a kiss and a hug
from Lady Margaret.

And the kitten.

At the top of the stairs, she glanced casually to her
left before turning right, then went very still.

Some slight distance down the hall she saw Fortescue and pretty Patricia, standing much, much too close.
Even as she watched, the stern and impassive butler
broke into a blindingly handsome smile, matched only
by the stunning one from Patricia herself. As they
leaned closer still, Sophie closed her eyes against their
joy, though a soft laugh, vibrant with affection, danced
down the hall to her ears.

Everyone had love, it seemed. Everyone but poor,
plain Sophie Blake.

Damn Sophie Blake, anyhow!

FORTESCUE WASN'T SURE how it happened. One moment, he was standing with Patricia in the upstairs hall
discussing the possibility of finding a suitable play-
mate for Lady Margaret, who seemed rather lonely in
the great house with no one but her kitten, and the next,
his hand accidentally brushed hers . . . and their fingers
caught . . .

The moment stretched on. He could scarcely

breathe as Patricia's slender freckled fingers slid between his. He gazed helplessly down at the top of her
head, her maid's mobcap as always losing the fight to
contain her masses of fiery hair. She seemed unable to
take her gaze off their entwined fingers, yet she made
no move to pull her hand away. Then, astonishingly,
she slowly allowed their hands to clasp fully.

Only then did she look up, her green eyes brilliant
with a mixture of wary confusion and desperate longing. Fortescue closed his hand on hers and tugged,
very gently, never taking his gaze from hers.

She stepped forward slowly, tilting her head back,
her pride and her yearning evident in the very curve of
her long neck. "What is it you demand of me, sir?"

He shook his head and let out his breath slowly.
"Demand?" *Oh, my beauty . . . so prickly, so proud . . .*
"I have no right to demand anything." He reached his
other hand to stroke an ever-wayward strand of flaming
hair away from the soft curve of her cheek. "I can only
request . . ."

Her eyes softened then, warming as the wariness re-
ceded. A smile tugged at the corners of those astonishing lips. She moved a step closer. "What is it you
request, then?"

He couldn't breathe. He couldn't speak. He only
shook his head, helpless in the face of what he most
desired in the world. *Could you ever love me?*

She laughed then, soft and fond and teasing. "You're
a great actor, sir. A man of granite and ice, they say be-
lowstairs . . . what if they could see you now?"

He looked down at their hands, still clasped. She

had not released him, even as he had not released her. Lifting his gaze to hers, he let himself fall at last into those green Irish dreams, danger be damned. "Marry me, Patricia."

There was a small satisfaction, even in the midst of his whirling panic and glee, in seeing those green eyes widen in shock.

"YOU, CINDERELLA!" THE stepmother said. "You're all dusty and dirty, and yet you want to go? How can you go dancing when you've got no clothes or shoes?"

Sophie swallowed, took a breath, then continued to read the story aloud.

He's going to marry Lilah.

Yes, he was. And if she had an ounce of sense, she would turn around and find someone of her own.

"Go on, Sophie!" Meggie jiggled with impatience. "What happened then?"

Catching herself on the winding trail of self-pity yet again, Sophie found a smile for the little girl. "Sorry." She went on, reading the story she knew so well she could shout it from the rooftop blindfolded.

Before Sophie had encountered little Lady Margaret, she'd never spared much thought toward children. Other women had them—women with husbands—but Sophie hadn't actually known any since she was a child herself.

Now, with Meggie snuggled up close beside her, bony elbows in Sophie's ribs, pointy knees pressing to her side, silky head tucked to her shoulder, the kitten a sleepily purring ball between them, Sophie experienced a longing so deep it took her breath away. For the first time in her life, she allowed herself to dream a child of her own into her vague, foggy future. All it required was to find a man she thought worthy of duplicating into the world.

How strange that not so long ago she might have taken any man who asked and thought herself fortunate, yet now she found it difficult to accept the attentions of more men than she'd actually been able to count yet.

That's Graham's doing.

Absolutely. All she needed to solve this little dilemma was to find a man more intelligent, more charming, more handsome and at least as tall as the new Duke of Edencourt.

Is that all? Why not pick something hard?

Sighing, she bent her head to kiss the top of Meggie's shining crown. "Nutmeg, you're fading. Go on to bed now." She untwined Meggie, then stood. The skinny little thing didn't weigh more than a pail of water, so she simply lifted her and carried her to her bedchamber. Once there, it was off with the shoes and stockings and dress and into bed. Sophie did a quick, lopsided braid to keep the girl's hair from tangling— with a silent promise to do better in the morning—and sent her off to sleep with one kiss for the girl and one for the kitten, snuggled on Meggie's pillow like a fuzzy, black-and-white hat.

Sophie pinched out the candle with a quick motion and left with only one lingering glance back as she closed the door. Deirdre would be a good mother to the poor child, Sophie knew. There was no reason to want to steal her away, just so she herself would never be without someone to love.

Go get your own.

Her own child, her own home, her own man. If she could, she would take the home and the child and skip the man. . . .

Oh, really?

Standing in the hall, her back pressed to Meggie's door, the silent house enveloping her, she knew there was no point in carrying on the lie, not in her own heart.

She wanted what she wanted, God help her. She wanted, out of some madness, to win Graham for her own. Lilah be damned, status be damned, secrets be damned. What was the point of this life, this breathing in and out, this beating of the heart, if it wasn't to matter to someone, to belong to someone, to live and breathe and beat heart to heart with someone else? If she couldn't have Graham, then her going on would have all the purpose and point of a machine, rumbling along, soulless and blank.

So go get him.

She would if she could —

Have you actually tried?

She stopped, her fingertips going to her lips in surprise. She *hadn't* tried, had she? Here she was, all dressed up and waiting for her prince to notice, instead of slapping him a good one and dragging him down for a kiss that would make him forget every other woman he'd ever known!

If she wasn't so giddy and thrilled by the thought, she'd have taken a moment to feel very, very stupid.

Chapter Seventeen

John Herbert Fortescue was a man in love. And, unlikely as it might be, the girl he loved seemed inclined to love him back!

Patricia had one hand to her cheek, stunned at his proposal. He'd kept the other one tight in his. "Marry you? But—" She blinked and fought for a real breath. "I—"

For a moment, he found hope in the growing joy in her face. She was going to say yes!

Then a shadow fell over her gaze, like a cloud over the Emerald Isle itself. She took a step back, shaking her head, blinking away the joy. "No . . . no, I cannot! I cannot stay here, in this cold gray place, far from my family—" She swallowed and straightened. His gut twisted at the bleak certainty in her eyes. "I'm sorry, sir. I could never wed an Englishman."

Oh, is that all?

Volcanic elation rose within him, hot and fierce. He laughed aloud, shocking her once more. "But you see, my darling Patricia, I *am* an Irishman!"

She shook her head, confused. "I fear that having a

bit o' the blood won't do, s—John." She looked down at the hand he still held. "I have no hatred of the English like many do," she said quietly, "but I wouldn't know what to say to a man who didn't ache for the very cliffs and sea the way I ache."

He leaned close, overjoyed to finally know the reason for her objection. "An' which cliffs would that be, lover? For meself, I pine for the Cliffs of Moher."

She froze at his lilting tones and he drew back, smiling. He nearly didn't recognize his own voice, so long had it been. "Ye didn't think I set my sights on ye for your face alone, did you, darlin'?"

Then she raised her gaze to his. The hard fury in her eyes drained his joy, filling him with alarm.

She stepped back, away from him, shaking off his touch as though it were slimy. "You're *hiding* your birth?" Her lips drew back in disgust. "Like a man *ashamed?*"

His empty hands dropped to his sides. "But . . . I had to! There's no work in service for us if we've still the mud of the potato fields on our boots—" No, wait. That was a slur, an English phrase he'd not ever uttered before. Had he been in this gray, grimy city for so long that he'd begun to believe such things himself?

The girl before him, the lovely creature born of home and dreams and everything he'd forced himself to forget, drew herself up tall, her expression steeped in disdain.

"I'd rather an honorable man, though English, than a shabby Irish traitor. I've no use for you at all, John Fortescue . . . you or your house of lies." She turned crisply and strode away, her rigid spine a testament to how useless any pursuit would be on his part.

Out of a decade of habit, Fortescue steeled his own posture and smoothed his face into an expressionless mask. Regaining his cool exterior did nothing to soothe the burn in his soul and his aching, desperate heart, but he would not chase down the halls of Brook House, howling her name like a madman—much as he might long to.

He'd made an honest, honorable offer. She'd refused him for reasons neither reasonable nor righteous. She didn't love him. There was nothing to be done about it.

His passion would fade in time. His pride would make sure of it.

GRAHAM TOSSED HIS hat and scarf to the footmen waiting outside Lady Peabody's and strolled into the house with a sigh. The last thing he wanted at the moment was to hear a flock of warbling virgins, all trotted out in identical muslin gowns with flowers in their hair and miserable obedience in their eyes.

Welcome to the auction block, my dears.

Why was he here? He ought to be at Lilah's, pleading his troth, making a case for her consideration, promising her the world as his duchess, etc. Instead, he was here, hoping for an opportunity to apologize to Sophie, unable to think of anything else but the pain in her gray eyes at his words.

I took pity on a poor, plain girl from the country! There's nothing to be jealous of!

Wincing at the memory, he paused at the top of the steps. He was an idiot. He knew that. He also knew that he was careless and thoughtless and wasteful. He'd never realized he could also be cruel.

Lusting after Sophie was his own difficulty. He shouldn't have taken his surprise and dismay out on her. The loss of her support and friendship would be . . .

He couldn't bear to think on it. He was already at a loss. He'd always avoided his family, for they drove him mad, but now he was beginning to realize what it meant to be entirely alone in the world.

Now his only family in the world was his cousin Tessa. *Lucky me.*

Of course, there was always Nichols, his loyal manservant. Graham sighed. What was he to do with the man? The butler's frenzied answer to Graham's immolation of the trophies had been to collect more from all over the house and place them in a sort of balding, desiccated assembly in the study, a fresh—so to speak—audience to Graham's betrayal of his father.

All the better to watch him suffer, he supposed.

The dunning notices had begun to arrive in earnest. Everyone wanted to get a piece of what he'd given his first creditor, it seemed.

There were only so many items of value left in Eden House. His family tended to collect death, not art. For the moment, Graham's method was to make piles of the bills, sorted by severity of the thinly veiled threats contained within. After that, there was nothing much he could do but continue in his plan to marry Lilah.

As he paused at the doorway to Peabody's ballroom,

temporarily converted to a music hall, Graham wondered if he could persuade any of the creditors to take the stuffed bear.

In his mind, he could almost hear Sophie's amused snort. *Only if it has a gold arse.*

SOPHIE TOOK LEMENTEUR's advice and arrived late. She greeted Lady Peabody graciously but without apology. That seemed odd, but Lementeur had ordered her to never, ever show doubt or diffidence. Leaving the Peabody ladies, mother and indistinguishable muslin-clad daughters, behind, Sophie enacted her obligatory meandering stroll through the crowd searching for a certain tall, fair-haired duke. The valet grapevine had claimed this as his destination. People were milling at the moment, for it was one of the extended social breaks in the schedule of performances.

How strange to move so freely, albeit carefully, among this glittering elite. How strange that no one else seemed to think it strange at all.

In deference to Lady Peabody's classical decor, Lementeur had put Sophie into a flowing, draped gown of creamy silk, with a simple hair band of gold-finished leaves twined around her braided and coiled hair. Sophie felt as though she'd walked straight out of an illustration of ancient Crete. She carried that with her as she followed instructions. Once around, with brief nods to an exalted few, a couple of languid curtseys to those atmospherically ranked present, and then she chose a Grecian pillar to pose next to.

Then she flicked her fan open.

As if it were some kind of hunting horn, the pack gathered at once. Sophie felt rather as if she'd been treed, the way they bayed at her. One asked her about Graham—apparently he'd claimed to be escorting her tonight—but Sophie only gazed at the fellow flatly until he blushed and looked away.

Poor boy.

She ought not to feel bad for him. He'd never looked at her twice when she was poor, plain Sophie.

Well, he's looking now.

It didn't matter. She could never marry a pup like that.

In the box the dress had arrived in, there had been a note from Lementeur. "Strike at the summit. Don't wait for the fall." In other words, don't waste a moment.

Cinderella only had until the stroke of midnight. Sophie's breath left her at the realization that her own midnight might very well be nigh. Graham could even now be proposing to Lady Lilah. Time to stop wasting the evening on these silly boys.

Where the blazes was Graham?

Then Mr. Wolfe appeared in Sophie's blurred vision. He bowed courteously, then leaned closer.

"I fear I am underdressed for such an occasion," he admitted.

Sophie spared his attire a glance. He was rumpled and his neckcloth was far too informal. "Just a bit," she said with a smile. Poor fellow. The fact that he found himself out of his element at such entertainments only endeared him to her more. The fact that the other younger gentlemen could scarcely hide their derision made her broaden her smile and bestow rather more interest on Wolfe than she truly felt.

Mr. Wolfe brightened under her regard and seemed to lose his shyness a bit. "I had hoped to see Lady Tessa this evening. I fear I did not pay my due respect to her this afternoon, especially considering my business responsibilities to the family." He flushed awkwardly and glanced away. "I was quite distracted."

A man who forgot to look at Tessa while Sophie was in the room? That was perfectly charming. Sophie tilted her head and smiled. "You flatter me, sir." Then she waved a hand. "Tessa's health is quite unpredictable these days, I'm afraid. Lady Peabody invited me to join her daughters under her chaperonage this evening."

Mr. Wolfe turned to gaze across the room at her ladyship, who was busily promoting her daughters to any and all gentlemen within the confines of the ballroom and not paying one iota of attention to Sophie. "I see."

Sophie took advantage of his distraction to glance swiftly about the ballroom. Where was Graham? Had he changed his plans and gone to Lilah's? Was it even now too late?

She turned back to find Mr. Wolfe gazing at her intently, that disturbing glint in his eye once more.

"May I help you find someone, Miss Blake?" He seemed terribly eager to please. "Are you perhaps looking for your cousin, the duke?"

"He isn't my cousin, not really," Sophie said swiftly. "Why, have you seen him here tonight?"

Mr. Wolfe nodded calmly, but his eyes seemed full of dark excitement. "Indeed. I saw him entering one of the retiring rooms just a moment ago." He gestured to the far corner of the ballroom. "Over there."

At that moment, the musicians began to play softly, guiding the guests back to their seats with a tune. If she wanted to search for Graham, she must slip away now.

She curtsied absently. "Thank you, Mr. Wolfe. I am in your debt."

Her attention focused on the far doorway, Sophie made her way against the crowd. Even through her distraction, however, she imagined she could feel that dark intensity following her through the room, like the heat from a furnace on the back of her neck.

IN THE CORNERS of Peabody's ballroom, there were small chambers, hardly more than alcoves really, furnished with fainting couches and mirrors to check one's hair, and doors to close on private moments. Graham had retreated to one in order to compose the perfect apology.

Sophie had finally arrived. Graham had watched her serene parade from a corner. He'd smiled to himself when he'd realized that her dreamily haughty gaze was partly due to the fact that she couldn't see a damned thing without her spectacles.

He'd hesitated, unsure of how to begin to make up for his cruelty, at a loss to explain his conflict and confusion—and then the slavering hordes had descended. The moment was lost. He'd retreated to this quiet place, determined to find the right words to repair their broken friendship.

Lilah, with the unnerving instinct of a predator, found him there.

"Hello, lover."

He whirled to see that Lilah had her back pressed to the door, cutting off his escape. She slouched there, one hip cocked, her fingers toying with the edge of her shawl, stretching it out before her in a langorous manner. "You're not kissing me yet," she pouted.

A pout on that beautiful, marble face was ludicrous. Graham fought back his repugnance. *Lilah is going to save my estate.*

He let out a breath. "I thought you were going to wait for me at your house."

She shook one long-nailed finger at him slowly. "That's not the correct response, my darling. You're supposed to be thrilled to see me. You're supposed to passionately pull me into your arms and kiss me like I'm the last drink of water in the desert."

She pushed off from the door and slinked nearer. "You're supposed to beg my permission to do nasty, naughty, dirty things to me in this little room, with the entire world on the other side of the door. You're supposed to apologize on your knees and promise never, never to keep Lilah waiting ever again."

Feeling very much like bait in a snare, he woodenly waited as she approached him. She slid her dainty, smooth hands up over his chest and around his neck.

"Did you hear me, Grammie? I waited for you," she murmured. "I was all creamy and damp from my bath

and I waited naked in my bed, just the way you like."
She stood on tiptoe and snapped at his chin. He managed somehow to neither quite flinch away nor be bitten. Lilah liked to use her teeth as much as her nails.

"But you. Didn't. Come." She emphasized her complaint with strategic tugs on his neckcloth. He allowed her to pull his mouth down to hers, where she promptly kissed him hard, hot and wet.

There was a part of Graham that liked it. Or perhaps he was merely remembering liking it. Or maybe there was something of his louty, lusty father in him, for as Lilah squirmed enthusiastically against him, he managed to stir up a small flame of the old arousal.

Yes, he was going to be all right, he realized with relief, ignoring the other, much larger portion of himself that claimed it was time to push her away and then wash his mouth out with a stiff whiskey.

He was going to be able to use Lilah as surely as she was determined to use him. Equally gainfully. Equally blatantly.

Equally reprehensibly.

"Tell me I'll be your duchess, Grammie," she urged as she tugged at his clothing and her own. "Tell me that I'll be the Duchess of Edencourt and that we'll be the most fabulous couple in all of Society and we'll throw the most magnificent house parties—" She paused in the middle of undoing his waistcoat. "Is Edencourt in very bad condition? I've heard stories that it's gone a bit dirty and dingy with nothing but men living there."

Graham managed to not quite laugh. "Dirty and dingy," he repeated noncommitally. If the rest of the world didn't know the true state of Edencourt, it was more due to his father's lack of hospitality than any real sense of secrecy. Still, best not to paint too grim a picture now, before he'd secured its future with the sale of his name.

"I'll be a good girl, Grammie," Lilah promised, panting. "At least until you get a son." She licked his lips. "The usual arrangement."

Abruptly, despite the general acceptance of just such terms amongst the *ton*, Graham found that he didn't want the usual arrangement. His mother's ring rested in his waistcoat pocket, ready to bring forth and offer to his betrothed. He imagined he could feel it between them, a small bit of gold-and-diamond armor keeping her at bay.

Could he even imagine putting it on Lilah's talon-tipped finger? She would sneer at such a paltry stone, no doubt. Yet what choice did he have?

As Lilah pressed him back to fall onto the fainting couch and then climbed astride him, false passion aflame on her lovely face, Graham did what thousands of reluctant partners had done before him.

He closed his eyes and thought of England.

THE USUAL ARRANGEMENT.

Sophie felt her gut go cold. She'd seen Lilah slip into this little room and not come out.

Needless to say, she'd found just the fellow she'd been looking for all evening. Her stomach roiling at the tangled limbs and skirts and long lustrous obviously false hair displayed before her, she waited.

For pity's sake, the two of them were so involved they didn't even realize they'd been interrupted!

Sophie couldn't resist the urge. She went forth and yanked. Lilah's fall came off in Sophie's hand, along with a shower of pins and a few strands of Lilah's real hair as well.

Lilah's screech mingled with the soprano's aria. Sophie quickly kicked the door shut on the assembly outside.

Lilah sprang off of Graham's lap to turn on Sophie. "*You?*"

"So sorry to interrupt, but I feared you were about to suffocate this gentleman with your ample breasts." Sophie sent a vicious non-smile at Graham. "Good evening, *Grammie*." Then she turned to Lilah and held out the fall. "I hate to be the one to tell you this, Lady Lilah, but you're losing your hair."

Lilah made a grab for it, but Sophie held it high.

Lilah's uncanny eyes narrowed. "I'll make you sorry, you . . . you . . . whinnying nag!"

Graham stirred. "Lilah, there's no call—"

Lilah turned on him with a snarl. "Don't you dare defend her, you puling maggot—not if you want my money!"

Sophie folded her arms, dangling the ebony tresses idly. "My goodness, Graham," she said placidly. "Think of the years of wedded bliss before you." She sighed dreamily. "Years and years and *years* . . . " She tilted her head. "Then again, Lilah's last marriage didn't last nearly that long." She smiled at Lilah. "Did it, pet? And we all thought he was such a healthy, vigorous man . . ."

"Sophie," Graham stood. "I'd rather you didn't interfere—"

But Lilah and Sophie had locked swords in earnest now. They ignored him.

"A dead husband is better than never getting one at all," Lilah said with a sneer. "I don't know who you stole those gowns from, but when I get through with you, everyone in London will know what a common little piece of country rubbish you really are."

Sophie raised a brow. "I've made no secret of that."

Graham moved forward then to put a hand on Lilah's arm. "That's enough!"

Lilah swung too quickly for him to duck. The crack of her hand on Graham's face was shocking, but the faint trails of blood on his cheek from her nails made Sophie sick with fury.

Stepping between them, Sophie advanced on Lilah until she loomed over the smaller woman. Even Lilah finally began to discern her own danger. Good. Sophie hadn't been nearly as gently raised as the world thought.

Now seemed the time and place to reveal that little fact.

"Stay away from Graham," she said, her tone easy but her eyes fierce. "You don't deserve him. No one speaks to him the way you just did. No one—" she emphasized her point with a hard poke to Lilah's shoulder "—insults or abuses this man *ever*." She leaned close enough to whisper. "Stay far, far away, Lilah, or I will, with my own two hands, drag your pretty, privileged Mayfair arse from here to Brighton." She raised her prize and shook it in the other woman's stunned face. "By the hair."

It was astonishing how fast Lilah could move that privileged arse when she really wanted to. The door slammed on the musicale once more, leaving Graham and Sophie alone in the silence.

Chapter Eighteen

Graham retied his neckcloth with hard, impatient jerks. "That was quite a display. For a moment there I wasn't entirely sure you were faking."

He saw doubt flare in her cloudy-sky eyes. *Neither was she.*

"It looked as though you needed rescuing," she said, giving a careless shrug.

He ran distracted hands through his hair to rearrange it. "I know you're trying to help, Sophie, but Lilah is better than some insipid virgin bride!" He shook his surcoat out with a flap and shrugged into it. "The last thing I want is to take some inexperienced infant to wife!"

He'd have to start all over again now. Lilah wouldn't be likely to forgive such a humiliation, not even to be his duchess. His head spun in circles with his heart, confused. What a sight Sophie had been when she'd fought for him! No one had ever fought for him in his life! Disturbed and unsettled and, of course, being him, he said the wrong thing.

"Duke to be had—cheap!—going fast," he snarled.

He saw her recoil, the disappointment plain in her expression. "But Graham . . . Lilah? No number of fine waistcoats is worth spending the rest of your life tied to that—that—*canine!*"

Miserable, he gave as good as he got. "That's easy for you to say. No one is giving *me* lavish garments for nothing!"

Her eyes narrowed. "I've been given gifts for approximately a week. You've been parasitical your entire life!" She threw out her hands. "God, Graham! When are you going to grow up? When are you going to realize that life isn't a toy-filled nursery where no one cares what you break? Is that really all there is to you—a three-inch layer of self-indulgence and arrogance, wrapped around nothing at all?"

Graham stopped short. "Is that how you see me?"

She went mulish, her arms folded, her eyes furious. "Is there any reason I shouldn't?"

No, actually, there wasn't. A careless man-boy, thoughtless and destructive. That was precisely who he was—or at least, who he had been.

Sophie misinterpreted his silence and rolled her eyes scornfully. Only then did Graham see the dampness in them.

"Soph." He took a step toward her.

She turned away, giving him her back as she swiped a secretive hand at her eyes. "Bugger off," she snarled. "I'm going back out there to find someone who has more on his mind than money!"

"You've turned into such a lady," he teased softly. He made a grab for that hand and caught it. He tugged her around. "Sophie, don't let's be angry. I didn't mean to upset you."

She kept her face turned away. "I'm not upset. I'm just dead sick of you, that's all. No time for this, I fear. Too many more important people waiting for me outside."

He drew her chin about with tender fingers. "Here now. You've mussed your fancy doings." He pulled out his handkerchief and dabbed at her powdered cheeks, smoothing the lines of her tears away. "There now, all pretty again." He dropped a quick, meaningless little kiss on her lips, so close to his own.

Except . . . it wasn't meaningless at all.

SOPHIE FROZE AT the brief touch of Graham's lips on hers. So did he.

Time hung there, sweet and long, each unwilling to move away, unable to think or protest or do anything but *stay.*

The little room was a haven, the gathering outside growing more distant with every pulse beat, the sounds faded and misted beneath the pounding of two hearts.

When she inhaled, taking in the heat and scent of him, it was as though she breathed some of his life and vitality into her spirit. Suddenly nothing was to be feared, nothing was to be hidden. There was no one in the world but the two of them, and she reveled in that isolation.

He was here and he could be hers. All she need do was reach out—

His solid pectoral muscle flexed beneath her palm and she realized she already had.

It was all he'd needed, it seemed, for in the next in-stant she found herself pulled roughly into his arms, against that rock-hard chest, into the circle of his scald-ing sexuality.

She made no sound of protest, not even a gasp of surprise, for there was no surprise here. He was pre-cisely as he ought to be and so was she, quivering for him, on fire for him—

Willing.

Nay, eager.

It was so easy to let go that it made her doubt she'd ever held on. She slid both hands up to lace them around his neck, moving slowly as if in a dream. He exhaled harshly at her voluntary embrace and she was ashamed of how much she'd held back from him. She vowed she would show him herself, in such a way he might never forget it.

She twined her fingers through his hair gently, then tightened them. His eyes widened and he opened his mouth to speak.

"Shh." It was stunning how sure she was, how she knew just what to do. She'd never kissed before but she knew just how to tilt her head to make their lips fit just so. She went up on tiptoe, sliding her body slowly up his hard stomach and chest, making no attempt to hide her enjoyment of the sensation.

He swallowed, hard. She felt the power surge through her, raw feminine power older than time. She claimed her seductress self, allowing her to well forth and play out the moment with slow, sure enticement.

He waited, his jaw tense, his eyelids heavy with

unexpressed desire. He hardened against her. She smiled slightly and rotated her hips to press the softness of her lower belly into his rigidity. A rocky shudder went through him and the cords of his throat throbbed, but he kept his silence, still pinned in place by her fingers entangled in his hair.

He could have broken free, but Graham was finally in the place he'd dreamed of since . . . how long? Just this week—or for months?

He dared not so much as breathe too hard, although he could be panting by now if he allowed himself. She was so innocently, wickedly sensual—this was not his careful, restrained Sophie. This was the woman who had fought for him, the woman who had stood fiercely between him and Lilah's vicious insults.

Then there was no more time for memory, there was only now, for she kissed him at last.

Her lips were soft, her nipples were hard, her fingers in his hair causing him pain he would not have forgone for a thousand nights of heartless pleasure. She was the one. She had ever been the one. He'd known, in some place he'd never investigated inside himself, he'd known since the first time he'd rescued her from running into a wall.

He stood there, taking her closemouthed kiss for as long as he was able to bear it, for he savored the innocence he tasted in it. She would never kiss so again.

Then he violated that sweet virginity with the tip of his tongue, a slow careful penetration that made her stiffen in surprise.

She wasn't one to quail. No, not his Sophie. At once

she was back in the joust, her own dainty tongue slipping into his lips, the soft sounds of her pleasure vibrating through his mouth.

God, so sweet, so strong, so powerful—

He couldn't get close enough to her. In two steps he had her down on the fainting couch, her willing body at last pressed completely to his. Beneath his . . .

Soft and pale, her breasts emerged from her bodice when he pulled at the neckline. The gift of her flesh filled his hands as he impaled her mouth again and again with his tongue. There were other things he would do with that tongue, things she would enjoy, things he would get to in just a moment, just as soon as he'd had enough of fitting his hands around her small, high, perfect breasts.

Oh, the things he would do to his magnificent Sophie . . .

Outside the alcove room, the audience broke into applause. Jarred, Graham broke the kiss.

"Oh God." Not Sophie! He was a monster. He was a rotter, through and through. "Oh, bloody *hell!*"

He backed off her, turning away—*tearing* himself away, in fact, an act which cost him more than he could ever articulate. He rubbed both hands over his face, straining for sanity through the aching, heart-pounding lust . . . and need. Need like nothing he'd ever felt before. Need that nearly had him turning back and flinging himself upon her once again, just for one more minute of that sweet, pure hearthfire light . . .

He forced himself away, as far as the tiny room would allow. Leaning his forehead against the opposite wall, he clenched his eyes tightly shut and beat back the aching loss until coherent thought returned.

Mostly.

Losing himself in Sophie . . . When had she become a pool of cool clean water? When had she become the unpolluted air in his lungs? Why hadn't he seen it sooner—why had she kept it from him, like a secret, like a treasure hoarded away for someone more worthy, someone less blind?

Too late.

No. Never. He needed this—needed her—needed—

You need Lilah's pile of gold.

No. He could not trade this . . . this pure, clean creature for a tainted harpy like Lilah!

Then trade her for the folk of Edencourt.

The pale, sunken faces . . . the blank, enduring eyes that held no faith in his promises . . . the rot and the waste and the damned, squandered years he'd walked right by . . .

Trade Sophie for his people? That . . . that he could do. Must do. To live without kissing Sophie would be torture. To live with destroying Edencourt . . . that would be hell on earth.

Resolute, he turned his heart to stone. Only then did he dare to turn back to her.

She was upright and dressed again, although her hair was down from its elaborate coil, falling untamed and coppery over her delicate ivory shoulders as she sat tensely on the fainting couch, her hands knotted in her lap.

He was an idiot. Looking at the girl before him, the

most lucid, non-babbling thought he could form was just that.

I am an idiot.

She gazed at the floor, her cheeks bright with flush. "This was not a mistake. Don't you dare say it was a mistake—I couldn't bear it."

"Sophie . . ." He wanted her but he couldn't. Ever. "That was a mistake."

He would not be his father. He would not please himself at the cost of Edencourt's people. He was only glad he'd managed to stop before he'd gone too far.

No, you aren't. Too far is precisely where you want to be.

She'd given him so much. Understanding. Friendship. Safe harbor from the unhappiness he'd been immersed in for so long that he'd considered it the natural order of things. She'd told him the truth, about himself, how he lived and greatest of all, about herself. Until he'd ruined matters, she'd been entirely and completely herself with no apology. She'd inspired him to see into himself, to want to be a different man than he'd been bred to be—a better man.

In his world of glittering facades, shifting loyalties and slippery deceit, a sincere friend who spoke the truth was worth more than gold.

What had happened to create Sophie the cynic?

I see no reason to allow the grimness of the real world to interfere with a desire to make things the way they should be.

He'd killed that. He saw that now.

He'd toyed with her affections. Thinking back with

disgust at his insincere flirtation and his indifference to the proprieties, he realized what he'd done to her in his boredom and caprice.

The fact that he'd entangled his own feelings did not matter. His heart was not his to lose. It belonged to Edencourt.

"So that is all, then?" She raised her chin and gazed at him evenly. He steeled himself against the stain of disappointment and hopelessness in her expression.

He gazed back at her solemnly. "Did you expect more?"

"Of course not. Who am I to expect anything in this world?" She lifted her chin proudly and stood. Shaking out her somewhat-the-worse-for-wear skirts, she moved to the door. "My congratulations on your imminent engagement, my lord."

With a dip and a careless tilt of her head, she was gone, striding back into the noise and crowd of the musicale as if she had more important business kept waiting.

Worry slithered through Graham's relief. Her gray gaze might seem calm and disinterested to others, had, in fact seemed so to him once upon a time, but he now knew what raged beneath that still surface. His Sophie was a hard-headed, fiery, unpredictable creature.

Who now seemed to think she had nothing to lose.

Chapter Nineteen

Everyone was enjoying a superior alto, absorbed in the best music of the evening. Sophie slithered sidways in the shadows of the back of the room, careful to walk lightly. If she could make it out of the room before the song ended, she could—

Her elbow struck a tall, Chinese vase on a side table. It teetered, then slid right through her desperately reaching hands.

Into those of Mr. Wolfe. Breathless with relief and quite frankly happy to see a friendly face, Sophie ignored the oddity of his lurking outside that particular room. Instead she merely helped him carefully place the vase back in position. Then she put a hand on his arm.

"Mr. Wolfe, if I might impose?"

He took one look at her, his hot eyes intent on her face, then tucked that hand into his arm and walked her from the room, keeping himself between her and any possible observers. Really, he was a very thoughtful man.

Once in the hallway, he waved away a footman who

stepped forward. "Fetch my carriage, can't you see she's ill?"

Sophie blinked, then suppressed a rising hysterical giggle. Ill? Yes, she was ill. Overheated, overcome, overwhelmed. Infected with lust.

Not only lust of course, but definitely, there was a very large portion of lust in the mix. Graham's lips, his heavy, hardened body, his *hands* . . .

Then her memory flashed on his eyes when he'd declared it all a mistake. The light had gone out from those eyes. The only thing she could see in those once-playful, teasing depths was sincere regret.

So kissing her—*among other things!*—was cause for regret, hmm? She wasn't worth it, apparently. She ought never to have kissed him so shortly after Lilah had. How could she compare with a lover as experienced and beautiful as Lilah?

You're running circles round the real problem here.

Problem? There was no problem. There was only a mistake. Graham would testify to that.

Sophie was barely aware of having reclaimed her cloak and being led out to a waiting vehicle. The footman helped her up and she found herself seated in a phaeton with Mr. Wolfe.

"Oh, yes please," she managed dimly. "Take me away from here."

He obediently clicked his tongue against his teeth and started his horses at a quick walk. Sophie sighed. It was such a relief to deal with reasonable man who simply did as she asked.

Her way home secured, Sophie wrapped herself in her cloak and lost herself in her thoughts.

IT WAS ONLY a moment later when Graham emerged from the Peabody house, but the phaeton identified by the groom as belonging to Mr. Wolfe was already nearly out of sight.

Graham didn't believe for a instant that Wolfe was taking Sophie properly home. The man was a bounder, a pouncer, lurking at the water hole, waiting to devastate the next helpless creature wandering by for a drink.

Graham would be damned if Sophie was going to be that prey.

Another groom passed him, bringing a fine saddled horse. Graham stepped forward. "I'll take that."

The groom blinked at him, then looked over his shoulder. Graham followed his gaze to see Somers Boothe-Jamison giving him a strange look.

"Ah." *Just stealing your horse. Sorry.* "Now see here, Somers—"

"You ought to go after her," Somers interrupted, frowning down the street where the phaeton was no longer visible. "I don't trust that Wolfe fellow. There are some very odd tales circling about him."

Graham briefly closed his eyes in relief. Thank God. Then he grinned fiercely at Somers. "So I'll just take your horse then?"

He was already mounting. Boothe-Jamison simply

waved him on with a weary hand. "Go on, then. I'll find another way home. Be good to that horse, would you? Not all of us are dukes, you know."

Graham settled himself into the saddle. "Try Lady Tessa," he called out as he dug his heels into the mount. "She always has room in her carriage for a bloke without transport." Only the young and handsome ones, of course, but Somers was a big lad. He could take care of himself.

The phaeton was well out of sight. Wolfe was really putting on the speed.

What in the hell was the man up to in such a hurry?

SOPHIE TUCKED HER face down against the chilly night air and contemplated the riotous mess she had created with her impulsiveness.

What was wrong with her? She'd never been so wicked before. She'd stolen money, lied and perpetrated a fraud but she had never lain beneath a man and let him touch her—nay, encouraged him to touch her! It hadn't been only Graham who had pulled at her bodice to free her breasts to his hands!

Yet in the end, she had allowed him to move away from her, to pull back that wonderful heated gift of passion and need he'd offered her. She could have stopped him—or rather, she could have started him again! She'd known that all she needed to do was to touch him, kiss him, press against him, and she would have been back down on that couch, willing clay in his hot hands once again.

Why? Why had she walked away?

Because in a few more minutes you were going to have to confess. In another second, you would have spouted your love like a fountain and spoken more truth than Graham is ready to hear.

Sophie truly hated it when that little voice was right.

With a deep breath, she ordered her thoughts to calm. There was no point in getting tightly wrought over the evening's events. Tomorrow she would figure out a way to either tell Graham or to make sure he never found out the truth. What she needed right now was a good night's sleep. What she needed right now was her bed—

Except that when she raised her face and looked about her, she wasn't anywhere near Brook House. Or Primrose Street.

She was in the middle of a wood! The road stretched out before and after them like a moonlit ribbon in the dimness. The lighted lanterns dangling from either side of the phaeton gave only moderate circles of light. The moon, nearly full, gave the rest.

"Where are we?"

At her question, Mr. Wolfe guided the horses to the roadside and pulled them to a halt. "It was nearly time for a stop anyway," he said cheerfully. "It's a long way to Gretna Green. We won't be there before dawn."

Gretna Green? Oh, dear. "Mr. Wolfe, please do not inform me that you intend to—" Surely the man wasn't that stupid?

But he only beamed at her, the darkness making him look oddly . . . sinister? Which was ridiculous, for

Mr. Wolfe was just like Mr. Stickley, a harmless, rather sweet fellow who had perhaps misread her attentions.

Wasn't he?

He smiled wider. He certainly did have excellent teeth. "Miss Blake, don't you see? We were meant to be together, in that place, on this night! All day I was trying to ascertain how I ought to do this properly—should I approach Lord Brookhaven for your hand, since you have no father living? But this—this is so very romantic! We shall be lovers tossed upon the road, two travelers seeking rest and respite on their weary journey, a man and a woman, getting married—"

"What?" Sophie drew back from him. "Mr. Wolfe, surely you can't be serious! How can you be in love with me? You've only known me for a matter of days!"

Wolfe grabbed her hand and pressed it to his heart. "It was your kindness, I think. The way you saw my nervousness and drew me out, the way you never failed to include me in the conversation, the way you looked right past those panting louts with all their fancy manners and poses, and didn't believe their blandishments for one moment!" He brought her hand to his lips and dropped kisses upon her knuckles. "You are a light among the dull and shallow, you are the only one who *saw* me for the man that I am—"

As he carried on, Sophie became more and more horrified. This was what she would look like and sound like if she ever confessed her true feelings to Graham. And this uncomfortable, guilty, but overwhelming desire to flee that she was feeling now? This would be Graham's reaction to such a confession.

Worse perhaps now because she ought to know better. She had seen the other side of this. She hated to think that she was just as thoughtless and careless as Graham!

Yet, how could she blame Graham, when he was only being kind, as she had only been kind to Mr. Wolfe? She had let herself get caught up in her imagination and damned fairy stories! And fooled herself into thinking there was more.

It was then that she saw the entire affair with crystal clarity.

Simply wanting to love someone because they were appropriate or deserving was as futile as wishing one could fly. Here before her was a man who seemed as perfect a choice for her as any she had ever met—and she could no more love him than she could soar through the air.

Just as Graham could never love her, simply because she loved him or because she deserved more than friendship.

What precisely did she deserve? She had lied and stolen. She had perpetrated an enormous hoax upon Society at large, pretending to be someone she would never truly be.

For someone who had always felt that her exterior did not do justice to her interior, it was a sobering realization that, perhaps, it did. Perhaps she was as plain and worthless within as she was without.

Perhaps she deserved precisely what she'd received. Nothing.

Wolfe's praises ran down a bit and now he was gazing at her with fire in his eyes. It actually made him look a bit demented, poor man. How she would hate to be reduced before someone this way!

Taking a breath, she tried to ease her hand from Wolfe's grasp before her fingers became completely numb. "Sir, I fear you've labored under a misunderstanding."

Oh, the words were awful, weak and spiritless, yet what else could she say? The answer itself would devastate him, that she knew with all her heart. How she phrased herself probably mattered very little.

Yet she could not help but try to ease the sting. "You are a very fine man, Mr. Wolfe. I've greatly enjoyed our conversations—" That was a vast overstatement, but it would do. "And I have nothing but the utmost respect for you—"

"Oh, my darling!" He pulled her to him, his arms overcoming her startled resistance so easily that she doubted he had even noticed it.

"Mr. Wolfe!" She squirmed, but he held her without difficulty. She'd never tried her strength against a man's. It shocked her how simple it was for him to subdue her struggles.

"Mr. Wolfe, let me—"—*go!*

His mouth came down on hers as he pressed her back in the seat, his weight trapping her helpless beneath him.

Chapter Twenty

Graham drew back on the reins of Somers Boothe-Jamison's splendid, lovely horse. The animal had maintained top speed through all of Graham's false starts and dead ends. Now, at last, he saw the phaeton ahead, its side lanterns bright even on this moonlit night.

Dismounting, he tied the horse several yards behind the vehicle and started forward. He didn't see anyone inside—had he misjudged that Wolfe fellow? Sophie could very well be safe at Brook House at this moment—

A rustle, a gasp. Sophie's strained voice, full of dismay tinted with fear. "Stop this!" The unmistakable sound of a fist hitting flesh and bone.

"*Sophie!*" Graham didn't recall running. All he knew was that he was on top of the man in the carriage in an instant, pulling his fist back to bloody the bastard's . . . the bastard's bloody nose?

Startled, he turned to look at Sophie, who was gazing at him with perplexity while shaking her right hand in pain.

"Where did you come from?" She flexed her fingers and winced.

Suddenly a bit weak in the knees, Graham dropped his chokehold on Wolfe's collar and sank to the padded seat beside Sophie. He looked back and forth, from the unharmed—if one didn't count bruised knuckles—Sophie to the vividly bleeding Wolfe, who now had his handkerchief pressed tightly to his nose. The man's eyes gleamed, but it was too dark to see with what.

Graham was fairly sure that his own were gleaming with amazed respect. "You defended your own honor."

Sophie shrugged. "Mr. Wolfe's . . . affections overwhelmed him." She frowned at the man. "I'm very sorry, sir. I didn't mean to harm you, but you simply wouldn't listen to me."

Wolfe warily slid himself up to a sitting position. His gaze flicked to Graham. "I meant no harm," he said, his voice muffled.

Graham didn't believe him for a moment, but Sophie simply waved a hand. "I know that. But seriously, sir—even if I had returned your sentiments, I would not have appreciated being accosted in an open carriage on a dark road."

This turn of phrase gave Graham decidedly improper ideas about accosting her in a *closed* carriage on a dark road. . . .

Then again, he'd likely wind up with a swollen nose of his own. He smiled at his brave, self-reliant Sophie. "Is there anyone else you need to assault this evening, my delicate flower, or are you ready to call it a night?"

For an instant, she smiled back, then her expression

chilled. "Graham, are you under the impression that I'm speaking to you again?"

He sighed. "You're angry, I know. At the moment, I think it's a bit more important that I take you back to Brook House safely."

She gazed at the man on the floor of the phaeton, crammed as he was in the narrow space. Then she looked up at Graham, her brow furrowed.

"What is it?" He was tired and sticky from his ride. It was time to go.

She rubbed at her sore hand. "I'm trying to decide who is the lesser of two evils."

Graham gaped. "You can't be serious!"

She glared at him. "Mr. Wolfe didn't do anything that you didn't do—and with rather more honorable intentions, in the end!"

Wolfe nodded. "I asked her to marry me!"

Graham couldn't believe it. "But I—!" He halted. What was he going to say? *I want to marry you . . . more?*

Not possible. There was nothing he could say.

She saw it in his eyes. Her elegant face became closed and cool again. "I will go home with Mr. Wolfe."

Wolfe was nodding. "Of course, Miss Blake!"

Graham considered giving the fellow another blow to the nose. *Smarmy bastard.* No, he wouldn't trust this lout with a one-sided pound note, much less with a treasure like Sophie. He swung down from the phaeton without a word.

Sophie leaned forward, calling after him. "Graham, don't take it so hard—"

Graham solved the entire matter by walking around the back of the phaeton, pulling Sophie out, tossing her over his shoulder, indignant cries and all, and striding back to his borrowed mount.

She kicked and pounded and even bit, but he had her wrists safely pinioned and his coat was thick enough to protect him from her teeth. Wolfe was another matter entirely.

The man roused himself to run after them. "Edencourt, you brute! Put the lady down at once or I'll turn the law on you!"

Graham swung about, causing Sophie to give an uncharacteristically girlish squeal of surprise, and glared at the man who'd tried to assault his woman.

"Wolfe, go ahead and call the law—if you really think they're going to look any more kindly on your actions tonight than mine." Then he smiled. "A solicitor's word against a duke's—how do you think that will play out?"

His bluff called, Wolfe snarled, his face ugly and hard. Graham wished Sophie could see the fellow now, but he didn't dare let her down long enough. She'd belt him one and escape into some other, even more dangerous situation, no doubt.

No, there was nothing to be done but protect her from herself. He warily turned his back on Wolfe and continued to the horse. Tossing Sophie up into the saddle, he swung up behind before she had quite sorted herself out.

Luckily, she wasn't a horsewoman. Instead, she clung rather gratifyingly to his arms as he held her close and kicked the horse into a canter.

"Wait!" Sophie cried. "You're going the wrong way! London is back there!"

Graham grinned into the wind and the flyaway banner of her red-gold hair. "We're not going back to London."

He aimed the horse at a hard gallop—

Straight to Edencourt.

Chapter Twenty~one

"You don't really expect me to continue to tolerate this treatment, do you, Graham?"

From where he walked ahead, leading the borrowed horse, Graham didn't answer. After the first flush of triumph when he'd stolen her away, he'd begun to wonder when exactly he'd lost his mind. Was it when he'd learned of his father's death? Or had it been the next day, when he'd placed Sophie's long, elegant fingers on his cheek and tingled with the electricity of her touch?

Or had it been a process more slow and sinister, brought on by long evenings of brandy and firelight and losing too many hands of cards?

Whenever the original lapse had occurred, he'd surely worsened matters now with his ill-thought-out kidnapping. Yet, despite the fact that he knew better, despite the fact that he was making the mistake of his life, despite the overwhelming logic of turning around and hot-footing it back to London with Sophie's reputation unbesmirched, he'd been unable to aim his feet in any direction than that of Edencourt.

It was interesting, being mad. As a man who'd never really had much purpose other than being as charming as possible to as many women as possible, having an undeniable compulsion driving him onward was a truly novel experience. Whatever the consequences, he must, at this moment in time, without pause, take Sophie away to Edencourt with him.

A shoe struck him just above his ear. Without pausing, he bent to retrieve it and thrust it into his pocket along with its mate, a hair comb, a fan, a reticule and a bit of decoration pried from his saddle. "You're running out of ammunition."

He heard her sigh from where she rode the horse he led. "I know. I was saving that shoe so I could strike at the perfect moment."

He grinned wearily but didn't turn. "Was it as satisfying as you'd hoped?"

He wasn't sure if the snort he heard came from the horse or from Sophie. It might have been either, for the horse was every bit as irritated with him as Sophie was.

It was a very nice horse, a real quality mount, but even such a fine beast was bound to tire while carrying two.

"Are you ever going to explain yourself?" Sophie demanded.

Graham kept walking. "I think it falls into the realm of saving you from yourself," he said conversationally. "That's what I have come to so far."

She made a noise. Yes, that was definitely a Sophie-snort. "I hardly think I'm a menace to Society."

He shook his head. "Oh, but you are. You're more

intelligent than most of them, so they cannot stop you. You're also more stubborn than any other ten women put together." He sighed. "You see what I'm up against."

She scoffed. "You're making no sense whatsoever."

"You're headstrong and reckless," he stated. "Not to mention wildly unpredictable."

A moment of peace. Then, "I am?"

He closed his eyes against the flattered pleasure in her tone. "That was not a compliment, Miss Blake."

She barked a dry laugh. "It was if you're me." They walked along wordlessly for a long moment. Then she started in again. "If I am such a brazen troublemaker, then why are you, of all people, the one who must rein me in?"

Graham didn't answer, for what could he say when he didn't understand it himself? At his continued silence, Sophie made another equine noise of disgust and fell quiet at last.

By the time Graham and Sophie made it to Edencourt, it was close to dawn. The moon had gone down some time ago and the sun was not yet up. After hours of galloping, then trotting, then walking, Sophie sat in the saddle, slumped in misery and exhaustion, her eyes closed and her hands clinging to the pommel as if it was the only thing keeping her from sliding to the ground.

It probably was.

Graham had been on foot, leading the horse, since they had crossed onto the Edencourt estate. That was more than an hour ago, yet the great crumbling house was not yet in sight.

Since both Graham and Sophie still wore their evening clothes, this made walking somewhat less enjoyable than clinging to the jostling saddle. Therefore, Graham walked and Sophie rode.

"I hate you," Sophie mumbled, her eyes still shut. "Just in case I forgot to mention that."

Graham kept walking. "I think you might have, just a few times or so." Nothing more than he deserved, he was sure.

She groaned. "As long as that is absolutely clear."

At last Graham spotted the bulky shadow of the house far ahead, just a grim dark shape against the slightly fainter darkness of the pre-dawn sky. "We're here, love."

Sophie shook her head. "I don't believe you anymore. I don't believe in Edencourt at all, quite frankly. I think you made the whole thing up and you're actually some sort of demon sent to torture me for my sins."

"Sins? You? That would take about three and a half minutes. Hardly any fun at all for a demon." The horse, sensing an end to its wearying journey, picked up its dragging feet. Graham picked his up as well, better to have this long night done. "Now, myself, on the other hand . . . I would take a thousand years to punish properly."

"No trouble at all," she snarled, her eyes still tightly shut against the pain in her posterior. "I'm looking forward to it."

Then they were there, on the great drive that rounded a circular garden—or that now rounded a circular patch of weeds—approaching the grand sweeping steps of Edencourt.

The horse jolted to a stop and refused to go any farther. Graham looked into the animal's eyes and decided not to push the topic. Even the nicest, finest horses had their limits.

Graham tied the beast's reins to an iron ring posted next to the drive. Then he moved to Sophie's side and put his arms about her. "Come on, love. Lean into me."

She whimpered in protest as her sore body refused to move, then toppled onto him. He caught her easily and hefted her fully into his arms. She wearily draped her arms about his neck and dropped her face into his shoulder. "Gray, I hurt," she whispered.

"I know, pet." He carried her into the great, cold, echoing house. "We'll get you warm and comfortable in just a moment."

His mother's bedchamber was perhaps the only room in the house not too devastated by the general disrepair, for it had sat unused since her tastefully demure death thirty years ago. Graham had often wondered if perhaps she hadn't been ill at all, but simply sick of her great brute of a husband.

It was just as Graham recalled it, filled with graceful furniture, well covered by a previously careful staff. If the chimney wasn't too bad, he ought to be able to make some sort of fire in there as well.

Once in the room, he was able to deposit Sophie into a chair while he moved about pulling the dust covers away. He piled them in a corner and went to inspect the fire.

There were no obvious signs of disrepair. When he peered upward, he saw nothing blocking the faint gleam of dawn at the top of the flue. He went to where Sophie curled into the chair, pale and drawn in the dimness. He pulled her cloak over her dangling limbs. "Stay warm," he told her. "I'll be back in a few minutes."

Sophie barely heard him. She'd missed a few nights' sleep in her life, but she hadn't spent them clinging to the back of a horse. In fact, she'd never actually been on a horse before tonight. At some point during the night she'd thought of mentioning that fact to Graham, but there hadn't seemed to be much point. Once upon a time, she'd rather thought she'd like to learn.

Now, with her body aching and harsh jolts of pain running up her back and down her legs, she couldn't imagine why someone had ever thought to climb onto the back of a horse in the first place! It was bloody unnatural, that's what it was!

The house was cold and dark, but it wasn't moving so there was definite improvement in her situation. In a few moments she was going to rise from this chair and leave this place under her own power.

After she murdered Graham, of course.

Poison or knife attack? Poison could be quite agonizing, but then again, knives were so satisfyingly bloody.

She fell asleep before she could make a choice.

When she awoke, she was warm. Not only that, the room was light with early morning sun streaming in through grand and beautiful windows. Sophie blinked against the assault of such golden glory and sat up slowly and gingerly.

What a lovely room! She instantly loved everything about it, from the delicate lines of the beautiful mahogany furniture to the ornate plasterwork running about the edge of the ceiling. Her eye followed that to the fireplace, where a bright fire burned cheerfully, gleaming off a large copper tub—

Oh, God. What a beautiful thing. Not only was it large and capacious, but it was full of gently steaming water and dressed with cloths and soap and what in heaven's name was she waiting for?

As quickly as she could, she stood and began to strip off the beautiful Grecian gown that could never be worn again after kidnapping, brawling and riding all night. Thank heaven it was more loosely draped than her fairy queen costume, or she'd never have gotten it off by herself. She meant no disrespect to Lementeur's genius, but she trampled it like the rag it was in order to get to that magnificent tub!

Naked, she cautiously slipped one foot into the water. Oh, bliss. Easing her raw, sore bottom into the water was a bit trickier, but it wasn't too bad if she clenched her teeth. The relief to her sore muscles made all the sacrifice worth it. She leaned back in the tub, stretching luxuriously, then lazily raised her hands to undo her hair.

Graham backed into the room trying to balance the tray that bore some of the last edibles left in the house.

He was in an impossible position. Last night he'd

compromised Sophie rather thoroughly by all this—if anyone ever found out.

Yet, if he did right by Sophie—this thought made him rather idiotically happy—and turned this outrageous kidnapping into a proposal, how would he be able to save the people of Edencourt?

His mind had churned back and forth until he'd had to stop thinking entirely. Preparing her bath, puttering in the larder, had allowed him to finally still the whirling doubts in his mind. As for their borrowed mount, he'd returned to tie the horse in the center of the circular patch of weeds before the drive, since the poor creature seemed unwilling to leave it.

In the kitchen, he found tea leaves that were still dry and still smelled of tea and some preserved pears in a jar. There had been a small barrel of pickled herring and several more jars of preserves, but the loot he was most pleased with was the ham he'd found hanging in the larder. Once he'd sliced away the rind—for he really didn't think Sophie would like to see the gnawed areas left by the many rats that now lived in Edencourt—and cut it into awkward chunks, he'd come up with the idea that they could stick them on skewers and brown them in the fire.

Proud of his hunting skills, he turned to present the tray of steaming tea, pears and ham with a smile.

She was quite simply and perfectly naked.

Her back was to him as she tipped her head back to to let down her hair, which streamed over the back of the tub and pooled on the floor like an amber waterfall. She was gloriously, outrageously surrounded by light.

The morning sun danced over her wet skin like diamonds on ivory, a glowing nimbus that highlighted the lean elegant shape of her arms, her delicately muscled shoulder, her long graceful neck. It shimmered in her cinnamon-gold hair like motes of magic. She quite simply took his breath away.

He could see just the side of one small breast when she raised her arms again. With his throat closed with stunned admiration, he watched the water sluice over that proud breast, enveloping it with reflected light. Abruptly Graham decided that anything more ample would be superfluous.

She ran her hands over her arms then, up to uncross at her neck and then down over her body with an easy self-caress. Graham's cock hardened instantly.

He ought to be ashamed of himself. In fact, he was. Sophie deserved better than to have his irresponsible lust inflicted upon her private moment.

That didn't mean that he had any intention of moving from this spot. She hadn't heard him come in. She was completely involved in the pleasure of her bath. He was helpless before that simple sensuality, guilty but riveted.

Rinse. Smooth away the water. Rinse. Smooth. Leaning back then, she raised a long achingly beautiful leg from the water and stretched it into the air. She soaped it with her hands, sliding her palms over and over her delicious skin, up and down that incredible thigh, calf, ankle—up and down—

Bloody hell, he was about to orgasm right where he stood, with his hands full of tray!

He couldn't stand it. All he wanted was Sophie, the way she looked at that moment—minus the expensive gowns, without the powder and the pearls and intricate hair and newly sophisticated manners. Just Sophie.

He hadn't seen her until it was too late, like a buried treasure that another man found first. She was not the easy beauty, not the obvious target, but required perception and wisdom—yet he now saw the truth. She was entirely beautiful to him.

Was the gemstone buried in the cinders any less valuable than that displayed in a fine ring? The only difference was the setting.

If only he could have what he wanted instead of what Edencourt needed.

He closed his eyes against temptation. Then he turned away, set down the tea tray, scooped up Sophie's gown and cloak and dancing slippers, and slipped out of the room.

He couldn't look at her and not want her . . . but he could keep her from leaving until he figured out how to keep her safe from his bungled rescue attempt.

Not to mention keeping her safe from his growing lust.

Chapter Twenty~two

Sophie didn't leave the bath until it was nearly cold. After washing the horse off her and soaking her aching bones until her fingers pruned, she was ravenous.

There were a few tattered but clean pieces of toweling, but nothing else. She would have to put on her gown again, unfortunately. The thought of putting the ruined thing back on her clean skin was dismaying, but not as dismaying as finding out that it was gone!

She'd dropped it right there in front of the chair, she was sure of it! She cast about the room, conceding the possibility that she'd instead flung it off in wild abandon as she capered naked to the tub. It was a beautiful tub, after all.

But the gown was truly gone. Which meant someone had taken it. Which meant that the scraps of toweling she now wore about her breasts and pelvis were the only clothes she had!

She was going to kill him! Poison and knives were too kind for him. Burning at the stake was the only answer! She dropped her head back and gave forth to her fury. "*Graham!*"

In the corner of the room she spotted a pile of dusty cover cloths. Winding one about her until nothing showed but her face and her bare feet, she paused to sneeze several times, then strode purposefully out of the room.

The purposeful effect might have been slightly ruined by the necessity of taking very tiny steps because of the confining wrapper, but that only made her shuffle along more quickly, her anger growing by the moment.

She couldn't find him. She wandered through several long hallways that never seemed to end, her feet growing cold and dirty and her wet hair chilling her neck and—wait! Was that the front door?

She shuffled quickly across the marble floor of the entrance hall and put her hand to the latch. It didn't move.

Locked? She was *locked in?*

Unable to believe it, she could only mindlessly jiggle the frozen latch. What was Graham thinking to leave her here like this? What sort of daft bucket-head took a woman to a deserted house, stole her clothes and *locked her in?*

She could see the line of sunshine come under the door and dance across her bare, dusty toes. She wasn't going to be able to get out into the sunshine. She wasn't going to be able to get out at all. Graham, the light-minded idiot, had probably already forgotten where he'd put her! He'd be knocking on the door of Brook House tomorrow, wondering where Sophie was!

Everything was ruined. She could hardly seduce

Society if she was locked in a madman's house, and she wasn't even sure if she wanted to be Society's darling anymore, for it had mostly been wearying and certainly boring. Nothing had turned out the way she'd thought it would. Her magical gown was gone and her face was unpowdered and her hair probably looked like an owl nested in it and she was "just Sophie" all over again!

All her life, she'd attributed her troubles to the fact that she was odd-looking. Plain girls weren't wanted. Plain girls shouldn't hope for more. Plain girls should be grateful for what little they had.

Now it seemed that her lack of beauty might not have been at fault at all—not if she could still end up empty-handed and humiliated! Perhaps it wasn't her exterior that was ugly. Perhaps it was her interior. Perhaps her life was unfortunate because that was precisely what she deserved for being a liar and a thief and a fraud.

She'd thought being beautiful would make life perfect and nothing had come of it but getting her locked up in this great, bloody cold empty house!

She kicked the door, hard. The door didn't seem to mind but her bare foot protested sharply. Limping and shuffling and shivering and using words she hadn't realized she knew, she made her way back to "her" chamber, primarily by following her own footprints in the dust.

There she found the tray. She frowned at it. Was this already here when she'd left? She hadn't noticed it, but perhaps she'd simply been too irate.

Or perhaps Graham was concealed somewhere, watching her, sneaking into the room when her back was turned. She glanced around suspiciously. Then she shook her head. "Hunger is making you odd, my girl."

The tea was cold, but she put the pot near the fire to warm it and dug into the pears and ham instead. Eating swiftly and neatly, she drank the tea, washed her feet again in the cold bathwater and rearranged her dusty toga until she could actually walk in it. Taking the portion of ham that she hadn't eaten, she wrapped it neatly in a napkin and, for lack of anywhere better to put it, tucked it into a fold of her robes.

Then she set about searching the house methodically, room by room. If Graham expected her to act like a weak, helpless princess in a tower, he'd chosen the wrong girl to play that part!

GRAHAM WASN'T SLEEPING. After his shameful bit of voyeurism, he'd taken a long walk through the Edencourt fields, trying to calm his mind and form some sort of plan. All that he saw convinced him that marrying Sophie was an impossibility. He'd never get Lilah back now, but that stupendously vapid milkmaid heiress might do as well. At least she wouldn't kill him in his sleep.

Probably.

Right now Sophie likely wanted to. He seemed to bring that out in women these days, didn't he? No more Graham the charmer. No more easy laughter and silly, shallow games.

He passed through a small gathering of cottages that had once been sturdy and comfortable enough, the people content at least, if not actually happy. Now they were rubble and rot, most likely deserted to their downward spiral along with the rest of the estate.

When he was a child, it had been a shabby but genteel estate. When he was a young man it had seemed to be growing poorer, but he'd put that down to his own increased sophistication and not to any true decay. Now it was worse than ever and there was no denying that his father had dealt the killing blow.

I think I actually hate you, Graham thought to that loud, brash man he'd scarcely known. *In fact, I know I do, as surely as I hate every drop of your blood that runs in me.* He'd thought he was so different from them. He'd thought he was above them in understanding and civility and intellect, but he was only a polished-up version of the same man. He'd just as heartlessly bled his people dry for his own amusements, never giving a thought to responsibility or self-denial.

Well, he was paying for that now. Denying himself Sophie was going to make him miserable for the rest of his life. Or perhaps he was too shallow to love properly? Perhaps his yen for Sophie was merely that of a brat who didn't want a toy until it was denied him.

God, let it be so. Otherwise the rest of his life was looking to be a very long time.

FINALLY, BY THE neat trick of following the *other* footprints in the dust, Sophie meandered her way into what had to have been Graham's bedchamber once upon a time. It was the only room in the house she'd seen, other than her own, that lacked the murderous collection of animal corpses and body parts.

There in a trunk at the base of the bed, she found clothes! Beautiful, wonderful clothes! They must have been Graham's when he was a growing boy, for they'd never fit him now. Fortunately, they fit Sophie very nicely indeed. Once she found a neckcloth to belt the huge shirt in and stuffed the toes of the boots to make them smaller and stuck her hair up under a discarded cap, she fancied she looked a proper boy indeed!

It was quite a rare feeling, swimming in too large clothing. It almost made her feel dainty! Her heart kindled a surprising spark of forgiveness. That wouldn't do!

Of course, if she hadn't been kidnapped, robbed and deserted, she wouldn't be dressing so ridiculously in the first place!

Angry and embarrassed anew about the whole mess, she made her way back down the stairs and to the entrance hall. Graham had locked this door, but had he locked them all?

Then she realized that her problem wasn't even that difficult to solve. All the rooms flanking the front door had windows that opened out onto the great terraced steps instead of dropping the usual twelve feet to the ground. With the flick of a latch and a nimble climb, she was out of the house and trotting down the steps.

If they could ride the distance in less than a night, how long could it possibly take to walk back to London?

She had no idea how far a horse could go in one night, but surely with long legs and most of the day left, she could manage it.

Sophie stopped short at the bottom of the stairs. The horse from hell was tied in front of the house like a watchdog. If she took the horse, she could be back in London by nightfall.

After her first two steps, the horse raised its head and snorted at her. She halted. Had that been greeting or warning? She folded her arms and glared at the thing. "I don't need you, you . . . hellbeast!" She turned on her heel and walked away, around the garden and on down the drive.

She wasn't afraid of it. That would be silly. She simply didn't feel like riding again so soon. If she ran into someone on the road and they should happen to ask, that would be her tale.

The horse snorted again behind her.

"Such a lovely day for a walk," Sophie said brightly to no one at all. "I think I'll walk a little faster!"

GRAHAM HESITATED OUTSIDE the room he'd already begun to think of as Sophie's. He had no choice. He had to tell her his plan to take her back to London and slip her into Brook House under cover of darkness. He only hoped that general alarm had not been raised by the Brook House staff when she hadn't come home last night.

If he'd been thinking properly, he'd never have brought her here at all. Unfortunately, when she'd chosen that bounder Wolfe over him, his mind seemed to have slipped a few cogs. He could blame it on lack of sleep and the heavy thoughts on his mind and the full moon shining down on the amazing planes of her face when she'd faced him down and calmly refused him, but the fact remained that he'd done the single most dangerous thing he possibly could have.

He'd given in to his own desires.

Now he had to beg her understanding and her forgiveness and, worst of all, her help in bringing off this ridiculous scheme. *"Tell Brook House that you were at Tessa's and tell Tessa you were at Brook House, and then we'll pretend this never happened and we'll never, ever think on this again, I swear to it."*

Except that he would, of course. Every time he wished his vapid, bosomy milkmaid of a duchess goodnight and went off to his thankfully separate bedchamber, he would wish he would find lean, elegant, tart-tongued Sophie there, bathing naked before the fire, the water turning her hair the color of brandy.

Which, by the by, was no more and no less than what he roundly deserved.

His plan on his reluctant tongue, he tapped on the door. No answer. She was asleep, of course. He'd dragged her across the county last night, remember?

I'll wager she's beautiful when she's sleeping.

His hand pressed the latch without him actually commanding it to. The door swung open with a slow creak. The room didn't look quite like it had when he left it. For one thing, the fire was out. For another, the tray of food was empty. The bed was untouched, but the pile of canvas covers was disarranged.

She'd gone wandering the house in a sheet? Of course she had. This was Sophie, after all. He would not be at all surprised to find her somewhere, sewing herself a gown, shoes, and a carriage to carry her home!

Paying no attention whatsoever to the varying trails through the dusty halls, he began to search the house. At first he was amused. Gradually, he became dismayed. When he found his old bedchamber and the rifled trunk, he became alarmed.

When he found the front window wide open, he became frightened.

Gazing out the window, he could see nothing but Somers's horse lying sedately in the weeds, sleepily shaking off the occasional fly. The bucolic sight only worried him further.

If Sophie had fled him, why hadn't she taken the horse?

Because she didn't leave of her own free will.

No, that was ridiculous. This house had been deserted for nearly two years. Why would a criminal choose today of all days to randomly stage an assault?

Perhaps it wasn't random. Perhaps someone knows you're here.

No. No one knew they were here. The only person who even knew they were together was—

Wolfe.

Alarm turned to sickening panic in Graham's gut. That slimy bastard had stolen her once. What was to prevent him from doing it again?

The thought hadn't entirely crossed his mind before he vaulted through the window and ran for the horse.

SOPHIE WALKED FURIOUSLY for half an hour, her thoughts circling around her indignation and humiliation. Then as the exercise loosened her body and soothed her mind, she began to truly look about her for the first time.

The house of Edencourt had been grimy and shabby, but she'd dismissed that as having been full of men for too many years, without a woman's standards of housekeeping. The grounds around the house were a tangle, overgrown and wild, but she'd not paid much attention, for what else would one expect from owners who spent too much time chasing pleasure in London?

Then she came across the first group of cottages, a semicircle grouped around a small mill on the riverbank. The thatched roof buildings were small and square, obviously built of local stone many generations ago, much like the cottages near Acton. Unlike those, these had sagging roofs of moldy straw and desiccated gardens full of trash and rubble. And here she'd thought Graham was being shallow and greedy, marrying for money!

The need here was obvious. In fact, the cottages looked so grim that Sophie hesitated walking through the area. Should she go around? But they looked deserted. Surely no one lived in such disreputable homes?

Instinctively moving more quietly, and more quickly,

Sophie took the path straight through the settlement. She didn't want to leave the road in an area she didn't know.

Scarcely three steps into the clearing, she heard a sound like wood scraping on stone. Glancing warily about her, she hurried her steps. When she reached the center of the clearing, she saw a flash of movement to one side, a flutter of dark fabric that vanished behind one of the cottages. Icy threat seemed to climb the back of her neck. Though she wore Graham's clothing, she had no doubt that she appeared entirely female . . . and alone.

What to do? Stop and take a stand, grabbing whatever weapon came handy? Continue through the tiny hamlet and on down the deserted road beyond, to be followed easily enough? Or would the threat linger here in its home, allowing her to pass on?

The fact that turning to fight was her first thought would have surprised her if she'd given it a moment's consideration. Her entire concentration lay in the corners of her eyes, the blind spot behind her head, the vulnerability of her empty hands.

Unable to continue with such a feeling of menace at her back, she stopped to circle slowly, turning constantly to better watch behind her. Her spiral path took her near a pile of rubble, stones and broken planks and rusting iron bits. She knelt swiftly to grab up a bit of chain in one hand and a splintery length of wood in another. Shoddy weapons indeed, for the chain nearly crumbled to dust in her fingers and the dry-rotted board would likely shatter at the first blow—but perhaps it would be enough to startle someone into letting her be.

There was no one there, though the sense of menace blackened and grew. Could she be wrong? Had it been nothing but the creak of the breeze on an ancient shutter and the flutter of an abandoned bit of rag? Graham was always telling her she had too much imagination. Was she creating a dramatic pursuit when it was truly nothing but a boring walk?

Swallowing, she circled once more, her gaze hard on the shadows within the cottages and the gaping door of the mill.

Someone was watching . . . someone who meant her harm.

Chapter Twenty~three

Graham rode Somers's horse wildly, racing to and fro. There were two roads into the estate. He had no way of knowing which way Sophie had been taken, so he had to ride down all four tracks, east, west, north and south.

The roads were empty of life. The surrounding countryside was nothing more than a recriminating shamble of weeds, broken walls, tumbling cottages and a few hard-eyed and sallow farmers who only gazed at him blankly when he asked about a stolen woman.

His people surely didn't think well of him. He only hoped that basic decency would keep them from concealing Sophie's whereabouts.

But no one had seen her or a man fitting Wolfe's description.

"No one comes here, milord." Of course they hadn't learned of the former duke's death and his own ascension. Graham forbore telling them, for it could only harden them further against him. "No one ever comes here."

"Er . . . right. Thank you." Shamed and desperate at

once, Graham reined Somers's horse about and tried another direction.

Finally, on the south road, he saw an amazing sight. A tiny child played in the middle of a ring of tumbled cottages—he dimly recalled passing them on foot early this morning—and she wore on her dirty, golden hair something he immediately recognized.

It was his favorite boyhood cap.

She went very still as he approached, then turned to run when she saw him reining in his mount.

"No, wait! Please, have you seen a lady?" The child slowed at his pleading tone, then turned to stare at him, one dirty finger in her mouth.

Graham dismounted and moved forward slowly, trying desperately to project harmlessness and not his desperate intention to tie her up in a sack until she told him where she'd found the cap. "I've lost my lady, you see," he said softly. "She's tall, with red-gold hair—"

The child nodded. Oh, thank God. Graham moved forward, dropping the horse's reins and going down on one knee. *I am so harmless you could knock me over with one wave of your tiny, grubby hand.* "Can you tell me which way she rode?"

The little girl gazed at him with wide blue eyes, then slowly shook her head. *No.*

"You didn't see her ride by?"

No.

This was useless! The child hadn't seen a thing. She'd probably found the cap on the ground. He ought to leap back on the damned horse and continue south!

Graham took a deep breath, fighting down his panic,

reaching for patience. "Little one, did you see my lady or not?"

She nodded.

"Where did you see her?"

The child raised her other hand, the one she wasn't chewing on, and pointed neither up the road, north, nor down the road, south. Instead, her stubby little finger quite clearly indicated the cottage less than seven yards away.

"Oh." Graham stood, brushed off his knees and walked six quick strides to the door of the place. "Sophie?"

Sophie looked up from spooning something into the mouth of a woman who lay in a poorly made bed in the cottage's only room. "Oh, hullo, Gray. What do you want?"

Want? Well, to begin with, he wanted to run to her, drag her into his arms and kiss her blind. Then he wanted to shake her within an inch of her life for frightening him so. Then perhaps some more kissing. Yes, definitely more kissing. But there might be another bout of shaking later, as well.

"You worried me," he said in low voice. "I didn't know where you'd gone."

"I'm on my way to London," she said absently, now dabbing at the woman's fevered face with a cloth. "I only stopped to help Moira here. Her husband's in the city working in a factory. She's all alone here with the children. They tried to take care of her when she became ill, but they're so small . . ."

There were, he saw now, several more grimy blond

children in the room. It looked like dozens, but was surely more like five. Bloody hell, if he was their mother left alone with them, he'd have taken to his bed, too!

"Is Moira very ill?" He kept his voice soft, for the poor woman did look very ill indeed.

Sophie looked up with a quick smile. "She's mostly exhausted, I think. There hasn't been much food lately and I think she's been giving hers to the children."

"Sophie made food," someone said.

Graham looked down to see that his roadside nemesis had entered behind him. She pushed back his cap on her head to gaze up at him critically. "You're milord, aren't you? The one that Papa curses when he thinks we can't hear."

He returned the look. "Given up on your vow of silence so soon? What a pity."

"Graham, I'm so sorry," Sophie said, shaking her head. "I didn't know it was so bad here. I . . . I understand now, about Lilah, I mean."

Graham met her gaze to see that, like a miracle, the shine of belief and trust had returned to her beautiful gray eyes. She hadn't looked at him that way since he'd told her about gaining the title. Actually, she'd never looked at him in quite *that* way. Now it was as if her belief in him was not only restored but magnified by a thousand.

He had to swallow hard to send his heart back down from where it lodged in his throat. "Yes, well . . . er, what's for dinner, then?"

She smiled. "I made a nourishing soup from the ham you left me and some dried peas."

"And she found some carrots and bitter greens in the garden," the little girl piped up. "We thought we'd ate them all!"

Sophie shrugged at that, looking slightly embarrassed. "I just happened to spot them under the fallen timbers," she said. She gave the pot another stir. "There's enough for another day, but I wish I had more ham. The children need meat."

"Ah." Graham backed toward the door. "I'll be back in a pip and jiggle," he told the little girl. "You start counting and don't stop until you see me again."

She narrowed her eyes. "You'd best hurry then, for I can only count a little. One, two, three, four . . . one . . ."

Somers's Horse, as Graham had begun to call him, slanted Graham a disbelieving look when he tried to stir it to a canter. Then with a long-suffering sigh, the beast broke into a weary lope that still ate up the miles to the house.

Graham tied the horse back in its patch and climbed back through the window rather than bother with the key. In a few moments, he'd filled a cookpot with the last of the ham, all the jars of preserves and all the tea. He cast about for something more valuable to give them that they might sell for more food, but he feared that anything too precious might only bring suspicion down on them.

Then the shimmer of his own waistcoat buttons caught his gaze as he passed a mirror in the hall. Gold, of course. Only the best for the sons of Edencourt. He pulled them off one by one with a yank and a twist and tossed them into the cookpot. They could be sold off slowly and no one would think much of it.

Then he carried it all right back out through the window. "Handy, that."

The horse stared at him in frank dismay when he returned.

"Sorry, S.H., but we're on an errand of mercy." Graham grinned, feeling lighter than he had in a long while. "Besides, that little girl is counting to four again and again. We must get back before she drives Sophie round the bend."

When he arrived with his ridiculous pot balanced on the pommel before him, one would have thought he'd brought Sophie diamonds and furs. Her eyes shone with delight when she saw the tea. "Oh, perfect! I'll make some for Moira right away."

Then she turned to Graham and pressed her palm lightly onto his loose-hanging waistcoat. "Your buttons?"

He shrugged and glanced away. "I can always find brass ones. It's going to be a long winter."

She looked at him for a long moment, her head tilted to one side. "You absolutely devastate me, do you know that, Graham Cavendish, Duke of Edencourt?"

Because he'd given up some buttons? He shook his head, not understanding, but she only smiled mysteriously. "Let me fix Moira and the children up with some tea and preserves. Then I think we'd better return to the manor."

He blinked at her. "But we must get you back to London! You'll be missed!"

She shook her head and pointed behind him. "That thing isn't going to get us to London today."

Graham turned to see that S.H. had abandoned him and was nearly out of sight, trotting stubbornly back to its patch of weeds, reins trailing in the dust of the road.

He turned back to her. "I can catch him." Although he wasn't at all sure he could.

She shook her head again. "You might persuade him to do it all again so soon, but I fear you're going to have a much harder time convincing me."

With that, she turned and strode briskly back into the cottage. The place on his chest where her hand had rested felt cold without her.

WOLFE SNARLED FROM his hiding place in the darkness of the furthermost shack.

Foiled again. He almost had the gangling bitch—but he had no stomach for children, greasy little beasts. Besides, he probably couldn't have convinced her to come away before someone raised an alarm. Watching from the shadows as the two nauseating do-gooders fed the moldy masses, he snarled.

He wanted to kill them both, preferably with something white-hot and painful. Unfortunately, killing *her* was far too obvious. Stickley would be the first to point a finger.

Something niggled at the back of his thoughts. It had been so long since his head had been clear of liquor for several days in a row that it took a bit of work to bring the actual memory to the surface. He was clearly out of practice.

Then he had it. Sir Hamish's will!

"Should three generations of Pickering girls fail, I wash me hands of the lot of you. The entire fifteen thousand pounds will go to pay the fines and hardships of those who defy the excise man to export that fine Scots whisky which has been my only solace in this family of dolts."

The effort made his head pound, but Wolfe persisted. There was something there . . .

This was the third generation. One girl had already failed. One had married well, but her husband wasn't a duke yet. It was entirely possible that he wouldn't be by the time the Season ended. The last girl could still be stopped . . .

Then he had it.

"The entire fifteen thousand pounds will go to—"

Fifteen thousand pounds. Not thirty thousand. Stickley had doubled the trust, by gum—and after all the girls failed, the will only required that fifteen thousand pounds go to the smugglers!

The rest would be theirs, his and Stickley's!

All he had to do was to kill the Duke of Edencourt.

Stickley wouldn't like it—but then, once a man had killed a duke, what was to stop him from swatting an insect like Stickley?

Chapter Twenty-four

There was no point in hurrying, so Graham and Sophie enjoyed the long walk back to Edencourt. The time was later than he'd realized. He must have spent hours riding up and down these roads. Even now the day was fading, mingling long blue shadows with slanting golden light.

Sophie's hair fell unbound down her back, catching the light as the breeze played with the length of it. She walked with loose, open strides like the country girl she was, but her spine was straight and poised and her chin was high, like the elegant, polished "Sofia."

"This is my favorite time of day," she shared with him. "When the work is done and world starts to quiet."

"Not in London," he pointed out. "I know some people who are only now rising from their beds."

They looked at other with matching grins. "Tessa!" they said together.

Sophie's smile became rueful. "How am I ever going to return to Primrose Street?"

The very thought of this new, shimmeringly confident Sophie returning to be imprisoned beneath

Tessa's heavy thumb sickened Graham. "Don't," he urged. "Stay with Deirdre. She'd love it, I know she would. She's very fond of you, you know."

Sophie frowned slightly. "She is?" Then she shook her head. "I can't. I can't live as someone's permanent, useless guest for the rest of my life."

He frowned then himself. "You aren't her guest. You're her family."

She looked away, her gaze resting on the low stone wall alongside the road. "Hmm."

They walked in silence for a time. Then Graham's stomach rumbled, loudly. "We won't have any supper," he pointed out mournfully. "I gutted the larder thoroughly."

Sophie laughed. "That was man-thoroughness. I imagine there will be different results from woman-thoroughness."

He scratched behind his ear. "Could be. I'd never actually been in the kitchen before. I didn't even know that larder was there."

She gazed at him, her brow furrowed. "Graham, you do realize that a house that size has several kitchens, don't you? And each kitchen probably has more than one larder?"

He cheered immediately. "Really? Because you ate my breakfast."

She clapped a hand over her mouth, then ruined her guilty dismay by laughing out loud. "So that was why you gave me an extraordinary amount of ham! I assumed it was some sort of verdict on my unfeminine appetite."

He smiled sideways at her. "Sophie, no one in their

right mind would ever dream of calling you unfeminine."

She turned to him with a sudden, devastating smile. "Why thank you, kind sir!"

Graham, when he could breathe again and the dazzle had faded from his vision, couldn't for the life of him remember what they'd been speaking of.

No matter. Perhaps it was enough that for now, at this moment, he was strolling along a country lane with the only woman in the world he would ever love: his valiant, clever Miss Sophie Blake.

Sophie's mind was not so serene. She was forming a plan—a wonderful, terrible, frightening plan.

What if she took her charade to its farthest possible extreme?

What if she did more than steal two hundred pounds of dress allowance and travel money and pose as a poor but genteel long-lost cousin for a brief moment of freedom and change?

What if she continued the lie forever—for all the rest of her life!—and never, ever confessed to anyone that she was not, in fact, Miss Sophie Blake, great-granddaughter to Sir Hamish Pickering? What if she never went back to being who she truly was, a mere servant girl, a lady's companion to the fretful, demanding Mrs. Blake—who was, in fact, mother of poor, sickly, long-dead little Sophie?

What if she married Graham and won the Pickering fortune for him and all his desolate, neglected people?

There was no time to hesitate, to mull over her choices. Just as before, when she'd opened the post as usual and found the money sent from Lady Tessa for Sophie's debut, the moment called for immediate action.

Deirdre was about to become the Duchess of Brookmoor. It might already have happened, which thought brought new panic to Sophie's chest. No, she had to believe that she'd been brought here to see this place, this need, for a reason.

Deirdre didn't truly need the money. Calder was a wealthy and generous man.

You can diminish it all you like, but there's no avoiding the fact that you'll be stealing from someone who trusts you. You'll be robbing one of the few people on this earth who has ever cared about you at all.

Moira's thin face appeared in her mind, gray with fatigue and wear, though the woman had confessed that she was actually younger than she herself was!

No, it was necessary, all of it. If she didn't force Graham to wed her before the elderly Duke of Brookmoor died and made Calder duke in his stead, she wouldn't be able to help any of them.

Not even herself.

BY THE TIME they reached the manor the day was gone. All that was visible was the long white drive in the moonlight and the dark lump that was the sleeping horse in the green sward. Graham laughingly helped Sophie back through the open window, but when the walls rose hushed and vast around them he became silent.

His helping hand slid from hers slowly, as if he were being pulled away. Sophie didn't cling, though she felt colder without him next to her. There was time enough, she hoped. Together they walked up the graciously curving stair in the darkness. Graham walked her to "her" door, then stopped.

She couldn't see him but she could feel his tension as if he were tied to her. When he spoke, his voice was low and full of regret.

"This isn't right, Sophie. Tomorrow we must return to London. Perhaps we can persuade the Brook House staff to believe you've been at Primrose Street all along."

Sophie closed her eyes to better feel his mood. Was it regret that they must return, or regret that they were there in the first place? It didn't matter. Soon enough they might both have something to regret. She only hoped he would forgive her when she won the inheritance.

"Goodnight, Graham."

He hesitated, then she felt his palm, warm and large, cup her cheek. It was a kiss, of sorts. Her hopes rose. Perhaps he might forgive her sooner than later?

Then he was gone, a mere shadow in darkness. She heard the next door open, then shut behind him. Only then did she put her hand on her own latch and let herself into the duchess's bedchamber. Once inside, she could see very well, for the moon poured through the window much the way the sunlight had this morning. In that light, she rinsed her face in the cold bathwater and used a bristle brush she found in the vanity to tame her tangled hair. She ought to have been cold without a fire, but her plan heated her through every time she contemplated it.

At last she deemed enough time had passed. Stripping herself of all but Graham's shirt, which fell nearly to her knees, she shook out her hair and straightened. She didn't have Lementeur's magic to dazzle him with, or Patricia's skill to hide her flaws, but the darkness would hide most of that. She would have what she truly needed.

Loving Graham had come so easily to her that she wasn't sure precisely when it had transformed from a longing to a fantasy to a need so powerful that she would toss her already shabby ethics into the chamber pot in order to have him. She could lie to the world, but she was done lying to herself. Her heroic mission to save his people was a dim flame next to the inferno of her own selfish desires.

So be it.

At the last moment, she stopped to kneel next to her hearth. After a search with the poker, she found a live coal among the ashes. She scooped it out with the ash shovel and dropped it into the half-filled scuttle Graham had left there earlier. She may not have been feeling the cold but Graham might.

Then she eyed the adjoining door set into the elegant paneling of the wall, the one a duke might use to visit his duchess. Taking a deep breath, she put her hand on the latch and pushed.

GRAHAM HAD GONE to bed cold and hungry and desperately conflicted. The combination was enough to give him the strangest dream.

First and foremost, he was warm. Delicious heat shimmered on his skin, making him stretch languorously. Then there was a delightful soft weight upon him, stretched along one side of his body. Soft against his hardness—and by God he was hard!—a touch stroked over his pectorals, teasing the hair there, then traveled slowly and tantalizingly down . . . down . . .

It slowed, then stopped short. He writhed upward, pressing into it, impatient for those long, teasing fingers to wrap themselves around his throbbing cock.

This was one of his favorite dreams ever.

The hand spread warm and gentle over his belly, but didn't truly retreat. Yes, anticipation was better. *Make me wait. Make me ache.*

Then the lips came to his. He moaned then, the sound echoing strangely through the dream. What?

A soft wet mouth opened over his and he forgot his uneasiness instantly. So teasing, so giving and wet—damn, he loved Sophie's mouth!

In that instant he realized that he'd had this dream before. In the past months he'd dreamed it again and again, but it had never been so real, so hot and damp and breathless until the sound of their mingled panting echoed from the high walls of the duke's bedchamber—

What?

Wait. No, don't wake up. Don't be an idiot. Keep dreaming.

Too late.

Awareness came crashing in like a cold ocean breaker. He was at Edencourt with Sophie. Worse yet, he was in bed with Sophie.

No, it got worse. He was *tied up* in bed—trussed by both wrists to the bedposts, by God!—with Sophie spread onto him like jam on toast, her hands roving shyly but hungrily over him while her mouth teased his.

He drew back from her lips, his expression aghast. "Sophie?"

The horror in Graham's eyes could not be mistaken. Sophie's insides turned to ice.

A plain stick like you—who'd want you?

No man wants a giraffe.

No, of course he wouldn't. Her skin crawling at the revulsion he must be feeling, she slid from the bed, pulling the coverlet off to wrap about her. She wanted to blurt apologies, she wanted to cry, she wanted very much to not be standing in his room in the middle of the night with the silk cold against her bare, repulsive skin.

Her borrowed shirt lay pooled on the floor at her feet. She knelt, awkward in her haste, to pull desperately at the wad of linen. It tangled instantly in her hands, of course, then blurred completely. She stopped pawing at it and let her head drop to her bent knees, her eyes burning in defeat and humiliation.

Sophie Blake had done it again.

God, she hated Sophie Blake.

"Ah . . . Sophie . . ."

She flinched at Graham's voice. "Never speak of this. Ever."

"Sophie—"

She flung up a hand, her head still bowed. "I'm serious, Graham."

"God damn it, Sophie, untie me this instant!"

It was a rasping whisper, not a bellow, but it had much the same effect. Startled, Sophie overbalanced completely, sprawling on the carpet in a tangle of coverlet and nudity.

From where he lay on the bed, Graham saw a stunning flash of long elegant limbs leading up to a deliciously pert bottom, all bound in porcelain skin and amber silk. The momentary glimpse of sinuous waist and small, high perfect breasts came as a delightful second course as she scrambled to cover herself with the shimmering curtain of her ginger hair. The erotic jolt to his already taxed self-control made his eyes glassy and his breath come short.

Then he clenched his eyes shut against the sight of Sophie—his *Sophie!*—naked on the carpet of his bedchamber.

When he felt cold fingers fumbling at his bonds, he dared to crack one eye open—no, no good. She'd bound herself so tightly in the coverlet that her bosom pressed high, right into his vision as she leaned over him to reach the bedpost opposite. Praying that God would have mercy on him and dilute his raging erection sometime in the next several seconds, he kept his eyes dutifully shut against all the things he should not be seeing.

That didn't help against all the things he should not be feeling, like the way she pressed one knee between his in order to reach across, spreading his thighs apart and ensuring that the dragging silk of the coverlet swept across his swollen cock with her slightest movement.

Or the way her skin smelled of plain soap and water—practical, no nonsense Sophie—and how that crisp scent did absolutely nothing to hide the darker perfume of heated, aroused woman.

Would he ever be able to smell soap again without an immediate rush of heat to his groin?

Would he ever be able to look at Sophie in her demurely sweeping skirts and not remember how long and lean her thighs were, or how her small breasts were topped with the most delicious ruby pink nipples he'd ever have the pleasure to dream fruitlessly about for the rest of his life?

And what about that age-old question, the one pondered by men the world over, the one he'd shut his eyes before answering to his satisfaction—were the silken curls between those lovely thighs composed of the same ginger gold as on her head?

It might not be too late to find out.

Lecher.

Oy! I'm the one tied up here. It wouldn't be my fault if I had to open my eyes, just for a second, and the silk slipped again, just for a second—do you think she'd drop it again if I startle her?

Reprobate. This was *Sophie.*

Yeah, I know. Naked, damp, stunningly assembled Sophie . . . in my bedchamber in the middle of the night of her own volition. Who'd know?

He would.

Well, there's that. And I suppose Sophie might remember it as well. I suppose I'll just have to list this one under "Opportunity Missed."

Bloody right.

It's a pretty short list. I'm not actually all that honorable, you know.

He was now.

Am I going to keep this inner argument up for long?

Only until she finished untying him and was safely off the bed.

Good, because the old pistol is pretty close to firing.

Don't remind me.

Then he felt the loss of her heat and scent and felt her slight weight leave the mattress, mere seconds from causing him to embarrass himself rather thoroughly. His hands, now unbound, were still clenched in fists of sheer will not to touch her. He kept them that way as he slitted his eyes to make sure she was safely away.

She was across the room with her back pressed to the door and her bundle of shirt and coverlet clutched protectively before her. Her head was turned, her face hidden by shadow, her hair reflecting the coals with copper glints. She looked both fierce and captive, furious and demoralized.

Sweet stubborn Sophic.

Delicious Sophie.

This was, indeed, a pickle.

Chapter Twenty-five

Graham threw back the remaining covers and swung one leg over the edge of the bed, putting one foot to the floor. At his sudden motion, she startled like a deer.

And like a deer, long-legged in its fright, she scrambled suddenly for escape.

He tackled her, catching her in mid-flight and swinging her around to trap her against the door, his hands pinning her wrists over her head. He didn't wish to hurt her but he knew that if she made it out of the room, her imagined rejection would harden to stone and become permanent in that stubborn mind of hers.

She struggled fiercely, writhing against him. She wasn't weak but he merely used his big body to capture her resistance. Pressing her to the door, he laughed. "Play nice, Sophie. Don't force me to tie *you* up!"

She went perfectly still but her heart began to race next to his. He felt her nipples harden in a blink, poking into his pectorals like faceted rubies. An image filled his mind of Sophie, clad in something skimpy and trimmed in lace, her long, elegant limbs tied spread-eagle on his giant bed, blindfolded and submissive while he had his wicked way with her over and over again. His cock hardened, pressing to her belly with only the silk of the tenuously lingering coverlet between them.

Would she like that? The faint sound that came from her throat made him think perhaps she might.

I am surely going to hell.

Then enjoy the ride. Grab the reins and race into the night. Stop stalling and fidgeting and pretending there is anyone else in the world you could spend your life with. Mount and ride, lad.

Could it be that easy?

Why . . . yes, it could.

His conflict melted away like snow in the sunlight. He had no choice. She had, with one act, quite efficiently decided the matter for him, hadn't she?

Thank God.

With nothing more than a slight movement away from her, he let the meager obstacle of the coverlet slip from between them, leaving her bare and shivering and completely in his power.

Or perhaps it was the other way around.

Without setting her free, he took another step back and gazed at her nakedness frankly. Even in the firelight he could tell she was blushing furiously.

Sophie shut her eyes tightly and waited. She'd humiliated herself and assaulted him and now she must pay the price. As the moment lengthened and nothing else happened, she couldn't help but twitch impatiently. She felt the gust of Graham's laughter warm against her cheek.

"Open your eyes, you rapist."

Shocked, she opened her eyes to glare at him, her mouth open to defend herself—

He was naked. Golden and muscled, he stood mere inches from her, his chest flexed from pinning her hands, his rippling belly tight with tension, and lower still, his thick organ jutting proudly, aimed at her like an arrow in the bow.

Oh, yes. Skewer me. Please.

She didn't say it out loud. She had a little self-control, at least. Only the slightest hungry whimper betrayed her.

"What are you thinking?" His voice was low and husky.

She tore her eyes away from that magnificent stallion part and met his gaze somberly. "I'm thinking it might not fit," she said seriously.

He dropped his head but not before she saw the white flash of his smile in the fire-glow. After a moment of helpless laughter, a moment she spent steaming silently, he lifted his head and gazed at her with something entirely new in his eyes.

Her heart nearly stopped. The light she saw there . . . it wasn't affection or friendship or even lust. Her lonely soul rose to expand in pure joy. She knew that light.

She'd seen it in the mirror.

She felt the smile grow, the one she kept mostly to herself, the one that made everyone blink so oddly and stare at her. With Graham she could show herself. With Graham she needn't fear anything at all.

Graham felt his breath leave him at the glory of her smile. She glowed, pinned there naked in his hands, her splendid hair adorning her nudity like a benediction. His stunning, magnificent Sophie.

His.

Slowly, as if he feared to break a spell, he moved closer. Knee touched knee. Thigh pressed to thigh. His rigid cock nestled in the trim softness of her belly as if coming home at last. Her high breasts pressed to his hard chest, softly giving yet firm. At last, his lips met hers.

It was less a kiss than a promise.

Always.

Always was. Always would be. Love without end.

His fingers relaxed from her wrists. He slid his palms down over her arms, down to her shoulders to her neck, then cupped the delicate edge of her jaw as he kissed her more deeply.

Had any kiss ever filled him so? Had another woman's mouth ever satisfied anything more than superficial lust?

He couldn't remember. He couldn't even remember being that man who totted up the women he'd seduced in a year to determine if it had been a good one. That fellow was nothing but a watery reflection, distorted and blurred, washed away by the love of the truest, most honest woman he had ever known.

Then she slid her cool fingers over him, from his shoulders, down his back, to cup his hard buttocks in urgent hands.

Desire, which had never cooled but only simmered, flared once more.

That's when Graham realized the difference.

Passion was about the body, the senses and the skin and the pounding blood. Love was about something much less easy, much less simple. Love was seeing someone for exactly who they were—the strong and the weak, the fearless and the vulnerable, and knowing that the sum of it all, the total of the person, was worth more than all the passion in the world. To see the truth of someone, and have them see the truth of you—that was something more rare and beautiful than any simple affair.

Passion simply made the entire matter more exciting.

With a single motion, he swept her up into his arms and spun them both to land on the bed, naked and tangled and laughing out loud.

He went up on one elbow and found her face beneath all that hair, sweeping it back with one hand as he gazed into those infinite smoky eyes. "I'm marrying you tomorrow."

She quirked a brow. "Why not tonight?"

He shook his head in wonder. "You're always going to have the last word, aren't you?"

She grinned. "Not always. I promise, once a year I shall let you have it."

Ducking his head to nuzzle her into laughter, he breathed her in. "That's all right. As long as I get the last kiss."

She wrapped her fingers into his hair. "I find those terms acceptable, Your Grace."

Then the giddiness turned golden and languid. He

kissed slowly down that long exquisite neck, following the arch of it to her breastbone, pressing his lips against the heart that thudded so close. Her breasts were small but ripe, her nipples straining upward in excitement as he brushed his lips over each of them once, twice, thrice.

She squirmed, so helplessly responsive that he resorted to pinning those writhing hips down with his hands cupped over each hipbone as he let his mouth travel onward, tasting the hollow between the arches of her ribcage, dipping his tongue into her navel, nibbling his way over the feminine swell of her taut belly until her legs churned restlessly.

He solved that by sliding between them and tossing her calves over his shoulders. The scent of her arousal rose sweet and exciting. He dipped his head and took a taste.

She yelped in surprise. "Graham!"

"I'm a shocking fellow, I know," he said soothingly. "Now, let a man work."

Sophie clapped her hands over her eyes in embarrassment. She knew a bit about mating from her life in the country, but she was certain this was not normal!

Then he slid his nimble tongue into the parting of her flesh and she forgot all about her shyness. He played her like a flute. His mouth was always in motion, always with skill and control. The wet slickness of his tongue, the sharp but gentle nip of his teeth, the soothing warmth of his lips and the rough abrasion of his beard combined to tease her damp, sensitive flesh to a heated, swollen throbbing she'd never known before, not even in her own tentative exploration.

She dropped her hands from her face to drive her fingers into his thick hair, mindlessly urging him onward with animal whimpers of excitement. Hot dark pleasure swallowed her whole. Then he slid his hands from her hips and used his thumbs to part her lower lips. This time she didn't quiver in mortification but only obliged by opening her thighs wider in willing surrender. *Please.*

His tongue found her most sensitive nub and gently rolled it, hot, wet and swollen, into his mouth. *Oh yes.* He sucked it softly, tenderly, flicking his tongue over the unprotected tip until she jolted in unison, shocking pleasure firing off more and more quickly until her body shook with huge tremors of unnerved ecstasy. She strained upward, tossing her head, crying out for something hot and bright and aching—

He slid one long finger deep into her, his sudden violation swift and perfect and *please, please, yes—!*

Her hands flew out to grip the sheets, clenching them, holding on for dear life as the crashing wave of rapture overwhelmed her, tossing her high into the stars to fall madly, helplessly, wildly. She dimly heard her own keening but didn't care. She was nothing but white-hot sensation—burning alive—the combustion of her willing, obedient flesh the only possible outcome.

So be it. She would gladly die at the hands of her lover, her love . . .

Yet her heart continued to pound and at last the

breath returned to her lungs. Her body still trembled, damp and quivering as she panted in confusion.

Graham returned to her and took her into his arms, holding her gently while the tremors racked her still. Suddenly shy, she buried her face in his chest and fought to catch her breath.

"What . . . was that?"

She felt rather than heard his understanding chuckle. "That was your first orgasm, I think."

Rubbing her face into his hot skin, she moaned in embarrassment. "I think I made noise."

"No, not at all," he reassured her. "Not a peep. Silent as a mouse."

She laughed at that. "A very large mouse. With friends. And all their tails caught in a trap!"

He kissed the top of her head. "Don't worry. There's no one here but us. You can trap as many mice as you like."

"Do you—"

"Do I what?"

She rolled her forehead against the hard muscles of his chest. "Do you trap mice, as well?"

"Hmm." He caught her chin in warm fingers and tipped her chin up to gaze into her eyes. "Not quite in the same way. Are you frightened?"

She blew out a breath, stirring the strands of hair that refused to stay out of her face. "I am not. You might recall whose idea this was."

He smiled, but his eyes remained on hers. "I recall, dimly." Then he sobered. "I want you desperately, but only if you're ready."

She traced the chiseled edge of his cheekbone with her fingertips. "I'm ready. No matter what."

His eyes crinkled. "It isn't a firing squad, Soph. It will only hurt for a moment, I promise."

She rolled her eyes. "Well, for goodness' sake, why didn't you say so in the first place?" She flung her arms above her head, offering herself. "Go on. Deflower me already."

He laughed and moved to lie above her, his long legs between hers. "Your pillow talk could use some work."

"What would you prefer? 'Oh, pray be gentle with me, manly knight! I am but a simple country maid, pure and chaste, my limbs tied shut at the knees'—"

His brows rose. "That's not precisely the attitude I would wish."

She blushed, ashamed. "I'm nervous," she whispered. "I sometimes wax sarcastic when I'm nervous. Or break things."

He bent to kiss her softly, sweetly. "My darling, I want you to put your arms around me."

She did so, slipping them over his broad shoulders, stroking the hard muscles there. Heat stirred within her.

He breathed warm into her ear. "Now wrap your lovely thighs around my hips."

Trembling now in mingled anxiety and anticipation, she did so, gripping him with her ankles crossed behind his buttocks.

"Now kiss me," he whispered. "Kiss me like you did against the door."

That she could do, eagerly. She slid her hands into

his hair and pulled his mouth down to hers. She threw everything in her heart into that kiss, releasing all fear, trusting him fully.

When his thick organ slowly began to press into her wet softness, she closed her eyes and forced back the instinct to fight the pain. Instead, she concentrated on welcoming him, loving him inside her, granting him the entry to her body she'd already given him to her heart.

Rigid and solid and relentless, his erection pierced her slowly until she couldn't bear it. She tossed her head from side to side, lost in gasping pleasure-pain, the moment endless, his length and width devastating her even as it stretched and defined her.

At last he stopped, holding himself above her on his elbows, his head down, his breath coming fast as he held on, waiting for her. She began to fight the stretching pain that wouldn't end, writhing beneath him, trying to ease the sensation that she might tear in two and die, impaled upon his massive fleshy spear.

"Oh, hell," he groaned. "Oh, Sophie, be still, please—"

She couldn't. It was too much, too thick, too deep. She clung to him with her arms and legs tight and squirmed, panting in pain and aching pleasure, unable to take him, unable to let him go.

He was gasping. "Sophie, please—let me go!"

"No!" she cried, and held on with all her might. "I need—I have to—"

With a roar, he pulled away from her, his desperate strength too much. Then he was back, driving into her powerfully, fully, hard and fast. Something gave, sending a fiery bolt of agony through her. She shrieked, but still clung to him.

Then it was gone. He'd torn through the last resistance. Now it was only pleasure, slick and sweet and darkly hot as he drove helplessly into her again and again, his male growls of untrammeled lust drowning out her own trilling sighs.

His dominance and his heat and his very loss of control thrilled her. She exulted in her feminine power to excite him, in being beautiful and desirable to him. Each hot, powerful thrust and each dragging, exquisite withdrawal swept her away with tidal strength.

He cried out her name when he sank into her one last time, his orgasm ripping the breath from him.

It was only too bad it was the wrong name.

She ignored that flicker of pain, reaching instead for the pleasure of his release throbbing inside her. Ecstasy spiked again, mingling her cries with his groans, melding their hot breath and pounding hearts until she could not tell where she ended and where he began.

It was absolutely perfect. Though the manor might be crumbling about them, it might as well have been heaven.

He fell upon her then, dropping his face into her hair, easing himself to one side as his fading erection slipped from her body. She whimpered.

"I'm sorry," he said, breathless but full of remorse. "I should have been more careful. I shouldn't have—"

She lifted a weary hand to press her fingertips to his lips. "Shut it, Gray. It was splendid. You were splendid."

She thought about it for a moment. "I'm fairly sure I was splendid, as well."

He laughed damply and pulled her into his embrace. "You were indeed splendid. You were splendidest."

She sighed happily. "I expect I was." She snuggled into his arms and lay her head upon his chest. "You're mine now," she whispered sleepily.

Just as she faded into exhausted sleep, she thought she heard him murmur in response.

"Always."

Chapter Twenty~six

Sophie roused slowly, gradually becoming aware of every throbbing ache in her body. Make that her hard-ridden, hard-walked, hard-loved body. She stretched beneath the covers, sliding her hands over her naked-ness, testing her limbs. Nothing seemed permanently damaged. She opened her eyes.

The chamber was dark but for the fire. The room's grimy shabbiness was hidden in shadow, leaving only the gracious proportions and lovely ornate details to please the eye. With a bit of love and work, such a room could be a work of art—a room fit for a duke.

This duke. Her duke. The one she'd most wanted.

He was awake, looking out the bedchamber window at the moonlit estate outside.

He was naked and beautiful. No renaissance sculptor could have brought forth a finer creation.

"Gray?"

He turned to her with a smile, but the desolation in his eyes alarmed her.

"What is wrong?" Although she rather thought she knew.

He shook his head, still smiling. "Nothing."

"Horseapples," she declared firmly. Rising to her knees, she sat back on her heels with the sheet absently clasped to her bosom. His gaze warmed with desire and she was glad to see it—always!—but she held up a restraining hand when he came toward her.

"Gray, do you trust me?"

His eyebrows went up wickedly. "Implicitly. Are you going to tie me up again?" His smile slid to a comical leer. "Will you wear your corset this time?"

So arrested was she by a wave of lustful curiosity that she almost let him change the subject. She shook off the distraction just in time. "Wait." She scrambled back, away from his open hands. "I want to know: do you trust me?"

He stopped his forward rush and drew back a little. "I trust you, Sophie. I've always trusted you. You're the truest person I've ever known."

Oh. Well . . . best perhaps not to venture *there*, at least not quite yet. *I'll tell you the truth soon, my love, I promise.* Or would she? Graham thought he was a terrible rogue, but in truth he was the only man in his family who took honor and responsibility seriously at all. Would he even accept the money if he knew she'd stolen it by trickery?

Little faces, sunken and mournful . . .

Right. If it was wrong, then it was wickedness in good cause. She took a deep breath. "I want you to believe in me, Gray. I can—*we* can save Edencourt. I know it seems hopeless now, but you'll see. We'll have everything that we need."

His smile took on a curious twist and he tilted his head as he gazed at her. "Sophie, I know you're exceptionally clever—"

She took his hand and brought it to her heart, pressing it there. "I *promise* you, Gray." She tried to convey it with her eyes and her entire being. "Everything will be *perfectly fine*."

He frowned slightly over his smile. "Everything will be perfectly fine? How can anyone promise that? Life is never perfectly fine."

She squeezed the hand she held. "Believe. If you can't believe in the future, can you at least believe in me?"

As he gazed at her, his brow cleared and his eyes brightened for the first time. "I believe in very little," he said slowly. He brought her hands, still clinging to his, to the warmth of his lips. Then he smiled at her so unguardedly that it took her breath away.

"But I absolutely believe in you, Sophie Blake."

You're never going to be able to tell him. The secret will lie between you always.

So be it.

They made love again, softly and slowly this time. He was careful with her bruised flesh, so sweet with his gentle touch and his easy, cautious thrusts that it brought tears to her eyes to be so cherished.

"Don't cry, Sophie," he whispered in her ear. "I'll make sure you never need to cry again."

The tears came in a flood then and she clung to him, not sobbing but not able to stem the steady leaking from her eyes. Alarmed, he tried to slide from inside her, but she locked her legs about his waist and held him there.

"Love me," she whispered. "Please, I need you."

So he loved her, slowly and carefully, until her orgasm lifted her effortlessly into a shimmering sky and overwhelmed her there, turning her into a mindless scattering of stars. Her cries echoed throughout the empty halls, followed shortly by his harsher, deeper one.

Afterward, as he lay breathless upon her, his face tucked into her neck, she confessed one of her many secrets. "I love you," she told him. "I have loved you since the first time I beat you at cards, or perhaps even before . . . but I never believed in you. I am sorry for that. You deserve better."

He made a sound, then lifted his head. "No, I really don't—"

She stroked her fingers into his hair, then pulled gently. "Shut up, Gray. I'm proposing."

"Oh." He shut up, a grin forming.

She shook her head. "Stop smiling. This is serious."

"Right." The grin widened.

Her own smile tried to fight forth, then she sobered. "I always knew there was a good man inside you—the one who spent time with a lonely girl, the one who put her at her ease when she was doing her best to rid the house of breakables."

Graham winced, thinking of how he put her at ease, by making her realize his indifference.

"I believed that if someday you had the chance to

prove that man, you would," she went on. "You took your bloody sweet time doing it, but you have indeed proven yourself to me. I, on the other hand, behaved very badly indeed. I thought that if I became Sofia, that I could change my destiny with the shallow tools of allure and seduction. I—how shall I put this?—I turned into *you*."

"Oh," he said faintly. "Ouch."

"Precisely. However, I am happy to inform you that I am no longer you. I am no longer Sophie the Stick, either."

He gazed at her, his brow furrowed. "I never called you that."

"To my face."

He put his hands over his face. "Right."

She laughed. "Don't despair, Gray. You are no longer Graham Cavendish, layabout dandy. We are both changed."

"I like the new Sophie. I especially liked the new Sophie in nothing but my shirt."

She smiled. "I like the new Graham. I especially liked the new Graham in nothing at all."

He smiled back, slowly. "So are you going to propose, or shall I have my way with you again first?"

She rolled away from him and sat up on her knees. She held out one hand. He took it and knelt on the bed facing her. "I propose that we both propose again," she said.

He kissed her nose, for they were nearly of a height. "I propose that we accept that proposal."

She pushed him back slightly so she could gaze into his eyes. "I love you. I believe in you. I trust you. I want to be your duchess and help your people and have lots of tall, skinny fair-haired, green-eyed children and love them as fiercely as I love you."

He swallowed, for his throat had become tight. "I love you. I believe in you. I trust you. I want to be the finest duke I am able, with you at my side, and I want to father lots of tall, skinny reddish-haired, gray-eyed children and love them as fiercely as I love you . . . and I want you to believe that."

She smiled. "I believe, Graham. I will always believe in you."

THE TRIP BACK into London that morning was uneventful, if one didn't include spending a good half an hour persuading S.H. to allow two riders on his back once more.

"He used to be such a nice horse," Graham said, shaking his head. "I can't understand what's happened to him."

They mostly rode in silence, unwilling to let go of each other even for a moment. Despite the fact that Sophie found herself on horseback again so soon, for the first time in her life she allowed happiness to sweep her away, unguarded and unwary. After all, just as she'd assured Graham, everything was going to be perfectly fine.

All too soon, the dirty horizon of London came into

view. Then they were riding into the city itself. Cart-wheels clattered on cobbles. Shouts of laughter and anger rose above the clamor of rubbish bins and the calls of sellers. After the eerie quiet of Edencourt, the assault on Sophie's ears reminded her of that long ago day—only three short months ago!—when she'd arrived in London with two gowns and a trunk of stolen . . . er, unwanted books from Acton.

So much had changed since then. She had changed the most. Never again would she allow anyone to oppress her. Never again would anyone try! She would be the Duchess of Edencourt, rich and influential, with powerful friends and family!

Edencourt was not the only entity to be saved this day.

They came upon Brook House all too quickly. "I'm sorry to even stop here," she told Graham, "but Fortescue must be going out of his mind with worry. I only hope he hasn't sent word to Deirdre yet." And then there was the matter of her clothing. She could hardly get married in boys' trousers and shirt!

She kissed Graham good-bye and ran into the house. At the door, which promptly opened to a very relieved-looking butler, she turned to wave at him once more.

"I'll meet you at Eden House!"

Then she was inside, feeling half-naked without Graham at her side, reassuring Fortescue that of course she was all right and no, she hadn't been robbed by bandits, she'd been just fine, she'd been with His Grace the whole time, etc.

Fortescue only nodded at that. "Yes, miss. I knew he'd gone missing as well."

Sophie smiled. "The valet grapevine?"

He raised a brow. "Indeed, miss." Then he looked worried once more. "However, when I didn't hear from you yesterday, I did send a rider to their ladyships to see if you were possibly with them."

Sophie bit her lip. Oh, dear. Deirdre and Phoebe would be so worried. "We had best send more riders at once. Hopefully we can catch them before they panic."

Fortescue nodded. "Yes, miss."

Time was ticking away. "I must change quickly," she said, heading for the stairs. She flashed a smile over her shoulder. "I'm getting married today. Will you send Patricia up?"

At that, Fortescue turned to stone. "Patricia O'Malley is no longer employed at Brook House, miss. However, I hope you will accept my congratulations."

Sophie turned, alarmed. "Is she all right? Where did she go?"

Fortescue lifted his chin. "I'm sure I don't know, miss. I shall send a housemaid up to you, if that meets with your approval?"

He was certainly not happy about the situation, but Sophie hadn't the time to delve further. After the ceremony, though, she was determined to get some answers. The last time she'd seen Fortescue, he'd been a quivering pile of love-struck livery with perfect hair. Now he was a stiff, rigid poker of a man whose hair looked as though he'd been running his hands through it for days.

On her way up the stairs, she prayed that Patricia was all right and that Deirdre and Phoebe were not rushing home to save her.

GRAHAM LEFT THE bishop's office with a light heart and a special license in his hand. With his mother's ring still residing safely in his waistcoat pocket, he was one highly prepared bridegroom. Obtaining the license had been even easier than he'd thought.

He laughed to himself, thinking of what Sophie said when he told her where he was going.

Her eyes had widened. "Doesn't that require an enormous bribe?"

"For other people, perhaps." He'd grinned. "For me, only a tiny bit of blackmail. Himself happens to visit a certain girl at Mrs. Blythe's Palace of Pleasure—and I happen to play the occasional card game with that girl's rather indiscreet secret lover."

Sophie had smiled slowly. "Bad bishop. Good Graham."

S.H.—whom Graham was tempted to rename "Savage Horse"—stood outside the gates, sullenly submitting to his reins being held by a wary junior acolyte. "Take care, Your Grace. He bites."

Graham tried to defend the beast. "He's really very tired, you see."

The young man only stared at him uncomprehendingly and rubbed furtively at his robed arse.

"Right." He'd better return the thing to Somers.

Somers wasn't pleased. "What did you to do my

horse?" He walked around the beast as the three of them stood in the mews behind the house where Somers kept rooms. The horse put his ears back and bared its teeth at its owner, who stepped back in dismay and looked at Graham in horror. "Did you *beat* him?"

"Of course not!" Graham was truly offended. "I only rode him double out to Edencourt and then around the countryside for four hours yesterday and then double back to London this morning!" He thought for a moment. "He hasn't had anything but grass, though."

Somers looked as though he were about to cry. "Oh, you poor baby," he whispered to his horse. "It's all right now. Papa's here."

S.H. let go a long shudder and then planted his forehead wearily in Somers's chest, who then proceeded to murmur rather sickening endearments as he shot scathing looks at Graham.

"Ah . . . I'll just leave you two alone." Graham retreated swiftly. Really, he'd only borrowed a horse, for pity's sake!

The walk to Eden House wasn't terribly long. Graham cut through a few of the alleys to speed his way, whistling happily and thinking of plunking Sophie into yet another giant copper tub this evening after the simple ceremony was over. This time he'd feed her himself!

When he heard footsteps behind him, he paid no attention, distracted as he was by thoughts of soap and water and simply miles of long, elegant legs . . .

Abruptly he became aware that the footsteps were

running at him! He turned just in time to throw his arm up to deflect a blow.

"What the hell!" Without thinking, he reacted by throwing a fist wildly in the direction of his assailant's head. The fellow dropped the plank he wielded—dear God, the thing had nails sticking out of it!—and pressed his hands over his nose.

"Bloody hell!"

Graham saw then that the fellow had a cap pulled low over his brow and a black cloth tied over the lower half of his face. All that was visible were a pair of furious, pain-maddened eyes.

This wasn't good. Graham quickly glanced about. They were in an alley, far back behind several great houses. The grounds were extensive and the occupants and their servants weren't likely to respond to cries from the alley.

He should run. Of course, the fellow could simply run after him. He looked like a strong enough lout.

Graham balanced on the balls of his feet, ready to take action as soon as he knew the best course. Damn his father's excesses! If his wedding was interfered with by those damn creditors, Graham was quite prepared to bury the old duke's body in a pink silk gown as revenge!

"Tell your bastard employer that I'll pay what I owe someday," he told his attacker furiously. "Killing me won't make it happen any sooner!"

The man's eyes widened in surprise, then he shook it off. Reaching into his coat, he pulled out a long, gleaming knife.

Graham couldn't believe it. "I said, *not now!*" In a

swift motion given added speed by the absolute end of his patience with money troubles, he bent to retrieve the dropped plank and swung a single mighty blow at the damned thug's knees.

The man went down with a heavy thud, then began rolling around the filthy alley clutching his shins. "Aiii!"

"I'll bet those nails stung," Graham said without sympathy. He threw the plank down in disgust. "So by God, *leave me alone!*"

With that, he turned his back on the writhing minion and strode back to the street and on to Eden House.

On to Sophie.

Chapter Twenty~seven

When he arrived, out of breath and eager, he found Sophie was standing in the study, her arms crossed over her wrinkled bodice, her head tilted to one side as she studied the bear in the corner of the room.

She smiled at him over her shoulder, but then turned back to the bear. "It's missing a little something."

Graham smiled and leaned one shoulder on the door frame. "I couldn't agree more."

Sophie reached behind her neck to untie the strip of silk that had been pressed into service as a hair restraint.

She fussed with the bear for a moment, then stood back.

The fierce and brutal reminder of the old duke's lust for death now grinned clownishly over the giant pink bow now flopping about its neck.

Graham came forward and clasped his hands about Sophie's waist from behind, pulling her close to his chest. "Perfect."

Sophie leaned back against him and heaved a great sigh of happiness.

" '*Now the prince approached Cinderella, took her by the hand, and danced with her. Indeed, he would not dance with anyone else and would not let go of her hand. Whenever someone came and asked her to dance, he said, "She's my partner."* ' "

"She's my partner," Graham whispered into her ear. "Always."

She turned her face into his cheek. "I'm so happy that it simply doesn't seem real. It's a magic moment, a spell, a dream come true . . ."

Graham held her close. "It's real. I have the special license to prove it."

And he had Sophie, the truest thing he'd ever known. He had believed in nothing and no one—but he now believed in her. With her at his side, even with no money, he felt able to restore Edencourt with his bare hands, brick by brick if necessary.

Loving someone as good and true as Sophie might just possibly mean he'd been redeemed.

"I sent word to Tessa this morning," Sophie admitted. "She might even appear at the ceremony this afternoon."

Graham nodded. "She is the only family I have." Even resignation seemed too meager an emotion to cloak his glowing happiness. "Just picture it. You and I in front of the cleric, making our vows in an empty church—but for Tessa."

Sophie sighed. "She'll overdress and make rude comments and probably fling rotten tomatoes."

Graham laughed. "Why on earth would she object so strongly to our wedding? She stands to lose nothing by it."

But Sophie only moved away a step, out of the circle of his arms. "Your butler is a horrible man," she said. "Do you know he tried to make me go around to the servants' entrance?"

Graham laughed. "The next time you walk through that door, you'll be lady of this house. I can't think of a better revenge than that."

She smiled at that. He rejoiced to see it. Someday he was going to get to the bottom of the complex creature that was Sophie Blake.

He looked forward to every moment of exploration on the way.

"My love," he called softly. "Are you ready to get married?"

She swung around and blessed him with that blinding brilliant smile. "You bet your arse I am!"

THEY WERE TO be married in St. Mary of the Abbots Church. It was a quiet but gracious structure tucked deep into Kensington, on the far side of Hyde Park from Mayfair. A tall tower in the medieval style presided over the spacious gothic hall.

It was the traditional place of worship for the Cavendish family, though Graham hadn't set foot in it for decades. Still, his parents had wed there. As far as Graham knew, it was the only time his father had ever entered the place. His mother, however, was rumored to have been a frequent visitor. Perhaps, if such a thing existed, the spirit of his mother might linger to witness this day.

Would she have liked Sophie? For that matter, would she have liked him?

Surprisingly, the church was full. At the door Sophie hesitated, stunned by the shifting, fan-waving masses of apparently bored people she barely knew.

"Tessa told *everyone*."

Graham shrugged. "I am not displeased to have the entire *ton* as my witness. Besides, it might save hours of explanations later. We'll just let the gossips tell the world for us."

Sophie didn't look terribly reassured. "I don't like this."

Graham tightened his hand on hers. He simply couldn't seem to let go of her! "What harm is there in it? We haven't any secrets, after all."

Sophie lifted her chin and took a deep breath. "You're absolutely right. We have no secrets."

They walked up the aisle together, hand in hand. When the first head turned, a double wave of faces swung their way. So many faces—Sophie felt a little dizzied by it. She was glad she'd left her spectacles at Brook House.

"Everything will be perfectly fine," Graham whispered to her.

She laughed then, to hear her words turned back at her. He was right. She'd done it! She was here, in London, marrying an astonishing, handsome man she loved more than her own life and was about to become a wealthy duchess to boot!

Fairy stories did sometimes come true, it seemed.

Chapter Twenty~eight

There was something in the air between the couple at the altar, something perfect and pure and magical. Even the cleric, who had begun his task this afternoon with irritation and disapproval—the bishop handed out far too many of those special licenses!—began to feel the depth of the rote ceremony he'd repeated so many times. His reedy voice slowed and deepened and the vows grew in solemnity.

The crowd, composed as it was by the easily bored and the terminally distracted, became oddly still. Rapt, even. Hardened dowagers brought lace handkerchiefs to their eyes. Insouciant dandies dabbed at their cheeks with lace cuffs. The most jaded of women and the most dissipated of men all sat in spellbound silence, witness to something they had despaired of ever finding themselves.

True love.

In the far back of the church, Mr. Stickley wiped at his eyes without shame. Miss Blake had stepped out of the shadow of her shyness and had changed her life. Stickley wasn't worried in the slightest that Lord Eden court would use her shamelessly and waste her money. Any idiot could see that the man was entirely and deeply smitten. And she—why she glowed like ivory and fire, alive with love!

Her shimmering happiness filled Stickley with inspiration. Enough with his closed, dreary life of adding columns and collecting bits and baubles! In a few hours he would be handing over the Pickering fortune and then he would be free!

What he meant to do with that freedom was to find meaningful work and possibly, someday, even someone of his own to love!

The first thing, however, would be to rid himself of Wolfe forever.

"God, this is sickening."

At that gravelly and derisive voice, Stickley froze, then slowly turned to his left. As if conjured by the merest thought, Wolfe was even now making his way rudely down the row, ruthlessly stepping on toes. Of course, he was heading straight to Stickley.

Stickley shook his head in disapproval. "For pity's sake," he hissed. "Don't you know anyone but me?"

"Sod off, Stick," Wolfe growled. "I need to bloody sit down."

He forced himself into the sliver of space next to Stickley. Several neighbors gave whispered protest. "Sod off to you lot, too," Wolfe said with a sneer. "I'm an injured man."

Stickley slid as far from him as he could get, for Wolfe smelled none too lovely, even for him. "Where have you been sleeping, in a cowshed?"

"Stick, I hate you. I've always hated you. Shut up and watch the sickening duke take his horse-faced bride already. Rotting blue-blood bastard!"

Wolfe was never precisely cheerful, but this was foul-tempered even for him. Stickley determined that he could bear the rotter for one more hour. Then he would refuse to acknowledge his existence for as long as he lived.

Unfortunately, Wolfe continued to mumble obscenities. Finally, Stickley turned to him. "Wolfe, shut your ridiculous face!"

Wolfe, who had run rough-shod over Stickley for more than forty years, dropped his jaw and frankly stared at his partner.

Then acrid clouds of fury began to gather in his eyes. "Why you—"

A sudden murmur in the crowd caught Wolfe's attention. He rudely stood to get a better view of what caused such distraction in a crowd so recently sitting in enraptured silence.

Stickley watched his face change from sneering fury to amused anticipation.

"This," Wolfe stated with certainty, "is going to be good."

SOPHIE FELT LIKE her heart was flying right out of her chest. "I, Sophie Blake, do take this man . . ." *Oh, yes, please. Let me take him. Let me keep him forever. If only I can have him as my own, I shall never lie again for the rest of my life.*

A wave of whispers passed through the crowd. Sophie ignored it as she gazed into Graham's shining green eyes. If there was a heaven, then she was fairly sure she already knew what it looked like.

Then Graham broke their locked gaze, glancing toward the door in irritation. She saw him frown. "Tessa?"

Sophie blinked, emerging from her trance of happiness. She turned her head to look as well. In the brilliant daylight now pouring in through the open doors, she squinted to see that one of the entering figures was indeed Tessa. The other—

Oh, no. Oh, dear God, *no*.

Clumping through the church door on her cane, out of her bed for the first time in Sophie's memory, her heavy body madly swathed in woolens over outdated silk and lace, came none other than Mrs. Blake, helped solicitously along by Tessa.

The cleric became aware that neither man nor almost-wife was paying any attention to his holy words of marital warning.

He shut his Bible with a sharp snap and glared at the door. "What is the meaning of this interruption?" His crisp voice carried across the rising whispers.

Mrs. Blake stopped in the middle of the long aisle. Sophie's gut had gone to ice and her mind had frozen. All she could do was to grab for Graham's hand. "My love, I'm so sorry," she whispered.

Graham took her hand calmly. "I think I'd like to know what is going on as well. Who is this woman, Tessa?"

Sophie dizzily contemplated a strategic faint. It would hardly require any deception at all for she felt as though her body had ceased to exist but for the pounding of her heart. It was all very clear now. The crowd of spectators, the impeccable timing—all orchestrated by Tessa to achieve the moment of maximum impact.

Then it was too late.

"I am Mrs. Blake, the last surviving granddaughter of Sir Hamish Pickering." Mrs. Blake leaned all her weight on Tessa and raised her cane to point at Sophie. "This woman is *not* my daughter!"

MOMENTS AGO GRAHAM had been completely happy. He'd never been prouder of anything than of this day. For a man like him to earn a woman like this? It was nothing short of magic.

Now, the rising babble swirled about them. The cleric, who had no idea what the woman's claim signified, was still objecting to her rude interruption of His Grace's wedding. The crowd was chattering madly to each other, wildly curious, already gossiping as if this was the biggest scandal of the year.

"My Sophie is dead!" the strange woman was saying stridently, intent on making her point above the chaos. "This girl—" Frustrated by the lack of concentration of the masses, the woman brought her cane down onto the back of the nearest pew with a mighty crack. The report silenced all but the most determined tattlers. Shrugging back her shoulders, the woman looked about her disdainfully. "As I was saying—"

She raised her cane to point at Sophie again. "This girl is nothing but a servant in my house! A thief who stole my daughter's name and my money to bring herself to London!" She sneered. "She's nothing but a penniless orphan who turned on me viciously in return for my kindness!"

Graham turned to look at Sophie, his lips prepared to quirk in laughter at the absurdity of such claims. She didn't answer, but only stared back at him, growing paler by the second. The storm of guilt in her eyes should have told him, but he still couldn't bring himself to believe.

"It isn't true," he said slowly. "You would never— not you!"

He felt a tremor move through her and it shook him as well, the truth moving into him by way of her hand in his.

Graham's hands were icy and unfeeling. Did he still hold Sophie's hand in his?

Moments returned to play again in his memory. Tessa deriding Sophie's arrival in London, alone, shabby and oddly without possessions for a lady gently born. Sophie's surprising ability to take care of herself, even against the roughest customers.

Sophie coming to his room in the night, forcing a terrible, wonderful choice upon him.

"Sophie—" But of course, her name wasn't Sophie, was it? Graham blinked and shook his head, desperately trying to turn the world back to its rightful position.

She lifted her chin then and the answer was there, in

her fathomless gray eyes, swimming in guilt and regret and hope—really, that was ridiculous! Hope?

He dropped her hand and stepped back from her. "You *lied?*"

She moved toward him. "Graham, I can explain!"

He held up his hand sharply. *"Don't* speak to me." He couldn't bear it. The vast and billowing happiness of a few moments ago was revealed to be precisely what he'd always suspected until he met Sophie: complete and utter shit.

No. Not Sophie. Not Sofia either, obviously. Graham gazed into her damp, shattered eyes. *"Who the bloody hell are you?"* he bellowed over the din.

The room quieted instantly. Everyone who was everyone held their breath, waiting for more delicious scandal. Graham saw the liar before him swallow hard.

"She is Sadie Westmoreland," Mrs. Blake announced. "An orphan, taken in to be paid companion when my dear Sophie died from influenza."

"That's not all," Tessa said quickly. She prodded the woman's story with a whisper in her ear.

Mrs. Blake reddened righteously. "Yes, that's right! She robbed me! Call the watch! I demand justice! She stole two hundred pounds from me!"

Tessa's voice rang out again, her tone one of razor-sharp scorn. "So that she could come to London and *pretend* to be a lady!"

Sophie lifted her chin, but the curse of the red-haired smote her down. Her fair skin burned like a scarlet beacon, betraying her humiliation and shame.

The titters began from the area of the church where

Lilah was, but she could hardly be blamed for the fact that the laughter spread like a contagion, until the entire room rocked with laughter, either openly or guiltily, but laughing just the same.

Except for Graham.

Graham had gone as white as paper, with only his green eyes shining fury and humiliation at her.

Sadie—for she could own her name now, even in her own mind—watched the love she'd found writhe and die on the floor between them. She'd killed it herself, by filling it with lies.

She was Cinderella with a vengeance—Cinderella who lied, cheated and stole to get to the ball—only to have her own misdeeds shatter her dreams at the stroke of midnight.

She turned from her prince then, for she couldn't bear to see what she'd lost—or rather, destroyed. Instead, she lifted her chin and gazed down the aisle at the woman she'd learned to despise.

"Mrs. Blake has mistaken one little detail," she said clearly. "I was *never* paid."

Chapter Twenty~nine

Behind Graham, the cleric cleared his throat. "Your Grace . . . the ceremony is unfinished. What do you wish me to do?"

At first thought, all Graham felt was blinding relief. He wasn't married to this creature at all! It wasn't too late to find a rich wife and save Edencourt and put this whole horrendous day down to muddled thinking, poor decisions made in the devastating grief of losing his entire family. No one would blame him for a thing.

Except that he'd spent last night with Sophie in his bed. He'd lain with her and taken her virginity—she hadn't lied about that, he knew!—and that left her ruined.

He could almost hear his father's voice in his mind. "To hell with her then! It's not as though she's a lady! She's just a friendless, nameless girl who tricked you into it. Toss her into the street and think no more of it!"

True enough, as it stood.

Being broke and wed to a thief would destroy him. And Edencourt. He could beggar his house and sell off all his buttons, but that would only feed his folk for one winter. He needed to restore the estate entirely or it would always be a money drain!

Yet, being ruined and unwed would destroy *her.* Sadie.

When he'd taken her into his arms, he'd been making a vow of sorts, hadn't he? In his own mind, he'd committed to wed her in that moment.

In sickness and in health. For richer or for poorer.

Lifting his gaze, he stared at the stranger before him who wore Sophie's beautiful face. She gazed back at him, her finely carved features pale as death.

She must have seen his decision in his expression, for she held up a hand to stop him.

Of course, that was only because she didn't know what the decision was.

"Continue," he barked at the cleric.

Astonishingly, instead of subsiding now that her cause was won, Sadie Westmoreland only protested further.

"Graham, no! You mustn't! I can't help you anymore!"

He ignored her. She tugged her hand, prying at his grip with her free one, trying to liberate herself. "Graham, do not do this! I haven't a farthing to my name! You need to find someone else, someone rich who can help you save Edencourt!"

Her words meant nothing to him. It was as if she spoke another language altogether. The language of lies, perhaps. It didn't matter. It was all lies, every word ever spoken on this earth. Nothing was true.

He took her by the arm and turned them both to fully face the priest. "Continue!"

When she protested further, he silenced her swiftly. "Everything is going to be *perfectly fine.*"

A tiny sound escaped her, like the gasp after a death blow. Then she went still and silent. Graham kept his gaze straight ahead, refusing to believe in the tears that flowed unceasingly down the exquisite planes of her face.

He remained there, grimly mouthing his vows, until it was over. The cleric blinked at him hesitantly. "Is there a ring, Your Grace?"

His mother's ring. Graham's hand went to his waist-coat. He could feel the ring there—the ring he'd so eagerly looked forward to placing on Sophie's hand, making her his forever and always. It was the perfect "Sophie" ring, simple and elegant and unpretentious—except that Sophie didn't actually exist.

The damned thing even *fit* the lying, thieving creature, for pity's sake!

He dropped his hand as if the ring had burned him. "No," he stated firmly. "I do not have a ring for this woman."

The cleric hesitated. "Then . . . you may kiss the bride."

Kiss the bride. The words took a long moment to sink into Graham's brain. Then volcanic fury erupted through his icy shock and loss. Yes, by God, he *would* kiss the bride!

There, before God and two hundred witnesses, he pulled his adversary roughly into his arms. Thrusting his fingers deep into her silken pile of hair, he tipped her head back and brought his hard mouth down on her soft one. For a long, passionate moment, he bestowed upon that beautiful stranger all his rage and pain and thwarted, lost, betrayed love—

And kissed her good-bye.

Then he released her, spun on his heel and strode out of the church without a word.

He had to get away from her, away from those eyes, from that hauntingly elegant face, away from the magnetism that drew him, had always drawn him, had made him feel more alive than he'd ever felt before, had made him believe for the first time that there might be more to people than only sin and selfishness.

You wanted her to be real. You wanted to believe that she was good and true because she was the only person you've ever known who didn't think you were a bloody poor waste of air.

Who was worse—the liar, or the fool who chose to believe the lies, despite all evidence to the contrary?

His future in ruins, he had no plans but that of getting drunk and staying drunk.

Wolfe, sitting in the back, was doubled over in silently hysterical laughter. Tears of relief streamed down his face.

Stickley gazed at him in horror, but Wolfe only grinned at the partner he so despised.

"I've been sober for far too long," he wheezed when he found the breath. "I think I'm going to have a little drinkie to celebrate the nuptials of the Dukc and Duchess of Edencourt." He let out his breath on a long happy sigh.

No more worries, no more schemes. No plan at all, but that of getting drunk and staying drunk for days!

Chapter Thirty

Sadie slipped out the back of the church, her exit covered by the general hubbub and excitement. Since the St. Mary Abbots church was located solidly in the center of Kensington, it wasn't a terribly long walk to Mayfair and Brook House.

It only felt like a hundred miles.

As she approached the great house, it occured to her that they might not let her in. After all, she had no claim to relationship and had perhaps criminally defrauded them all in some way.

Yet everything she owned was in that house. She must chance that no one had yet heard the news.

She didn't have to knock. The door opened onto the sternly handsome face of Fortescue. "Your Grace."

What was left of Sadie's shattered heart slithered to her knees. Bad news certainly traveled like lightning.

Yet Fortescue opened the door wide and bowed her through. "Will you be staying long, Your Grace?"

She lifted her chin. There was no judgment in the butler's eyes. She wondered why. "I only came to gather my things."

He nodded. "Your dressmaker has already been here. He left word that you are to keep what you were given and that he wishes you well."

Sadie blinked. She'd not expected such kindness from Lementeur, for him she had defrauded worst of all, except for Graham. Then she remembered his words.

"A poor Cockney lad who dreamed only of beautiful fabrics and fine lace."

Well, perhaps Lementeur, the Liar, who slipped seamlessly into Society on talent alone, knew a bit about playing a part.

Fortescue was gazing at her evenly. There was nothing at all in his smooth face, but somewhere in the back of his eyes she saw . . . empathy? "Fortescue, what am I to do now?"

His lids dropped slightly, shuttering that glint of fellow-feeling. "I'm sure I'm the last person one should ask, Your Grace."

Should she go to Eden House and play at being its lady? Should she live with Graham in hateful silence for the rest of her life?

Well, it wasn't likely he'd be willing to live with her, was it? Perhaps there was an empty house, a small one, somewhere on the estate where she could live, a duchess in exile.

A princess in a tower after all.

The first step must be to go upstairs and pack. The next step she would think about when that task was done. Surely if she kept putting one foot in front of the other, she'd walk through all this somehow.

Oh, Graham. Why did you do it? Why did you make

me your duchess? Now I carry all of Edencourt on my conscience as well!

Then to her horror, Sadie saw Deirdre and Phoebe arrive at the rear of the entrance hall. She shot a panicked glance at the still open front door.

The knocker was back in place.

"Their ladyships came home in response to my first messsage," Fortescue informed her in a low voice. "They were very worried about you."

They didn't look worried now. Phoebe, who was sweet-faced and as kind as she was pretty, was blinking at her as if she'd never seen her before.

Deirdre, stunning, golden-haired beauty, was frankly glaring, her arms folded and her eyes narrowed.

Sadie debated running for her life, but since she hadn't anywhere in particular she needed to be for the rest of that life, she forced herself to put one foot in front of the other until she stood before them both.

Phoebe, who although she was good-natured should never be mistaken for a fool, frowned at her. "Sophie is dead, is that correct?"

Sadie didn't even bother trying not to laugh bitterly. "I didn't kill her, if that's what you're asking. I was brought to Acton nearly a year after the influenza struck. I never even met her." She tilted her head. "You did, however. When you were about five years old. Mrs. Blake talked about it. Do you remember Sophie?"

Phoebe shook her head regretfully. "No, I don't."

Sadie shrugged. "By all accounts, she was a very nice girl. Everyone used to talk about how quiet she was, but knowing Mrs. Blake, that might have simply been because she couldn't get a word in edgewise."

Deirdre made a derisive noise. "Is that how you talk about your benefactress?"

Sadie gazed at the woman she'd learned so much from. Deirdre had resisted Tessa's vicious oppression for many years, to emerge whole and victorious in the end. "She was never my mother, Dee. She was my warden."

Wary sympathy flashed in those sapphire eyes, but stubborn Deirdre wasn't one to give up that easily. "You lied to us," she accused. "You lied to *Meggie*."

Sadie took that blow directly to the heart, just as she deserved to. "I know. I'm sorry. I would not hurt Meggie for anything—"

"You already have!"

"—but since I didn't know she would take part when I began this, I had no way to prevent it once begun."

Phoebe leaned to Deirdre. "She has a point."

Deirdre shook her head. "She doesn't deserve a point!"

Sadie sighed. "Dee, Phoebe, I'm sorry. What can I do except to apologize?"

Phoebe tilted her head. "I think I'd like to hear the whole story. Dee, tell your magnificent butler to serve us some tea and cakes, will you? I'm absolutely famished and S—the duchess looks as though she's about to faint."

Deirdre grimaced. "She always looks like that." But she waved her fingers at Fortescue anyway. "Put us somewhere quiet, Fort. I have a feeling this will take a while."

It didn't, not really. After all, her life had very little to recommend it.

"I was orphaned at the age of seven. I don't remember my parents at all. I know their names and where they had lived, but it is only information from a piece of paper. I don't know why that is, but all I remember is the orphanage."

Phoebe leaned forward sympathetically. "Was it very bad?"

Sadie shrugged. "I had nothing to compare it to. It was very cold in the winter, but we slept two by two. We didn't go hungry, but the food was very plain. Every day we worked to maintain the orphanage, cleaning and gardening and washing, but it wasn't brutal work. We weren't beaten especially, but neither were we educated. I could already read very well, I think, for I used to borrow books from the staff and read whenever I could."

She gazed at the fire, her thoughts streaming back years. "The worst of it was always the knowledge that we weren't wanted. Now and then people would come to choose a child for their own. The youngest and prettiest went first." She tilted the corner of her mouth at Deirdre. "You'd have been gone in a flash."

Deirdre's face took on an arrested expression, as if seeing her own status clearly for the first time. "I'm an orphan, too."

Phoebe smiled slightly. "There but for the grace of God go you," she misquoted.

Deirdre looked grumpy. "Blast. How am I supposed to sustain my righteous anger now?"

Phoebe patted her hand. "You'll survive." She turned to Sadie. "Go on."

"There isn't a great deal to tell, I'm afraid. One day, Mrs. Blake's housekeeper came to take me away. I was very excited. I thought I was going to have a new mother. Instead, she used me as an unpaid servant, a pair of feet to fetch whatever she needed, whenever she needed it. For years I truly tried to please her. Then I stopped attempting the impossible. I began to dream of ways to leave. Four months ago, Tessa sent Sophie's portion through the post."

"Which you stole." Phoebe's tone didn't accuse. She merely sought confirmation of fact.

Sadie nodded. "Which I stole. And spent to come here to London and play the part of Sophie Blake."

Deirdre nodded. "I like it. A clean, simple plan. Those are the best."

Phoebe turned to look at her. "Deirdre!"

Deirdre shrugged. "What? I told you I couldn't hold on to a good mad."

"It was a simple plan," agreed Sadie. "Especially since I had no intention of vying for a duke. All I did was take money from a girl who didn't need it anymore. It was only a ticket to London and perhaps some new life other than unpaid servitude to a woman who could care less if I lived or died. Theft, yes, but since I still have most of it, I'd be happy to give it back to Tessa."

Deirdre waved a hand. "Don't bother. It wasn't hers. It was parceled out by Stickley and Wolfe as per the will."

"Right. Of course." Sadie smoothed the skirts of the pink silk she'd chosen to be her wedding gown. "I journeyed to Primrose Street to live with you all there."

"And you met Graham." Phoebe's wise, sky-blue eyes met hers in sympathy. "And fell in love."

Unexpectedly, Sadie's hot, dry eyes filled. She pressed both hands to her face, forcing the tears back. There was no use crying as if she hadn't done all of this to herself with her eyes wide open.

"I wanted to win the inheritance for Graham," she said dully. "So that I could have him and he could save his people. I never thought to even try before then. It simply wasn't for me."

She lifted her face and gazed at them without the slightest pretense. "I'm not sorry I lied. I'm sorry I hurt you, but my alternative was to rot in servitude for the rest of my life, not even able to save a few pennies, always fearing that I was about to be thrown out without pension or references. It was better to risk all than to continue thus."

"I should say so!" Deirdre declared stoutly. "I'd like to give that Mrs. Blake a piece of my mind right now!"

"And we had no idea that Edencourt was so badly off, did we, Dee?" Phoebe shook her head. "Those poor people."

"I don't think Graham realized it either, until he got his hands on the estate records. He blames himself so, thinking that every coin he tossed away on shallow entertainments stole the bread out of some child's mouth."

"Well . . . but it did," Phoebe said slowly. "And now he must live with what he's done. And so must you."

Sadie straightened. "I know that. Graham had one chance to change everything and I stole it from him."

Deirdre laughed out loud. "Sadie, are you under the impression that Graham Cavendish is some sort of innocent *victim?*" She shook her head. "Any guilt he might be feeling, he's certainly earned the right to it."

Phoebe nodded. "I'm assuming that you weren't alone in that bed last night."

"What?" Sadie blinked. "How did you—"

Phoebe smiled. "I was guessing, but it looks like I was spot on." She glanced at Deirdre. "You owe me a bonnet and two reticules."

Deirdre stuck out her hand absently. Phoebe shook it with satisfaction. Sadie crinkled her brow. "You're betting on Graham?"

"On you, actually," Deirdre said. "I told Phoebe you'd have him by the time the Season ended. She wagered you'd never take that long!"

Sadie looked at Phoebe. "Thank you . . . I think."

Phoebe stood. "Sadie, go upstairs and go to bed." She held up a hand when Sadie started to protest. "Don't be an idiot. You may not be our cousin, but you saved Deirdre's life and you've been a good friend to me. We aren't going to toss you out on the street over a little matter of twenty thousand pounds."

"Twenty-eight thousand pounds," Deirdre corrected. "At last count. Those solicitors must be feeding that account the good oats."

Stunned, Sadie let herself be directed up to her old room. A tray with more steaming tea awaited her and, yes, a steaming bath as well.

It wasn't over yet. Fortescue brought a summons from the Marquis, as soon as she had freshened up.

Her wedding day had lasted a year at least. Exhausted and drained, she bathed in silence, drank the tea and changed into the simplest Lementeur frock she had.

SADIE HAD NOT been looking forward to facing the powerful and influential Marquis of Brookhaven or his fiercely protective half-brother Lord Raphael. Lying to the women loved by men such as these had surely been one of her more foolish mistakes.

She raised her chin and entered the marquis's study in a swinging stride that was nothing like Sophie's shamble or Sofia's saunter. "Good afternoon, my lords."

Calder was seated behind his giant desk. He did not rise, but only gazed at her for a long moment. "She's still here," he said to his brother, who stood next to him with a scowl on his face and his arms folded.

Rafe nodded. "I can see that. What I don't see is why your butler ever let her in your house."

Calder quirked a brow. "I've been meaning to have a word with Fortescue about that."

"Be there somethin' I can do for ye, my lord?"

Sadie didn't jump when Fortescue appeared at her elbow, apparently called to materialize from the ether by the very murmuring of his name. Sadie was quite used to the butler's penchant for eavesdropping—and she had noted him lingering in the hall before she'd entered the study.

What she hadn't expected was to hear the dignified and somber fellow speak to his master with a pitch-perfect Irish accent. She didn't turn to look at him, thank heaven, or she would have missed Calder's priceless reaction.

The mighty marquis gazed at his loyal manservant as if the man had insanely burst into song. Lord Raphael slid the fingers of one hand over his lips as he watched his brother, but his twinkling brown eyes betrayed his laughter. He and Sadie exchanged a reluctantly amused glance as Calder sputtered.

"B—er, really . . . what?"

Fortescue only gazed at the marquis with cool expectation. In response, Calder seemed to feel as though he were required not to notice anything amiss. If his reaction was laughable, his throat-clearing, panicked attempt to do just that was nigh unto hysterical. "Er, yes, well . . ." He gazed desperately over Fortescue's right shoulder. "That will be all, Fortescue."

Sadie gave up and laughed out loud. What difference did it make when the marquis was surely about to have her tossed from the house, duchess or no?

Rafe openly snickered as Fortescue left the study with his dignity unmarred. "That point went to the butler, I believe, Calder."

Calder wiped his hand over his face. "Is he Irish? I didn't know."

Sadie gazed at him in speculation. "Does that matter to you, my lord?"

Calder blinked. "Eh? Oh, no, not as such. It was simply so . . . *bizarre*. It was as though my horse erupted into French curses." He shook his head. "I wonder what else I don't know about the man?"

If Sadie was not mistaken, what Calder didn't know was that his faithful household manager was about to take himself off after a certain fleeing housemaid. Still, it wasn't her business to say. She had her own worries at the moment.

She folded her arms and gazed at the two men before her. It suddenly occurred to her that she outranked them both. Poor she might be and currently unsure of precisely what lay in store for her, but she was legally and most securely the Duchess of Edencourt. With that thought in mind, she tilted her head and smiled more brightly than she felt. The two men blinked as if blinded by a bright light. Why did people keep doing that?

"I have just left the marchioness and her ladyship," she said congenially. "They seem quite happy with the both of you."

Calder and Rafe shook off their bedazzlement.

"I should hope so," muttered Rafe.

Calder looked at her speculatively. "You look very different, Miss Blake."

Sadie tossed her head. "I can't imagine why, Mr. Marbrook."

A twitch at the corner of his lips was Calder's only reaction to her heavy-handed correction. Rafe behaved somewhat better. He bowed deeply. "My apologies, Your Grace." Then he grinned at her, very much the old Rafe. "You look smashing, Sophie."

"Why thank you, my lord." She curtseyed. "But my given name is Sadie."

"Rafe, don't be drawn in." Calder's gaze was still cool. "This woman has lied to us all."

Sadie nodded calmly. "Indeed I have, although I assure you it was out of no desire to profit from you in any way."

"Truly?" Calder raised a brow. "Yet you moved into my house in my absence and apparently you've done something mystifying to my butler."

Sadie shook her head, her smile turning wry. "That part wasn't me. I blame that on a different redhead altogether."

"Ah." Rafe grasped it immediately. "The poor sod."

Calder looked sour. "I wish someone would explain it to me." He held up a hand. "Later. At the moment, I would like to know why I shouldn't toss Miss Bl— Lady Edencourt into the street."

Sadie continued to smile. He really was a dear man. So protective of Deirdre—as if a spitfire like Deirdre needed such a defender! "You may try," she said sweetly.

Rafe held up both hands in surrender. "That tears it. She must be related."

Sadie gazed at him fondly as well. "Only in spirit, I fear." Then she frowned. "Although . . . if Tessa is stepmother and cousin to Graham, then . . ." She blinked. "I *am* family!" Was that right? "Hmm. Well, perhaps not."

"Close enough for us!" Deirdre came to stand beside Sadie, facing down her husband. "Isn't that right, Phoebe?"

Phoebe entered and took up position on the opposite flank. "Absolutely."

Calder and Rafe gazed at the three of them, posing with identical arch expressions and folded arms. An unassailable fortress of feminine clout.

Rafe swore under his breath. "We're outgunned, old man."

Calder scowled. "Don't cave so quickly."

Rafe shook his head. "Outgunned, outnumbered and frankly, out of enthusiasm." He shrugged. "I *like* Sadie."

Calder harrumphed. "I never said I didn't." He gave it one last try. "Deirdre, you must think of Meggie! Do you really want to expose her to someone you don't know the first thing about?"

Phoebe shook her head. "Ouch, Calder. That wasn't wise."

From behind their skirts, a smaller, slightly grubbier version of female ferocity came stomping to the fore. Meggie took a stand in front of Sadie, her arms folded and her snapping brown eyes fixed on her father. "Papa, be *nice*. Sadie has had a very hard day."

Sadie felt her steel melt just a bit, leaving her with a tremble in her belly that just might turn into tears. She dropped her pose to drift one hand over Meggie's jet-dark hair. "Thank you, Nutmeg. I was afraid you were angry with me."

Meggie twisted her neck to look up at her. "Sadie, you had to lie. You were an orphan. *I* know what it's like when no one wants you."

That did it. Calder went down like a felled tree. "But Meggie . . ." His face looked ready to crumple. "I always wanted you! I just didn't . . . I didn't know what to do . . ."

Deirdre snickered and Phoebe cleared her throat. Sadie had to smile.

Rafe shook his head. "Brother, you didn't stand a chance."

Meggie looked at her father with sympathy, a kindly conqueror regarding a devastated enemy. "It's all right, Papa. I know you want me *now*."

Sadie thought Calder might cry. She patted Meggie on the head. "That's enough, pet. Let the poor man come up for air."

Phoebe smiled. "It's settled then. Sadie may stay as long as she likes."

Rafe smiled back at his wife as if he had no choice but to do so. Likely he didn't, smitten as he was. "I'm glad we've resolved that, but what of Graham? From what we heard, he's in serious trouble with his estate."

Calder seemed to be recovering, for he nodded regretfully. "I'd be happy to help monetarily but I don't think Graham would take it. I know I wouldn't."

"Food," Sadie suggested quickly. "You can send food to the cottagers. He'll accept that, I know he will."

Phoebe's eyes brightened. "Oh, yes, that's marvelous. Even an idiot man can't turn down food for the children."

Rafe looked offended. "Oy!"

Phoebe waved a hand affectionately. "I didn't mean you, darling. You're hardly ever an idiot man anymore."

Rafe didn't seem all too sure he'd been complimented. "Er . . . thank you?"

Calder was gazing at Sadie in speculation. "Perhaps you'll do, after all," he murmured.

Sadie saw the gaze and raised him one eyebrow. "Perhaps you'll do, as well."

Deirdre clapped her hands. "Swords *down*, I say!"

Abruptly, Sadie felt every moment of her "very hard day." Her head pounded and her body ached from too many hours' unaccustomed riding and from . . . well, *Graham*. She raised a hand to one cheek. "Thank you all for your concern," she said. "But I'll only be staying long enough to gather my things . . ." The room seemed to tilt just a bit. It seemed like weeks since she'd slept.

Meggie peered up at her. "Are you going to faint? Because if you are, you should be sure to stand next to a sofa or something."

Deirdre put a supporting arm about her. "Calder, look what you've done!"

Calder gaped. "But . . . I . . ."

Phoebe came to her side. "Rafe, get some water!" Rafe took off at a run.

Then Fortescue was there. "Her Grace's room is ready. There's a bath waiting and I'll send up a tray at once."

Sadie, who in the last day had been loved, accused, wed, abandoned and now, at last, embraced, allowed herself to be ushered upstairs and put to bed like a child by the closest thing to a family she had ever known.

Chapter Thirty-one

The whiskey tasted like piss. Graham glared suspiciously at the decanter. What had Nichols been up to?

Frustrated and edgy, he threw the decanter into the hearth of his study. It shattered on the bricks, the whisky flaring in a momentary explosion of blue flame.

That decanter was fine crystal. You could have put food on someone's table for a month!

When had his inner voice become female—and always right?

Everything that could be sold would be sold. He should put the London house up for auction. He didn't believe it was included in the entail. Perhaps it would be enough to quiet the most vociferous—and violent!—creditors and purchase new roofs for the cottagers still determined to stick out the winter at Edencourt.

After that, he truly would be poverty-stricken.

He was not frightened for himself. He no longer seemed to possess an appetite and after the last twenty-four hours it was quite evident that he wasn't capable of ever drinking enough to shut out that tart, lying voice in his head. So he'd need no food or drink, only a roof over his head and chair to sulk in.

He'd be that mad, brooding duke in the crumbling manor, the one mothers used to frighten their offspring into obedience.

Be good or the duke will get you.

Shadows of his own childhood terror shivered through him. Spurred to restless action, he sprang to his feet—

But he had nowhere to go. There was no one waiting for him at Primrose Street but Tessa. There was no caustic strawberry-blond with endless legs and vastly too much brain for her own good.

Where did she go when you abandoned her at the church?

He hadn't abandoned her. She'd been safe and sound, in the middle of a crowd.

A crowd who despised her. Even the priest was casting her hostile glances.

Not his concern. Not his love, not his darling. Not his Sophie.

Just your wife.

He rubbed a hand over his face. His wife, Sadie.

Sadie.

He said it out loud, trying it out. "Sadie, Duchess of Edencourt." It sounded all wrong. A washerwoman's name and a title second only to the queen's. The combination was ridiculous.

He heard delighted laughter in his mind. *Ridiculous yet perfect.*

"See, I told you he was drunk."

Graham didn't bother to turn. "You missed my wedding, Deirdre."

"That's fair. You missed mine." She strolled into the room, followed by Phoebe. Graham waited for their smitten husbands to enter as well, then let his breath out in relief when they didn't. He thought they were all right most of the time, but the last thing he wanted around him now was love so thick in the air that one could hardly breathe.

I can't breathe. I can't feel my heart beating. I can't live without my Sophie.

Who didn't exist.

What a pickle.

He pressed both palms to his head, hoping the pressure would drive the voice out. Perhaps he should consult the priest. Didn't they do exorcisms from time to time?

The voice in his mind shut up, but there was no silencing Deirdre when she was on a roll.

"What are you doing, sitting here in the dark, drinking?" She strode to the window and whipped the curtains wide, letting in a horrible, harsh glare. She turned to regard him with her fists on her hips. "You have important matters to see to!"

Graham blinked at the sunlight currently piercing his brain with white-hot needles. "Shut that, would you? The carpet will fade. I might have to sell it soon."

Deirdre waved a sheaf of papers in his face. "You must do something to help Sadie!"

Phoebe took pity on Graham and shut the draperies partway. "Deirdre, why don't you take some of that fury out on Graham's execrable butler? I think we could all stand a cup of tea."

Deirdre exhaled in frustration, thrust her papers at Phoebe, then swept from the room in a righteous sputter. Poor Nichols.

Phoebe straightened the sheets as she watched Graham sink into the large chair behind the massive desk. "This is the strangest room," she said conversationally.

Graham grunted. "You should have seen it before the bonfire."

She smiled. "There's nothing like a good bonfire. I like the bear, though. That looks like something So— Sadie would do."

Graham closed his eyes. She was in his very blood and bones. What did it matter if traces of her kept appearing elsewhere? "She added the bow."

"Ah." Phoebe came to seat herself on the low stool at his knee. "Graham, I haven't known you that long. I've known Sadie no longer. Yet it seems to me that she truly loves you." She sighed. "She's so very sad."

She was at Brook House. Of course.

Safe and sound.

He didn't care. Not a whit. Still, something deep inside ceased its circling worry and settled down wearily to mourn instead.

Stupid loyal hound. Stupid loyal heart.

He tipped his head back on the chair. "Phoebe, what does it matter if she loves me? I don't even know the woman."

"Graham, if you don't quit that tuneless drone I'm going to dump this putrid tea in your lap."

Graham didn't open his eyes. "Oh, lovely. Deirdre's back."

Aren't you just a bit sick of yourself by now? He was, actually. He opened his eyes.

"I think you ought to be good and sick of yourself at this point," Phoebe pointed out.

"I know I am," agreed Deirdre.

Still, his aching heart seethed. "She ruined me!" In the financial sense, of course, not the other. Except that actually, she'd ruined him there as well.

Phoebe glared at him. "Sophie only did it for you, Graham!"

"She lied!"

Deirdre snorted. "One lie. One teensy little lie. Surely you've lied to someone, somewhere, haven't you, Graham?"

"But—"

Phoebe weighed in. "She was all alone!"

That struck him. He knew what that was like.

Phoebe continued. "You put her on a pedestal. That's not fair. Sooner or later she was bound to make a misstep and fall. She's only human."

He hadn't thought of her as human. He'd thought of her as . . . as . . . as some sort of icon—a symbol of truth and decency and blah, blah, blah—God, he was sick of his own circling thoughts!

It was easy to blame her for everything, but Edencourt had been in trouble since before she was even born and it was going to remain in trouble for a very long time. Even with some astounding influx of cash, there was no miracle cure for the estate. It was going to be hard, slogging, gradual work—work that he hadn't wanted to admit that he might not be up to.

He'd thought he needed Lilah's money—but that was simply the old Graham, hoping someone would take away the hard parts. He raised his head from his hands and looked at Deirdre and Phoebe.

Sadie Westmoreland had lied to them as well. She had tricked them and made fools of them and even tried to steal their inheritance!

Hell, she'd tried to *give* him his heritage, all wrapped up in a pretty pink silk bow.

All she'd stolen from him was his heart.

But then, he had given that willingly, hadn't he?

Deirdre was watching him closely. "Lementeur told us that you had your chance to back out of the wedding. Have you really asked yourself why you didn't?"

He ran a hand through his hair. "I couldn't ruin her."

Phoebe smiled at him. "But you could ruin yourself?"

Deirdre's satisfied smile would have put a well-fed cat to shame. "Sounds like love to me."

Love.

"Bloody hell!" Graham stood abruptly. "I forgot! That Blake woman told me she intended to press charges!"

THE BITTER, VENGEFUL Mrs. Blake had taken up residence at the house on Primrose Street. Tessa, having won the battle to save Deirdre's inheritance, had graciously allowed it, then within the hour had packed up her things and moved in with her new lover.

When someone was even more poisonous than Tessa, that someone bore watching.

Graham, Phoebe and Deirdre mounted the steps of the house in unison. When Tessa's slackard butler finally answered the knocker, he found himself face to face with three cheerful angels of retribution.

Deirdre stunned him with a glowing smile that didn't reach her furious eyes. "Good afternoon, Harrick. We've come to make a *family* call."

Chapter Thirty~two

In the parlor of the house on Primrose Street, Graham, Phoebe and Deirdre surrounded the stiffly quivering Mrs. Blake.

"You say she was a servant?" Phoebe exuded patient ruthlessness. "Yet you never paid her, is that correct?"

"I gave her a home, didn't I? Treated her like family! No need to pay her as well! That money came addressed to *my* daughter! And she stole it! That ungrateful, wicked—"

"Your daughter?" Graham spoke slowly, holding the gazes of Phoebe and Deirdre as he raised his brows with significance.

Phoebe's eyes widened, but Deirdre caught on immediately. "Yes," she agreed with Mrs. Blake, nodding sympathetically. "Your daughter, Sophie."

Mrs. Blake immediately leaned toward the only source of sympathy in the room. "Yes, my sweet darling, my precious—"

"Daughter." The corners of Phoebe's lips began to rise. "Your daughter."

Mrs. Blake began to catch on that something was

amiss, that her audience kept repeating the same phrase over and over again. "Yes," she said tartly. "My daughter Sophie! What of it?"

Graham looked down at his folding hands. "After you lost your daughter, you brought S—Miss Westmoreland home, correct?"

The woman's gaze was truly wary now. "Yes. I missed my own Sophie, so when she passed, my housekeeper brought me an orphan girl to keep me company. She said she chose her because she looked like my sweet darling—although I never saw the resemblance—"

From what Graham could see of the woman and the miniature she clutched dramatically to her chest, Sophie—er, Sadie, looked enough like them both to be naturally born in that family. Hair too red to be properly blond, eyes of a particular storm cloud gray, and the Pickering nose in full flower. He could see that Phoebe and Deirdre were drawing the same conclusions. The woman had intended to pass the orphan off as her own daughter to win the Pickering fortune!

"Hmm." Deirdre's smile was a bit too bright. "What is it called when someone takes a child from an orphanage and gives her a home?" She snapped her fingers in the air. "Graham, help me here. What's that word?"

Graham smiled. "I believe the word you're thinking of is 'adoption.'"

Deirdre's smile became like that of a satisfied cat. "Yes, that's the word. Precisely." She was all but purring as she watched Mrs. Blake through narrowed eyes.

Phoebe followed suit. "The money was meant for your daughter, as you said. Does adoption not make Sadie Westmoreland your daughter—and thus the rightful great-granddaughter of Sir Hamish?"

The woman's eyes narrowed. "I'm sure I don't know what you mean."

Phoebe tilted her head with a smile. "I think I know someone who can explain it to you."

Mr. Stickley, when he arrived, was ushered into the familiar parlor and confronted with the eerie tableau of the Duke of Edencourt, the Marchioness of Brookhaven and Lady Marbrook, all standing behind a chair like a handsome warden and his two beautiful guards. The chair was occupied by a subdued and uneasy version of the awful woman who had ruined Miss Blake's beautiful wedding.

Except she wasn't Miss Blake, was she?

"Oh dear," Stickley blurted. "What a pickle all this is."

He blinked in mystification when the three people standing broke into spontaneous laughter.

Once matters had been explained to him, however, Stickley was in his element. "In entailment, an adopted son is not considered a legal heir," he explained. "But an adopted daughter could most definitely inherit from an ordinary will, provided that said will did not stipulate blood relations."

He gazed at the marchioness in consternation. "Are you concerned that Miss Blake—er, the Duchess of Edencourt will be allowed to inherit before you?"

"Not in the slightest. I hope she does." The marchioness smiled at him, her eyes brilliant with momentary fondness for him. She truly was a beauty, wasn't she? That golden hair—those stunning eyes—

The duke snapped his fingers before Stickley's face. "Ease back on the candlepower, Dee. The bloke's not used to it."

Stickley cleared his throat and fiddled with his neckcloth. "Er . . . yes. Well. Excuse me . . . *what?*"

Lady Marbrook put a hand on Stickley's arm. "Sir, we *want* the duchess to inherit the Pickering fortune."

"She deserves it," the marchioness agreed stoutly. "I don't need it."

Lady Marbrook smiled. "Neither do I."

The duke nodded. "But most importantly, we need to obtain Mrs. Blake's assurance that she will not press charges for the theft of her daughter's money."

Stickley sniffed. That was a legitimate concern, for even a duchess could be accused of a crime. "Mrs. Blake ought to have informed us of her daughter's death immediately." Then he relented. "Or as soon as she felt able to, in her grief."

The marchioness muttered something like "which means never" but that couldn't be, for the marchioness was the image of ladylike propriety.

Mrs. Blake snarled. "I'm due what I'm due. No one steals from me, not even a stick-shaped orphan!"

Stickley shared worried glances with the duke and his two lovely companions. The entire arrangement wouldn't work if the woman wouldn't cease her vendetta and claim the duchess as her legal daughter.

* * *

WHEN SADIE WOKE in her room at Brook House, Deirdre's new maid, the one she'd taken with her on her journey, was brushing out the pink gown from yesterday.

Her wedding dress, to be perfectly accurate. She'd chosen it because it was that single pale perfect shade of pink that even girls with reddish locks could wear. She'd felt beautiful and feminine and desired in it.

It seemed like so long ago.

The new girl, Jane, smiled at Sadie when she saw her eyes were open. "Good morning, Your Grace. Would you like tea? Should I ask for breakfast to be served in here?"

Sadie blinked. *Your Grace.* She wondered how long it would take to get used to that.

Breakfast came and went. Sadie donned a morning gown of cool green silk and wandered downstairs. She hadn't the vaguest idea what to do with herself. Should she journey back to Edencourt by herself to help the cottagers? Should she wait here for Graham to send for her—which might never happen? Or should she hop the soonest ship out of port and be the Duchess of Edencourt in America, where everyone would be duly impressed and she could dine out on her title for the rest of her life without paying a dime?

Of all the options, she longed to go back to Edencourt. Not simply because Moira and her children needed the help, but because that single day and night at Edencourt had been the closest thing Sadie had ever known to being *home.*

Most women aren't afraid their husbands will throw them out when they are discovered at "home."

She was loitering in the front parlor when she heard the knocker. A moment later Fortescue came to the parlor. "Lady Tessa and Mr. Somers Boothe-Jamison, Your Grace."

"Really?" Sadie frowned. "How . . . odd."

"Darling!" Tessa sailed in and bestowed an auntly kiss on Sadie's cheek. Since it was the first such she'd ever received, Sadie could be excused for ducking ever so slightly, so that the kiss landed on her ear. For Mr. Boothe-Jamison, however, she had a sincere smile. "How is your fine horse, sir?"

Somers grinned. "He's just fine, Your Grace. The only reminder of his ordeal is a tendency to lie down whenever possible."

Tessa fluttered. "Sit down, So—er, Sa—darling! Somers insisted that I come to call on you today—to see if you are well and if you need anything." Tessa stared at her with intent cheer. "You don't need anything, do you?"

Somers cleared his throat. "Tess, we discussed this. I don't want to have to remind you again."

Tessa giggled and fluttered her eyelashes at Somers. "Yes, my love."

Tessa giggled?

Sadie abruptly wondered if she had, in fact, not actually woken up this morning but even now lay dreaming in her bed upstairs. No, it couldn't be a dream. She'd have to be mad to come up with something outrageous like a girlish, fluttering Tessa who *giggled*!

She blinked rapidly and turned back to Tessa. "Ah . . . what is it you wanted to tell me?"

Tessa sent Somers one last worshipful glance and then let out a deep sigh. "Somers made me come here today to apologize to you."

That wasn't very helpful. There were so many things for Tessa to apologize for that Sadie simply didn't know where her aunt ought to begin. *I'm sorry I plotted against you* would be a great start, but that would simply never happen.

"I'm sorry I plotted against you," Tessa said without a trace of irony or double-edged commentary. "I ought not to have sent for Mrs. Blake. I only meant to get you in trouble with your mother, not cause a nationwide scandal."

Somers folded his arms. "No excuses, Tess. Take full responsibility for your actions."

"All right. I might have been *hoping* for a nationwide scandal, but I had no idea the secret was that good." She shrugged. "Why in the world did you even bother to invite me?"

Sadie could only stare at her, stunned. One harmless-looking young man had the predatory Lady Tessa wound firmly around his pinkie finger.

"It wasn't personal, Sadie. Graham is family, but I had every hope of Deirdre winning, even then."

"But she doesn't need the money, Tessa," Sadie said.

"The money isn't the point, dear," Tessa explained

crisply. "Winning is. Winning is always the point."
Then she left, mooning at the new man in her life even
as they walked arm in arm from the house.

OF ALL THE people who had come and gone through
Brook House over the ten years of his supremacy there,
Sophie–Sadie Westmoreland, the Duchess of Edencourt, was one of John Herbert Fortescue's favorites.
Like him, she had risen by wit and resilience from bad
beginnings to a better place. Like him, she had made
mistakes along the way. People had been lied to—
people who had deserved to know the truth. Furthermore, like him, the strangely graceful and elegant
duchess had been abandoned by the person she'd most
wanted to stand by her.

Fortescue watched the duchess as she leaned by the
front window of the parlor and gazed unseeing at the
city outside. The man she waited for wasn't coming.
Everyone knew that, including the duchess herself.
The Duke of Edencourt had been publicly humiliated.
London was agog. The very streets and parks rang with
laughter at his gullibility. A man didn't quickly forget a
betrayal like that.

*How would you know? Patricia refused you because
you're a liar and fraud.*

And then she'd left, taking his cracked heart with
her into the night. He had no idea where she had gone.

*Start with County Clare. On the cliffs. How many
O'Malleys can there be in a hundred miles of coast-
line?*

In Ireland? Hundreds, probably. Yet . . . it was possible that he could find her. What would he say? How could he deny that he was a liar—that he'd been ashamed of his pedigree and had spent the last fifteen years eradicating it from his very thoughts?

Until she came, with emerald eyes and hair of fire and the sound of home in the lilt of her voice.

Home. He'd left so long ago, determined never to look back, to shake the "mud of the potato fields" from his boots forever, to seek a better life, a better route . . . to where? In the end, all routes led to the same place.

Who would mourn him when he died?

The silver will miss the hell out of you.

I don't think the brass knocker can survive the loss.

What was the point in being the best butler in London if no one stood at his side to give a damn? What was yet another day of impeccable servitude without that lilting, teasing voice giving him what for over his pomposity, or those shining eyes seeing to the needs and cares of those around her, or that magnificent hair tumbling down onto his pillows at evening's end?

"I resign."

At the window, across the parlor, the duchess didn't startle in the slightest at his sudden declaration. "I don't blame you," she said without turning. "You'll not find another girl like Patricia in this lifetime."

"I resign." Saying it again made it more solid. "I resign at once."

The duchess breathed a soft gust of laughter and leaned her head against the window embrasure. "I heard you. Now go tell the marquis."

"The marquis." Oh, hell. He turned away, his gut chilled at the thought of abandoning the lord he'd served for so long. It had been a privilege to serve such a man. It was a rotten trick to abandon him so suddenly.

"Fortescue?"

He turned back, grateful for the momentary reprieve. "Yes, Your Grace?"

"Do you think she'll forgive you?" She turned to him at last, her gray eyes damp and luminous. "I don't know what you did, but it must have been terrible for her to run away like that."

Fortescue nodded. "I did . . . what you did, Your Grace."

She smiled sadly. "I thought as much. Lementeur said that we always recognize each other, even when we can't recognize ourselves."

Can't recognize ourselves. "I know myself again," Fortescue said, the Irish boiling through his blood. The pull of home was so ferocious he could hardly breathe. *Home. Patricia.*

The words held the same meaning.

The duchess nodded. "I'm very happy for you. If you see me lying around anywhere, be sure to tell me to find me again, as well."

Fortescue gave her a crisp bow of respect, not entirely because of her title. "It would be my pleasure, Your Grace."

She waved a hand. "Go on, then. And don't worry. Calder is all squishy love-struck gumdrop these days. He'll hardly bite at all."

Fortescue straightened, then let the façade of perfect English servant slide away forever. He gave one of the most highly ranked ladies in London a cheeky grin.

"Ye're a grand girl, Sadie. He's a whiskey-blinded fool to let ye go."

She let a smile light those storm-cloud eyes for the merest instant. "Get on with ye, ye great flirt," she replied, her imitative Irish lilt so terrible it was almost right. "Go tell the master you've had enough of wipin' his gold-plated arse."

With a laugh, John Herbert Fortescue took his last order from an English aristocrat and, turning on his heel, promptly did precisely as he was told.

Chapter Thirty~three

After a time, Sadie wearied of her vigil at the window. Graham wasn't coming.

And even if he did, she couldn't bear to face him. What could she say to him but that yes, she was a liar and a thief and, yes, she had seduced him to force him to marry her.

All in good cause? That sounded a bit thin when there was no Pickering fortune to compensate for her transgressions.

No matter where she went or what she did, she knew she didn't want to stay here. She couldn't expect Deirdre to avoid Graham for the rest of her life. She certainly couldn't bear to see him taking mistresses over the years, yet what else could happen? She could stay and help at Edencourt, but her skills were paltry. Though she would gladly serve them, she wasn't sure she would be much good. She would only cause strife when she encountered Graham there, anyway.

Going to her room, she began to pack. Traveling clothes in one trunk. Her Lementeur creations in another. She was running out of room.

In the chest of drawers she found her translations. They were all there, from the story of Sleeping Beauty in the Wood, to the Summer and Winter Garden, and of course, Cinderella.

Overwhelmed with memories and sadness, she sat down to read Cinderella again.

She sat down on a stool, took her foot out of the heavy wooden shoe, and put it into the slipper that fit her perfectly. After she stood up and the prince looked her straight in the face, he recognized the beautiful maiden who had danced with him. "This is my true bride!" he exclaimed.

Why was she torturing herself with this story? She put it away from her. For a moment she was tempted to throw it and all her other translations into the fire, but then she thought that, if nothing else, she might bind them up and give them to Meggie.

A good-bye gift.

The room had been returned to its former unused state. Every sign that Sadie Westmoreland had ever existed had been erased. It had been altogether easy to do so, in fact. After all, she had always lived on the outside edge of true existence. Never a real home, never a real family, never a real love.

Oh, my love. My everlasting love.

She closed her eyes against the memory of the look in Graham's eyes the last time she'd seen him. She shouldn't have let him go through with the wedding ceremony. His honor wouldn't have allowed him to stop it, but she could have fled, or shouted "Fire!", or *something* to save that stubborn fool from himself.

And from her.

Annulment was still a possibility. She planned to pay a visit to that bishop on her way out of London. If blackmail worked for Graham, it ought to work for her just as well.

A footman knocked at the door. "His Grace has come to call, miss."

Sadie glanced up to be sure that the key had been turned in the lock. "Tell His Grace that he needn't bother ejecting me. I'm leaving London very shortly anyway."

"Yes, miss," the man said doubtfully. Poor fellow, having Fortescue's duties thrust into his untrained hands.

Then she heard Graham's voice in the hall, raised in protest. Hungry for the merest scrap of him, she rose and pressed her ear to the door.

"Damn it, don't you have the bloody key?"

The footman murmured something. Sadie hoped Fortescue had taken the keys with him and dropped them off a cliff. She loved Graham. She needed Graham.

She would not allow herself to have the tiniest bit of Graham. He deserved better.

Besides, she couldn't bear to face him.

There wasn't another sound out in the hall. Disappointed, Sadie stepped back from the door and dropped her face into her hands. "Oh, my love," she whispered.

Then she heard a thud and a muffled curse. She lifted her head and gasped at the man sprawled on the floor by the window, coatless, his sleeve torn and a sprig of leaves in his hair.

He winced, then grinned up at her. "Isn't this the way they do it in those stories of yours?"

She gaped, unable to speak. Then she swallowed harshly and moved back a step, though she longed to rush forward.

Yes, rush! Rush!

She shook her head, denying him, denying herself. "I can't see you!"

He sat up and brushed at his weskit. "Then you're not looking hard enough. I'm here and I can prove it. I've made a proper mess on the rug."

She laughed damply, then pressed her hands over her face, covering her eyes. "Stop! Stop making light! You know you shouldn't be here!"

"No, I don't," he said, his voice gentle. "Explain it to me."

She shook her head. "Don't you know there must always be a penance paid in these stories? The liar always comes to a bad end. Hoist on his own petard."

"Oh, *that*," he said dismissively. "Well, don't worry on that account. You didn't lie."

In her surprise, she forgot about not looking at him. She dropped her hands and stared. "I didn't?"

He didn't stand as she'd thought he might, but only remained relaxed on the floor, sitting tailor fashion with his hands draped easily over his knees. He smiled up at her, his green eyes alight. "I could explain it to you, but you're right—you must pay a price first."

She gulped air, hope and despair a warring tempest in her belly. "Wh—what price?"

He held out his hand. "You have to help me up. That climb was painful. I've hurt my . . . my petard."

Laughing shakily, she moved forward to tentatively take his hand. The instant his fingers closed around hers, he gave a mighty tug.

With a faint shriek, she fell into his arms. He pulled her close and rolled the both of them until he lay above her, toe to toe, nose to nose, on the floor. He smiled down at her astonishment. "See? We still fit." He pulled something from his waistcoat pocket and slipped it onto her finger. "You're the only one who fits."

Sadie blinked at the lovely ring. "Where did you get this?"

"It was my mother's." When Sadie gasped and made to remove it, he placed his hands over hers, stopping her. "She was the Duchess of Edencourt. So are you. It is your ring now."

Sadie protested again but her will was weakening. She loved the ring. She *wanted* the ring.

Besides, he'd climbed a tree to give it to her. *A man will do astonishing things for a woman he is ardent about.*

If he pulled away from her now and disdained her forever, if she stepped in front of speeding cart tomorrow, if the world ended this evening—she would always have this moment. Without an instant's hesitation, she wrapped her arms about his neck and pulled him down for a kiss that might have to last her the rest of her life.

She'd never been a wasteful sort.

A while—quite a while, in fact—later, Graham came

up for air. "Sophie—" He cleared his throat. "Sorry." He began again. "Miss Westmoreland, would you care to accompany me to the parlor? There's something there I think you should see."

Sadly, for the moment was gone and might never come again, Sadie smiled and let him rise. "Miss Westmoreland? Need we be so formal, Graham?"

He held up a restraining hand. "Now, now—we mustn't speak. We've not been properly introduced."

Giving a small, helpless bark of laughter, she rose as well and let him lead her from the room. At least he wasn't letting go of her hand.

Downstairs in the parlor, they found quite a crowd. Brookhaven and Deirdre, Marbrook and Phoebe, an excited Meggie, a string-tangled kitten . . . and Mr. Stickley, the solicitor.

Everyone was smiling, except for the kitten.

When Sadie entered, Mr. Stickley moved forward, his prim smile sincere and admiring. "Your Grace, I am so happy to see you again!"

Sadie cleared the surprise from her throat and managed to answer graciously enough. "Thank you, sir. It is nice to see you again as well."

He made a neat little bow. "And my sincerest congratulations on your excellent match, my dear! I knew that one of you ladies would win!"

Sadie frowned anxiously. "Oh, dear. No one has told you—I'm not really Sophie Blake."

Mr. Stickley chuckled indulgently and clapped his hands together. "Of course you aren't! My goodness!" He reached into his coat and pulled out a slip of paper.

"Nonetheless, here you are! May you use it in good health!"

Confused, Sadie took the paper—and then realized that it was a check. A very *large* check. Her fingers went suddenly numb and the check floated to the floor.

Mr. Stickley peered worriedly into her face. "Are you all right, Your Grace?"

The room threatened to tilt. Graham's arm came about her, strong and warm. She steadied at once. She reached out a hand for the check that Mr. Stickley had retrieved from the floor. "If you don't mind, sir . . . I should like to read that again."

The paper was cool and crisp in her hand. The amount was as she'd first thought—nearly thirty thousand pounds. This time, however, it was the name on the check that caught her up short.

Sadie Westmoreland Blake Cavendish, Duchess of Edencourt.

"Blake?" Her throat tightened. She looked helplessly at Deirdre and Phoebe. "What . . . what is this?"

Deirdre grinned. "Congratulations. You're not an orphan anymore."

Phoebe shook her head, smiling. "Actually, you haven't been for fifteen years. Mrs. Blake legally adopted you when she brought you home to Acton."

Deirdre's grin turned fierce. "That's her account and she's standing by it, by God."

"Adopted?" Sadie blinked. "Then . . . we truly are cousins?" *A real family.*

Phoebe gazed at Sadie with gentle understanding in her eyes. "Graham did it."

His strength and steadiness had never left her. She'd leaned into him as naturally as she'd breathed—without thought or hesitation. Now she turned to him, so many questions bubbling forth that she was mute with them.

He smiled down at her, then touched the tip of her nose with his finger. "You are Sadie Blake. Mrs. Blake will swear to it in any court in the land."

Sadie blinked. "But . . . she hates me."

His smile turned a little sad. "I'm fairly sure she hates everyone. I'm positive she hates me, since I am the one who pointed out that if you received the inheritance then you would be able to pay her back her two hundred pounds."

Deirdre snorted. "It wasn't hers to begin with."

Sadie looked back down at the check in her hand. "Shouldn't I give her some of this? I mean, she's the real Pickering, not I."

"Don't you dare!" Deirdre plunked both hands on her hips. "Do you know why she sent her housekeeper to that orphanage? She was looking for a girl to pass off as Sophie to win the prize!"

Phoebe nodded. "She finally confessed that she only gave up on the idea when you turned out to be . . ."

"Plain," Sadie finished without a hint of rancor. "It all makes sense now." She gazed down at the check in her hand. "Fair enough, then." She turned to Graham and offered him the check with a smile. "For your Edencourt."

His hand closed over hers, the check inside. "For our home, Sadie Westmoreland Blake Cavendish, Duchess of Edencourt." He raised their joined hands and kissed her knuckles. "It's very nice to meet you at last."

A real love.

She laughed and curtsied. "Likewise, Your Grace." Then she smiled up at him with all the love she'd never thought to show him again, a smile that brought wonder to his eyes and a gasp of astonishment from Mr. Stickley.

"But you may call me Sadie."

Chapter Thirty~four

Squinting against the afternoon light, gray and pearly though it shone through the clouds, Wolfe stumbled from the public house and wiped his foul-tasting mouth on his sleeve. Bracing one shaking hand against the doorway, he leaned to spit on the cobbles. The barmaid had let him sleep off his binge in her bed, though she'd been sorely put out this morning to discover that there was no coin to repay her generosity.

Wolfe's head rang and pounded and generally felt as if a crew of laborers were erecting a gallows within his skull. The image of a noose swung behind his dazzled vision for an uncomfortable moment. Then he managed to dispel it by dwelling upon the sizable assets of the aforementioned barmaid.

With such uplifting thoughts to bolster him, he managed to straighten his back and stand erect. He ran both hands through his unwashed hair and then smoothed them down his coat front. Still flat, even at his age. Forty-mumble was only the middle of his prime. He had many, many years to enjoy the fruits of his labors. For the time being, however, he needed to hit Stickley up for an advance on his retainer. There was still the matter of the Marquis of Brookhaven to dispense with. When that bloke lay cold, there would be no more chances for the great-granddaughters of Sir Hamish Pickering to lay hands on a nickel of the old bastard's gold.

With a somewhat less than upright, shambling motion, Wolfe began to wander his way through the winding streets and alleys of Shoreditch, making his way back to more respectable environs. Too bad. The very smell of the piss-and-soot–coated cobbles put a spring in his step that had never been accomplished by the scent of flowers or perfume of the finer life.

"Back to the office," he muttered to himself, then snickered. "Tick-tock, old boy, time is money." Who was it who used to say that until Wolfe wanted to brain him with a cricket bat? Oh, yes. Mr. Wolfe the Elder had been wont to spout that homily to his dear partner, Stickley the First.

Now there was a bracing thought. Imagining parting ways with Stickley forever brought a beatific smile to Wolfe's face that nearly eradicated the reddened eyes and greenish pallor.

The squalor of Shoreditch behind him at last, Wolfe paused before a Fleet Street shop window to adjust his cravat. Oh hell, where was his cravat? Recalling that he'd used it to bind the hands of the barmaid at some point in the last few days, he shrugged. The wench could burn it, for all he cared. Soon he'd be swimming in luxury, the happy and hard-working recipient of nearly fifteen thousand pounds of interest from the Pickering Trust.

Stickley would no longer be needing his half, of course.

While Wolfe tried to force his fumbling fingers to do something useful with his collar, two ladies passed behind him. He could see their fine bonnets and shawls reflected in the mirror and the bored footman trailing behind with the parcels. Wolfe twitched with irritation. Ladies were parasites, too uppity to pay their own way with honest whoring. Soon he would have enough money to surround himself with eager prostitutes and like-minded friends for the rest of his life.

Such sybaritic pleasure almost distracted him from the ladies' conversation—that is, until he heard the name "Edencourt."

"Oh, no! It's her money, not Edencourt's! Nearly thirty thousand pounds they say."

The other woman sighed enviously. "Can you imagine? A young, handsome duke and all those riches. She'll be sleeping in Lementeur nightdresses, I expect."

The other woman snorted, no less enviously. "With that inheritance, she'll be gowning her *maidservants* in Lementeur!"

"But isn't it romantic? I heard that he stole her away to his estate and wouldn't let her leave until she promised to marry him."

I should have killed that scrawny bitch when I had the chance!

It wasn't until Wolfe felt the heavy hand of the footman on his shoulder that he realized he'd growled those bitter words out loud.

"Sir, I think you'd best move along now."

Wolfe found himself turned by force. The footman—damn, he looked more like a bodyguard than an simple manservant—stood firmly between Wolfe and the shocked gazes of the two ladies. The two very wealthy, likely very highly placed ladies. Wolfe fought down the volcanic rage searing his gut long enough to smear an apologetic smile on his features and mouth some banal obsequiousness. The footman released him at last and Wolfe backed away, bowing and smirking and generally making himself sick with his own desperation.

How could it have happened? When he'd left this world only a few days ago, that horse-faced bride of Edencourt's had been exposed as a fake! Now she had the inheritance? Wolfe strode to the nearest newsboy, who was tying up the last of his unsold sheets for the day.

Wolfe shoved the fellow aside and grabbed up a gossip rag.

"Oy! That's a farthing!"

Wolfe turned the full force of his rage at the sniveling worm. The fellow paled and backed away from Wolfe's red, maddened eyes, making a small superstitious motion against evil as he did so.

Wolfe ignored him then, ripping the sheet in his urgency to read it. There it was, in the Voice of Society's column.

"If the Duke and Duchess of Edencourt weren't previously the most fortunate couple in England, already having the grace of fine looks and true love, then they surely are now. The Duchess, it seems, is the lucky winner of a charming contest between herself and her lovely cousins, now both wed to the brothers of Brookhaven, the marquis himself and his brother Lord Raphael Marbrook. Lady Edencourt has inherited a vast fortune for wedding her duke. Your Voice of Society now wonders if this will become the latest vogue in bequest—the legacy goes to the one who makes the best match of all!"

Gone. Evaporated. Sucked away by that prancing duke and his sponging relic of an estate.

Wolfe's hands began to shake once more. This time the rage was nearly swallowed by the panic and fear. He had people looking for him—people who now knew he had no more expectations of even his paltry retainer.

Oh, damn. His gut went to ice at the memories. He'd held his creditors off for months with stories of the wealth due him from the Pickering Trust. Lies, mostly, but everyone remembered how rich old Hamish had become. Wolfe had flung that name about with comfortable abandon, relishing the respect that had risen in the eyes of everyone who heard that he was executor of such wealth.

Never mind that it was Stickley who—

Stickley.

Wolfe pressed the heels of both hands to his aching forehead. There was something he needed to remember about Stickley . . .

It's what my father would have expected of me.

Ah. Yes.

Wolfe drew in a long, shaken breath. That had been a close call there for a moment. He'd thought he might have to run for the West Indies or, God forbid, the Americas.

But there, as always, as dependable and useful as a boot scraper bolted to the doorway, was Stickley. Reliable, loyal Stickley, who had so thoughtfully arranged for Wolfe to be kept in the style to which he'd become accustomed.

Wolfe smiled, his thoughts resting fondly on Stickley for the first time in his memory.

He really was a fine old stick. Wolfe almost regretted having to kill him.

A FEW HOURS later, Mr. Wolfe was staring down the barrel of a very large, very black hunting rifle that lay perfectly poised in the arms of his erstwhile partner, Mr. Stickley.

"I should put that silly little pistol down if I were you, Wolfe," Stickley said with more panache than Wolfe would have credited him with. "You're outgunned."

Wolfe rapidly calculated his chances of killing Stickley before he himself was killed. The hell of it was, rifles just worked so much better than pistols! Pistols were forever jamming and if one had to shoot very far, they were distressingly inaccurate.

Deciding to live to fight another day, Wolfe bent to set his pistol on the floor. The rifle remained aimed at him for several long moments.

"What is the meaning of this outrage?"

Outrage. Wolfe's nerves twitched. The prissy little sod's very language grated on Wolfe's ear like the sound of a saw.

"I'm sorry, Stick, old man." Apologize. Lap it up.

Convince the smarmy little bastard to let his guard down. Then kill him and break into the safe.

It was a hell of a plan.

Not as good as the one that didn't include Stickley armed and ready for him, but beggars couldn't be choosers.

"I didn't mean to hurt anyone," he pleaded. *Oh, how I want to hurt you.* He opened his hands wide to demonstrate his helplessness and took a step forward. He had the reach on Stick. He could probably rip that rifle out of the smaller man's hands if he chose to.

Then he would pound the little bastard's face to mush. When the body was found, he'd be sure to cry all the way to the Bank of London.

Stickley seemed to be buying it. He lowered the rifle slightly. "You said you weren't going to harm Miss Blake or the duke."

Wolfe shrugged. "Are they harmed? I came out of the matter with a bloody nose, I'll remind you! And that duke won the day in the alley as well. Kidnapping Brookhaven came to naught and I never personally laid a finger on Lady Brookhaven. I simply encouraged Baskin's infatuation." While he spoke, he eased forward a fraction of an inch for every word. Then he lunged for the rifle.

There.

With a mighty wrench, he pulled the gun out of Stickley's grip, then quickly switched it to aim at him. "Ha! You're dead now, you little sod!"

Lamplight flared in the darkened room. "No, he isn't," a voice said pleasantly.

Wolfe turned to see a full audience of—blast it!—witnesses. Standing in the room were the Duke of Edencourt, the Marquis of Brookhaven and that literal bastard, Lord Raphael Marbrook.

"How thoughtful of you to recount your sins to us, Mr. Wolfe." The marquis's tone was dry. "There were some there I hadn't even known of."

Witnesses or not, Wolfe was the only one who was armed. He pointed the rifle at the gentlemen before him. "My lords, Your Grace, I'm sorry to inform you that you've all just purchased tickets on the 'Make My Wife a Widow' ship—" He smiled nastily. "Which sails immediately."

Stickley was shaking his head. "I always thought you were simply drunk most of the time. I never realized that you were in the process of becoming the stupidest man alive. If I knew you were coming with enough certainty to assemble this esteemed panel of witnesses, don't you think I would have used similar forethought to remove the bullets from my rifle?"

The three gentlemen opposite him pulled rifles of their own from behind their backs. "These, however, are quite loaded. Aren't they, Mr. Stickley?"

Wolfe turned on his partner in fury. "You're just as guilty of all that as I am, Stick. If I hang, you hang with me!"

He turned back to Brookhaven. "Do you want to know who attacked your fiancée and kidnapped your brother just before your wedding?" He raised one finger to point at Stickley. "This man right here was by my side all through that adventure."

Brookhaven narrowed his eyes. "Are you saying that Stickley was there, helping you stage a highway robbery on my carriage?" He moved nearer. "Are you saying that he held a gun on my brother's wife, my fiancée, and that he locked him in a rotten basement for days without food or water?"

Wolfe nodded vengefully. "He did!"

Stickley shook his head wearily. "So much whiskey, Wolfe. I knew it was only a matter of time until you lost your mind."

"What?" Wolfe looked from one man to the next but saw not an iota of suspicion about to fall on Stickley. He waved the rifle in frustration. "Ask your wife, Marbrook! She was there!"

"Oh, my, yes," Stickley nodded and made for the door to the kitchen. "My lady, if you please?"

When Lady Marbrook came out, Wolfe gaped. Then he smiled at her, his last hope. She drew back, her brows rising in alarm.

"Rafe, make him stop."

Lord Marbrook put an arm about her. "It's all right, darling. Mr. Wolfe seems to have experienced some confusion about the night before I was kidnapped. He'd like you to clear something up for us all."

Wolfe raised his hand to point at Stickley. "There were two of us that night, weren't there?"

Lady Marbrook blinked at him. "Two? Are you sure?"

Wolfe's jaw dropped. "You saw us both!"

She shrugged. "I can't really recall. I was so terrified, you see—a helpless lady alone on a dark road

with a highwayman . . ." She shook her head regretfully. "I'm not sure what I saw."

Wolfe saw it all now. Stickley had made a bargain
with them. His capture in exchange for sheltering beneath their protection and probably a bit of something
on the side.

Then the watch piled into the room, rough men
swearing and shoving him, all eager to claim the
bounty for his crime.

As Wolfe was taken away he could only glare hotly
at Stickley through the barred window of the wagon
like a caged animal.

MRS. O'MALLEY WAS a woman of great wisdom and
tolerance. She knew that if her eldest daughter, Patricia, claimed to have returned from England because
she'd been fired from her job for slacking work, then
the real reason was best left unspoken for the moment.
As if one of her children had ever slacked a day in their
lives!

It was a man, of course.

Mrs. O'Malley had five sisters and three daughters.
She could tell the difference between the strained pallor of heartbreak and the despair of failure.

Even the boys, bless them, knew that someone had
broken their beloved sister's heart. They cast worried
glances and muttered dark words about the "damned
English"—but not in Patricia's hearing, for it only
made her paler yet.

Mrs. O'Malley dried her hands of dishwater and

moved to where Patricia sat peeling potatoes for the noon meal. A family of seven hard workers could eat a fair pile of potatoes, but Patricia had peeled enough for an army.

Inhaling, Mrs. O'Malley cast her eyes to the heavens, hoping for aid. She was going to have to open a deep wound, but if she didn't cauterize it quickly with some common sense and practicality, they were all going to drown in tearstained peels.

Then movement caught her eye through the small front window. Someone was coming down the cliff road, walking with the loose, easy movements of one who'd been walking for a long while. A man, in sturdy homespun wool and linen—a tall, good-looking fellow with his cap tipped back to better enjoy the rare day.

"Who is that, d'ye think?"

Her daughter joined her at the window, gazing dutifully out at the world she'd retreated from. Then Mrs. O'Malley heard a gasp like that of a woman struck to the heart. She turned her head sharply to see that her fine Patty, always one of the prettiest girls in County Clare, had never looked so beautiful.

Mrs. O'Malley turned her gaze back to the man on the road. "That's never the Englishman!"

Patricia laughed, a trill of pure joy. "Don't be silly, mum. That's my Irish Johnny, come home at last."

Mrs. O'Malley watched as her eldest daughter ran lightly down the road to meet her man, the white wool ends of her shawl flying out behind her like the wings of a seabird soaring in to solid land at last.

Epilogue

Graham walked through the front door of Edencourt without having to touch the latch with his own lordly hand. Of course, that was because the doors had been removed and taken by the carpenter for some much needed repair. They ought to be back in a day or so. When more workers arrived, the progress on the house would go faster.

Graham hoped so. He'd promised Sadie the doors would be back on before the first snowfall.

"Windows!" She'd wielded her scrub brush at him. "Don't forget to hire a glazier! We have too many broken windows!"

It had been Sadie's idea to hire Mr. Stickley for the general organization and repair of the main house, and the fellow had turned his zealous efforts to spending the Pickering fortune nearly as fast as he'd grown it.

"I've secured the principle," he'd reassured Graham. There had been some other words in there, like "amortization" and "percentages" so when Graham's eyes had glazed over he'd waved the man onward in his efforts.

"Good show, old son."

Stickley had beamed. "This is highly rewarding, Your Grace. I hope I'm to be a guest here someday."

Graham had gaped at him. "As if we'd ever let you leave!"

The little fellow had become positively misty-eyed. Graham for one couldn't wait to turn him loose on the rest of the estate!

Still, at the moment, the estate looked worse than before. What had been sagging had been torn down. What had been broken was boarded up. What was repairable had been removed, leaving great gaping holes and rubble everywhere.

They were on their own with the whole mess. He'd cordially invited both Brookhaven and Marbrook to help. They'd regretfully declined. Since then, the old Duke of Brookmoor had died and Calder and Deirdre had taken Meggie and her kitten, Fortescue Minor, and journeyed to take up residence at Brookmoor. Rafe and Phoebe had immediately taken off for Brookhaven, panting to make it their own in custody for the first male son to be born to Calder and Deirdre.

Deirdre had confessed that she was expecting already. Phoebe had demonstrated a previously unnoticed competitive streak by immediately getting into that state herself.

Sadie had smiled happily for them both, then dragged Graham home to get a bit of practice in. Graham dutifully gave it his all. And then some.

Now, standing in the entrance hall, Graham coughed on a cloud of plaster dust. Moira's husband, John, was gleefully shaking out a tarpaulin from the upstairs balcony. "Sorry, Your Grace!"

Ah, the joys of homecoming. Graham made his way up the stair, avoiding the pitfalls where the crumbling marble steps had been ripped out and were awaiting the new order, which was very late.

Sadie hadn't been in the kitchens or in the gardens or even in the stables. He snickered at that. Sadie had declared that there was no need for her to learn to ride, for she was never getting on another horse again for the rest of her life. Yet she was always in the stables, sneaking sugar to the sturdy ponies that did the majority of the hauling at the moment.

At the top of the stairs Graham gazed down at his domain. It was astonishing how little memory of his old life here remained. With the ritual bonfire cleansing of every musty, desiccated hunting trophy, less and less of the old duke's brutality seemed to linger in these gracious halls.

Instead, Graham felt his mother's presence like a benediction. Was she here? He didn't really believe that. Perhaps it was only that he sensed the presence of a woman's touch. Every project Sadie turned her attention to achieved exceptional results, as if the house and the estate longed to be cared for, to be nurtured, to be loved—

Don't we all?

Finally, frustrated, Graham tossed his head back and roared her name over the din of hammering, sawing and general mayhem. *"Sadie!"*

"I'm in here, Gray!"

He followed the sound of her lusty shout into the old duke's bedchamber. She was kneeling in the hearth, cleaning years of ashes from the grate. She looked overworked, exhausted, grubby and grimy and utterly, entirely blissful.

"Sadie, you shouldn't be doing that yourself! You're getting filthy!"

She turned to look over her shoulder, then laughed at him. "Look at you!"

He looked down, plucking at his workman's clothing covered in pitch. "I've been directing the roofers at the north cottages," he explained. "I *had* to get dirty."

She sat back on her heels. "Hmm. You loved it. Like a boy in the mud."

"That's me, I'm a dirty boy!" He leered at her.

She leered right back. "Want to watch me take a bath later, dirty boy?"

He swallowed. Hard. *"Irk."* He cleared his throat. "Yes, please." Then he remembered why he'd come upstairs.

"Time for your riding lesson."

She rolled her eyes. "Horses are very useful. They can pull carriages and everything. I hear some people even eat them. I don't think it's necessary to burden them with riding as well."

He knelt before her. "They are very enjoyable to ride, I promise. You needn't be afraid."

She snorted, sounding very much like a horse, actually. "I'm not afraid. How could I be afraid of something that is thrice my size and has giant teeth and hooves of iron—"

"Yes, I'll admit, it's a fearsome sight when they attack those defenseless flowers and I shudder to think of what the bale of hay goes through—"

The filthy coal-brush struck him in the chest, but she was laughing. "Oh, all right! I'll come for my riding lesson as soon as I've finished here."

He looked around him dismissively. "What's so important about my father's room?"

She tilted her head. "This isn't your father's room, you idiot. This is *your* room."

He made a long arm and dragged her across his lap. "Our room," he growled into her ear. "If you spend every single night with me for the rest of our lives, I'll sleep wherever you like."

She laughed when his unshaven cheek tickled hers, but sobered as she gazed up at him. "I love you, Gray. I loved you before you were duke."

He smiled down at her and rubbed at a smudge on her cheek with one finger. It only moved the soot around. "I love you, Sadie, my lady. I loved you before you were one of the richest women in England. I also loved you before you were the most beautiful woman in England. I'm fairly sure I loved you before you were the maddest woman in England, but that's a close call."

She smiled then, bestowing her now famous brilliance on only him. That was just the way he liked it. He kissed her, dirty as they both were, using his lips and hands to drive her to gasping.

They made love in the cinders, a duke and a duchess in a happily ever after of their very own making.

Don't miss the first two novels in the beloved Heiress
Brides series from *USA Today* bestselling author

CELESTE BRADLEY

Desperately Seeking A Duke

Only a duke will do. But will it be "I do"—or adieu?

The Duke Next Door

When fate comes knocking, there's no turning back…